Chapter 1

It was the feel of her presence in my room that woke me —
again. I rolled over in bed and squinted at the clock on my
nightstand. "What time is it?" My voice slurred. The blurry
numbers came into focus. Two thirty-three. "Two thirty-three?
Don't you ever sleep?"

She didn't respond.

I scooted my pillow against the headboard to sit up, see what
she was doing. "What is *that?*" I asked.

"Like it?" She shimmied in front of the mirror. The layered
fringe on the dress she was wearing swayed in waves. "It's an old
flapper dress I found at Goodwill," she said. In her stockinged
feet, she performed a little Charleston for me. "It's vintage. Totally retro. Don't you think? I'm wearing this baby to prom."

I snorted. Her eyes met mine in the mirror and sobered me
fast. She couldn't be serious.

Examining the length of herself, she hooked her long hair
over her ears and wiggled her hips again. She'd chosen the
blonde wig tonight. It wasn't her favorite, since she thought it
made her look cheap. Like a slut. It did go well with the red
dress, though. She caught me looking at her and smiled. "I'm going to run for prom queen, too."

I burst into laughter, then clapped a hand over my mouth to
smother the sound. Wouldn't want to wake the parental units
upstairs.

She wasn't laughing.

She *was* joking. Wasn't she? "Lia —"

"*Luna,*" she said. "I've taken the name Luna." Her eyes fixed on mine. To gauge my reaction, I guess. Or seek my approval. What did it matter what I thought?

"Why change?" I yawned. "You've always been —"

"Lia's too close. Lia Marie. It's just too close." She crossed my bedroom, blazing a trail through the layer of clothes and other crap on my floor. As she passed under the window, she stopped and pivoted. The moon cast an eerie glow through my basement window. A spotlight. A spray of luminescent beams.

"Luna," she repeated softly, more to herself than me. "Appropriate, wouldn't you say? A girl who can only be seen by moonlight?"

Exhaustion overwhelmed me suddenly. Or my weariness of it all. "Go to bed, Luna." I snuggled down into my comforter and punched my pillow, willing myself back to sleep. It'd take me hours to drift off again, especially if she stayed to do her makeup. And she would.

I studied her through a slit eye. Something was different. A change had come over her. Nothing physical. More a shift in her cosmos — or maybe a crack.

"I can see your bra straps," I told her. "You need to buy a strapless."

"Really?" She twisted her head to peer over her shoulder. "Do you have one?"

"Get real. Even if I did, you're not wearing my underwear."

"It wouldn't fit anyway. I'm at least a C cup."

I blew out a puff of air. "You wish." Rolling over, I muttered, "You're such a freakshow."

Her hair splayed across my pillow, tickling my face. "I know," she murmured in my ear. "But you love me, don't you?" Her lips grazed my cheek.

I swatted her away.

As I heard her slog across the floor toward my desk — where she'd unveiled her makeup caddy in all its glory — a sigh of resignation escaped my lips. Yeah, I loved her. I couldn't help it. She was my brother.

Chapter 2

"**D**on't tell Mommy when she gets home," Dad says. "I want it to be a surprise." He smiles at me and Liam. Liam's six and I'm four and we're sitting on the couch watching Dad slice through the cardboard around Mom's new washer and dryer. He pauses to loosen his tie and roll up his cuffs. "Did I tell you guys I got a promotion? You're looking at the new appliance manager for Sears. Next stop, King of the World." He winks at me.

"Yay, Daddy." I clap.

Dad looks at Liam and frowns a little. Liam's found the instruction booklet for the washer and is poring over it. He reads everything now. He tries to teach me, but it's too boring. I just want to watch TV.

"Liam!"

His head shoots up.

"Here, take these boxes out back," Dad tells him as he carves out a door flap in one. "You and Regan can play fort."

Liam slides off the couch and the two of us drag the cardboard cartons through the sliding glass doors to the yard. We set them up next to the overturned kiddie pool. I can stand inside the boxes, but Liam's already too tall.

"Go get your Samantha doll," he orders me. "Get all her clothes, too. Bring the crib out and her bottles and diapers. Bring everything."

"You help."

"No." His eyes dart around the interior. "I have to set up."

By the time I get back, Liam's hooked the two boxes together and *lugged my play table inside. He's got my Little Tikes Kitchen in the corner and he's setting the table. "Put the crib over there." Liam points to the opposite corner.*

On my way past, he takes my Samantha doll from me and cradles her in his arms. Smiling sweetly down on her, he informs me, "I'm the mommy."

"No," I whine. "I want to be the mommy this time."

"You can be it next time."

"You always say that." I throw all the baby clothes on the ground and stomp out the door.

"Wait, Re." Liam runs after me. "You be the daddy. Daddies are cool. You can come home with a surprise for Mommy. Like you won a million dollars, so you bought me a new house and a car. Better yet — you can pretend my Big Wheel is a Harley. Vroom, vroom." He mimes revving up the handle bars.

I fold my arms, thinking about it.

"Come on, Regan. Just this once?" He retrieves Samantha's pink dress from the grass. "Please?" he asks real soft.

I drop my arms. "Okay."

Liam re-enters our playhouse. I know what he's going to do now — change her clothes. That's all he ever does when he's the mommy, dresses and redresses the babies . . .

My alarm blared and I bolted upright. Blindly thrusting my arm toward the nightstand, I punched off the buzzer. Was that a dream or a memory? It was too vivid to be imagined. Too real. Was his fascination with playing house the first indication I had that Liam was different? In his head and heart he knew he was a girl? That he was transgender.

No, there was something else. An earlier event, when we were even younger. My mind was too fogged with sleep to conjure up the image. Either that or I didn't want to remember. There were a lot of things I didn't want to remember.

I stumbled to the shower in a coma. The bathroom was still steamy, which meant Liam was up and dressed. I let the warmth seep into my body as I stripped. Then, bracing for the shock, I wrenched the cold water faucet on and plunged in face first.

Dad was chuckling at the comics when I trudged up the basement steps and into the kitchen. Next to him, at the dining room table, Liam absently spooned Wheat Chex into his mouth while scanning a textbook into his mega brain. Advanced Placement Physics, I noted with more than a twinge of resentment. He couldn't share a few IQ points with his only sister, could he? Liam was dressed in role, as he called it. Boy role. His long-sleeved shirt was pressed and buttoned to the chin; tucked into his khaki Dockers, which were ironed with military precision.

I couldn't even spell iron. My outfit consisted of faded carpenter pants and whatever shirt from the heap on my floor was closest to the door.

"Morning," Mom greeted me at the refrigerator with her perfunctory removal of the juice carton from my mouth. "You look like a zombie," she said, returning the OJ to the shelf. "Are you sick?"

"No. Just tired. From lack of sleep." I widened my eyes at Liam as I slid into my chair across from him. He flipped another page, soaking up quantum physics at Pentium speed.

"Why aren't you sleeping?" Dad asked, glancing up from the paper.

"No reason," I mumbled.

Mom took her chair at the other end of the table. She punched buttons on her cell phone and put it to her ear while Dad said to me, "You need to sleep. Girls have to get their beauty rest."

Liam's eyes met mine. I expected him to smirk or something, but instead he glared.

What? Dad was joking. God. Liam was so sensitive some-times.

"Yeah, hi Andy," Mom spoke into her cell. "It's me. Did we ever get our reservations confirmed on the Hartford house for the Sorensons' wedding? I can't seem to find the paperwork." She stirred her coffee.

I caught Dad rolling his eyes. He wasn't crazy about Mom's job. Specifically, her elevating her own status from Wife and Mother to More Significant Other. Not that he was sexist or anything, just boring and conventional. How could he resent her working? Since he got downsized by Sears and had to take a flunky job at the Home Depot, somebody had to earn our lunch money.

"Hmm." Mom sipped her coffee. "Maybe I'll call again just to be sure. Did you hear that Yarrow girl ask if she could order black frosting for her cake? Black. On a wedding cake." Mom listened for a moment, then burst into laughter. "Oh, Andy," she wheezed. "What would I do without you?"

My eyes cut to Dad, who bristled.

In an effort to drown out the sudden static in the air, I re-trieved my chemistry book from my backpack and set it on the table. The thought of what we were doing today in class made me queasy, so I put it back. Out of sight, out of mind. My phi-losophy of life in a test tube.

I snatched a bagel off the lazy Susan in the middle and smeared a glob of strawberry cream cheese on it.

Dad said, "A guy goes to the doctor for a checkup and the doctor says to him, 'I have bad news and worse news.'"

Liam and I groaned in unison. Dad folded the newspaper closed.

Mom continued, "I wrote up the cake order, but I might hold off a while before sending it in until I talk to her mother. She'll be mortified, I'm sure. I can't wait to see the wedding gown. What?" She listened, then laughed at Andy again. Nothing was that funny this early in the morning.

"'What's the bad news?' the guy says." Especially not Dad.

"'The bad news is you have terminal cancer.'"

"'Oh my God.'" Dad held his heart. He gasped and panted for effect. "The man asks, 'What's the worse news?'"

"The doctor informs him, 'The worse news is you have Alzheimer's.'"

"The guy breathes a huge sigh of relief. He says, 'Thank God I don't have cancer.'"

Liam chuckled. It took me a minute, then I cracked up. I tried to stifle it so as not to encourage Dad.

He beamed. "Good one, huh?"

"Andy, before I forget, I need to pick up a prescription on my way in, so I might be a few minutes late."

For some reason, that piqued Liam's interest. Mom disconnected and rose from her chair. Leaving her phone and Daytimer on the table, she bustled down the back hallway. To pop another upper, no doubt.

"I talked to Coach Hewitt yesterday," Dad said.

The hair on my arms stood up. Liam's hair would've too, if he had any there. Dad continued, "He says to come see him this week about getting on the team. Since that whole Diaz family moved back to Mexico, he's got a few open positions. He can't guarantee varsity, but JV for sure. Tryouts are Wednesday. Skip asked me what position you played, and I told him first base. Unless you want to pitch." Dad reached over and jabbed Liam's arm playfully.

Liam looked so brittle, I thought he'd break. He resumed eating his Chex as if grinding sand between his teeth.

Dad added, "Stop by his office after school today."

Liam swallowed. He said evenly, "I don't want to play baseball, Dad."

My breath caught. I looked at Dad. Liam had never said it out loud. Never.

Dad's expression didn't change, but his voice did. "Skip's doing this as a favor to me so you can participate in sports your senior year. It'll look good on your transcript, you know."

That made me snort.

Dad riddled me with eye bullets. I felt the shrapnel and squelched any smart remarks I might've considered adding. "All you ever do is sit on your duff downstairs and play those mindless computer games. No wonder you're so pale. Both of you."

I tried to send Liam a silent message like, Blow it off. But he was closed to the outside world, the way he gets. Staring into the depths of his cereal bowl, drowning.

Dad creased the newspaper in half lengthwise, then quarters. Slow. Deliberate. He said to Liam, "Do this for me."

That wasn't fair. That was so unfair. Liam's Adam's apple bobbed. If Dad made him cry —

"I'm terrible at baseball," Liam said quietly. "You know that. I'm terrible at sports, period."

"Aw, come on. You're not that bad." Dad whapped his arm again. Liam absorbed the blow like a deflated punching bag. "You just don't work at it," Dad said. "You don't stick with it. You've got the size and speed, you know. You could bulk up some, build your strength. We could go to the Y together and work out on the weight machines. Skip said he'd sneak us into the batting cages after hours. He says he's been trying to recruit you since your freshman year when he saw you play soccer."

Liam lifted his head and locked eyes with Dad. "Which I did for you."

Dad shoved himself away from the table, rattling the dishes

and silverware. He stormed into the kitchen. Liam and I eyed each other. Before I could say anything, Mom rushed back in, grabbed her cell and stuffed it into her purse, then opened her Daytimer. "I may be late again tonight." She flipped a page. "I have a hair appointment at four. Regan, why don't you throw together a tuna noodle casserole for dinner. You know the ingredients."

Sure. Eye of newt. Tongue of snake.

She added, "Since you're taking Skills for Living, it'll be good practice."

For what? I wondered. Poisoning my family? "I have to baby-sit," I said, a little too gleefully.

Mom opened her mouth to lecture me again about being more help around here, more subservient, less of a guilt trip on her, when Liam piped up, "I'll do it."

"No, you won't," Dad barked. "That's not your job." He loomed in the doorway between the kitchen and dining room, arms folded.

"Why is it *my* job?" I flared. Forget what I said about him not being sexist. "I hate to cook. Let Liam do it if he wants to. He's a better —"

"Regan." Dad held up a hand to silence me. "Your mother asked *you*. It wouldn't kill you kids to be more help around the house. Both of you."

"It might," I said under my breath. "We could choke to death on the dust."

Mom shot me a scathing look.

"I'll be happy to help," Liam jumped to my rescue. "Just tell me what to do." He turned to Mom. "What can I do?"

She sighed wearily. "I don't want to argue about it. I'll just reschedule."

"Who's arguing?" I asked. "If Liam's willing —"

"Don't reschedule," Dad ordered Mom, ignoring me. "Regan is more than happy to help."

"Dad, I told you, I have to work. What do you want me to do, quit my job so I can stay home and cook your dinner? Clean your house? Wash your clothes —"

I stopped. Why did that sound familiar? Mom and Dad both glowered at me, avoiding eye contact with each other, of course.

Mom shoved her Daytimer into her purse. "I don't need my hair done today. I can reschedule."

Dad's fiery eyes scorched my face. Why? He should be happy he's getting his freaking tuna casserole.

On her way by me to retrieve her portfolio from the kitchen counter, Mom placed a hand on my shoulder. I must've flinched because she said, "For heaven's sake, Regan. What's the matter with you? You're tense, not sleeping. Do you need something to help you sleep?"

"No." I twisted out of her talons. "I'm fine." She was the junkie, not me. Her medicine cabinet was crammed with uppers and downers and equalizers and mood stabilizers. I think she was going through the change — mental pause. I just wish she'd lock up all her pills.

Mom didn't leave. She lingered behind me, catching my eye in the glass patio door, actually looking concerned.

"I'm fine," I repeated, swiveling my head up to her. "I just have a couple of tests this week." Which was true, even though I wasn't sweating them. Not as much as chemistry today.

She continued on her mission, snagging her portfolio and hurtling toward the door, jangling keys. "Have a good day," she said to air, mostly.

Liam called after her, "You too, Mom."

Dad rose to make his final pit stop before heading off to Home Depot, where today he'd be demonstrating the joy of caulking.

"Can I get a ride?" I asked Liam.

He didn't answer. I took that to be a yes. We slammed down the rest of our breakfast in silence.

The sound of the toilet flushing signaled Dad's imminent return, so Liam and I packed up. Dad paused in the foyer, zipping up his jacket. "Don't take pills, honey," he said to me. "Just get to bed earlier." He pointed at Liam. "Go see Skip after school. Do it."

"Yes, sir," Liam said.

The door whooshed open and shut.

I crossed my eyes at Liam, which he missed because he was charging for the exit.

I snared my backpack and parka, hustling to catch up, but by the time I locked the front door behind me he was already backing down the driveway. "Liam, wait!" I flew across the yard.

He gunned the engine and swerved into the street.

I lunged for the door handle.

Slowly Liam turned his head. The look on his face — the sheer force of it — made me drop my hand and stumble backward.

We're down the street at the Walshes' for our weekly backyard barbecue.

No, it was more eventful than that. The memory jogged loose. A birthday. It was Liam's ninth birthday party. The day was warm enough to have the party outdoors.

We're celebrating Liam's and Alyson's birthdays together. Alyson is Liam's best friend — has been since kindergarten. Our parents and her parents have been friends for years. We do lots of stuff together, like celebrate both birthdays.

Except that was the last year we did birthdays. Why?

Liam and Alyson are jumping around, hyper about opening presents. They invited a bunch of kids from school to their party. All girls, Dad notices. I hear him say to Mom in the Walshes' kitchen, "How come there aren't any boys at this party? Doesn't Liam have any of his own friends?"

I climb onto a stool at the breakfast nook and spin around; pretend I'm not listening.

"He has lots of friends," Mom says, arranging candles on the cake. "They all just happen to be girls. What's wrong with that?"

Dad strikes a match and begins to light the candles. I count them to myself: one, two, three . . .

He shakes his head. "A boy his age . . ." Dad doesn't finish. "I found his birthday wish list on the dresser."

Mom jams her hand inside her apron pocket, like she lost something.

"A Prom Barbie? A bra?" Dad arches his eyebrows.

"He was kidding, Jack," Mom says. "It was a joke."

"A joke, huh? Why didn't he show it to me? I would've gotten a kick out of it."

Mom doesn't answer.

Dad exhales a long breath. "I don't get that kid. I really don't."

. . . seven, eight, and one to grow on.

Dad adds, "Sometimes I think we don't connect like a father and son should. Maybe I'm doing something wrong —"

"Daddy, can I put it out?"

Dad jerks around, like he's surprised I'm there. "Hey, my little Ray gun. Come on over here and zap it." He smiles and holds out the match to me.

I hop off the stool and run over, wet my fingers with spit the way he showed me, and smash the match tip between them. "Ow," I yelp when it hisses, even though it doesn't hurt.

Dad kisses my fingers. Then he clamps his big hands around my waist and lifts me over his head. Balancing me by my stomach on his head, he swings me around in a circle until I squeal and Dad gets dizzy. I know I'm too old, but I still like to play Daddy's girly whirligig.

I spy Liam in the doorway. He's watching us, watching me go round and round. Dad finally sets me down. We're both laughing and staggering. I see Liam's eyes fix on mine and he gives me that look —

Hatred.

That was the look. He hated me.

Why? Because of the way Dad treated me, treats me still, different from him? Dad never played favorites, if that's what Liam thought. In fact, since his birthday was in March and mine fell a week after Christmas, Liam always got more presents than me. What did Liam want, to be the girly whirligig?

It struck me like a hammer to the head. Well, duh, Regan. That's exactly what he wanted. It's what he's always wanted. If Liam could wish for one thing in the world, one birthday present, he would ask to be born again. Born right, in the body of a girl.

Chapter 3

*L*iam had stranded me in Siberia without a sled. It had to be a hundred below today, and the high school was two miles away. I'd only walked half a block and my feet were already ice floes. "Damn you, Liam," I seethed aloud. "I hate you."

No, I didn't. He didn't hate me, either. He was just angry about his life, which I could understand. It must be horrible to be in the wrong body, to have this dual identity. I knew he suffered. I just wished he wouldn't take it out on me. It wasn't my fault I got the body he wanted. I wanted Britney Spears's body. Did I get it? No.

Okay, so that was minimizing Liam's misery. But damn. It was cold.

As my toes cracked and fissured inside my frozen Nikes, the question lingered: Why was that the last year we'd celebrated Liam's and Aly's birthdays together? Something else had happened. What?

"Here we go." Mom pivots in place, balancing the sheet cake across her forearms. It's decorated two ways. One half is a football field with miniature players; the other is a pink ballerina twirling on a painted lake.

Liam's eyes light up. "Cool," he breathes. "Can I have her?"

I see Dad look at Mom. She avoids his gaze. "Get everyone rounded up," she tells Liam.

"Hey, Aly," Liam calls down the deck steps. "Wait'll you see this cake."

We sing and eat cake and I hear Liam pleading with Alyson to let him keep the ballerina. She doesn't care. She's into unicorns now. She'd give the ballerina to Liam anyway just because they're best friends. She likes to make him beg, though. Same way I do.

Liam and Alyson chant, "One, two, three, go!" They tear into their presents.

I sit by Alyson as she passes me everything she gets. Jewelry and clothes and hair scrunchies. Liam has to see, too. He oohs and aahs and touches and holds her presents. He keeps them too long because Mom has to say more than once, "Pass it on, Liam, so everyone else can see."

The gifts dwindle and finally all the packages are opened. But Liam's still riffling through the wrappings. Frantically.

"That's it, Liam," Alyson says.

"No, it isn't."

"I'm telling you, that's it."

Liam checks under the table, behind his chair. He turns to Mom. "Where are they?"

"What?" Mom asks.

Liam tilts his head at her. "You know. My presents from you."

"We got you the basketball hoop and the scooter," Dad says. "Isn't that enough?"

"No, because he's a greedy bastard," Alyson blurts out.

"Aly, really!" her mother scolds. Mrs. Walsh blushes and shields her face behind her hand. Dad and Mr. Walsh howl.

Liam stands up fast. He hoists his hands onto his hips and says, "Come on. Where are they?"

Dad bends over and grabs Liam's new basketball. "Let's go hang the hoop and I'll show you the O'Neill oopsy-daisy drop shot." He tosses the ball to Liam.

Liam catches it, but throws it on the ground. "That's not what I asked for. Where's my bra?"

A couple of girls behind me titter. Alyson giggles and covers her mouth. Mrs. Walsh does, too. I'm not laughing. I see Liam's face turn red. Dad's spine goes rigid.

Liam steps away from him. I do, too. The look on Dad's face . . . Liam whirls on Mom. "You asked me what I wanted and I told you."

It happens so fast it's a blur. Dad clutches Liam's hand and almost wrenches his arm from the socket. He yanks Liam toward the house. I hear Dad snarl under his breath, "We're going to have a talk, young man."

Liam whimpers, "No, Daddy."

Dad hauls him up the steps and into the house.

Mom and Mrs. Walsh start clearing the table while all the girls paw through Alyson's stuff. Aly takes me aside and whispers in my ear, "Liam's so funny. Isn't he?"

I nod. Force a smile.

She bites her bottom lip, gazing wistfully up the deck stairs. "I'm going to marry him, you know. Then you and me'll be sisters." She squeezes my hand.

I squeeze back, thinking, I already have a sister.

Had I really thought that? If I could see the girl in Liam, why couldn't Mom and Dad? Why couldn't everyone?

Whatever Dad had said in the house that day had caused a rift in Liam's universe. A black hole had opened up and swallowed him whole. Swallowed her — Lia Marie, her first chosen name. She'd receded, retreated, withdrawn.

But not forever. Not for long.

Weird. She was nine and asked for a bra? I was eleven before I got up the guts to ask Mom. But then Lia Marie always accused me of suffering from arrested development.

Tires screeched at my side and in reflex I hurdled a snowbank.

Liam's eyes met mine through his car window. He motioned with his chin for me to get in.

I considered making him beg. Oh, forget it. I'd already lost three toes to frostbite.

I climbed into his Spyder. At least he had the top up today. Sometimes he drove with it down, even in winter. As if he couldn't feel the cold; as if his body wasn't connected to his brain.

We rode in silence, me trying to coax circulation back into my fingers, Liam staring ahead with those uninhabited eyes. As we ascended Heart Attack Hill, Horizon High rose like the lost city of Atlantis. Then sank back into the sea as we roared past.

"Liam, drop me off," I said, panic rising in my chest. "I have to go to school today. I have a test first period and a paper to turn in in History." Not to mention Chemistry, which I didn't. "Liam!"

"I can't do this," he murmured, running a stop sign. "I want to kill him."

"Who, Dad? I'll help you. Just not this morning, okay?"

Liam switched lanes and veered onto the highway ramp. Great. Here we go again, I thought. He can ditch every other day and still get straight A's. His scores on the SATs have colleges recruiting *him*. I miss one day and flunk out. The only college that's going to be interested in me is F.U.

"Liam —"

"Not Dad," he says, merging into traffic. "Me. I want to kill me."

I sighed wearily.

I hated when he got this way — depressive, suicidal. His pain was so palpable, it made me hurt. Huddling inside my parka, which did nothing for the chill inside, I resigned myself to repeating my sophomore year. So what? How insignificant was school compared to saving my brother from himself?

Liam exited at Broadway Avenue and swung into a Starbucks. We sat in the car, neither of us making a move to get out. "What are we doing here?" I finally said.

Liam didn't answer.

I pointed to a sign on the door. "'Help wanted.' Is that a hint? I should be a barista? It's probably the only job I'll be able to get after I flunk out of high school."

He didn't take the hint. Instead, he removed the keys from the ignition and swung his long legs out the door to head inside.

As if programmed to be his lapdog, I heeled.

Liam ordered a latte and I got a mocha. Since he was paying, I went back for a blueberry scone. We sat at the window counter, sipping our drinks and watching the world go by. The real world as opposed to Liam's parallel universe. All I could think was, I need to be in school today. I need to go to chemistry. A woman lugging an overstuffed pillowcase shuffled into a Laundromat across the parking lot at the same moment a fat man exited. He dragged a little kid behind him. The kid was throwing a temper tantrum, stamping and wailing. We couldn't hear what the dad — or whoever he was — was screaming at the kid, but you could pretty much guess.

Liam said, "Watch. He'll grow up to make his father proud."

I exhaled a long sigh. "Liam —"

Like a sinking ship, he listed to the side. His head came to rest on my shoulder. "What am I going to do, Re?" he said. "I'm dying inside."

Oh God. Not this again. I looped an arm around his bony back and held his head. "It'll be okay."

"No it won't. It'll never be okay."

"Lia Marie —"

"Luna."

"Huh?"

"It's Luna."

"Oh, right. Luna." Her new name was going to take some getting used to.

A grungy guy at the end of the counter, who'd been keying into his laptop, stopped and stared at us. I met his eyes and widened mine, like, What? You got a problem?

He resumed working.

Liam lifted his head and straightened in his seat. "Every day, the same old thing. Hiding, lying, holding her in. It's too hard. I can't do it."

Don't cry, I thought. Please don't cry.

"When people look at me, they don't see the real me. They can't because I look like this." He swept a hand down his chest.

What was I supposed to say? How many times had I heard this? "I like that shirt," I settled on, trying to lighten the mood. "Is it new?"

He cast me a withering glance.

"Sorry."

"No one will ever know the person I am inside. The true me. The girl, the woman. All they see is this . . . this nothing."

"You're not nothing," I snapped. "You're a person. You're Liam."

"Liam." He let out a short laugh. "Who's that? A caricature I've created. A puppet, a mime, a cartoon character. I'm this male macho version of a son that Dad has in his head."

"Forget Dad," I told him. "What does he matter? You don't have to play baseball, okay?"

Liam closed his eyes and lowered his chin to his chest. "I need to let her out, Re."

"What do you mean? How?"

"I'm strangling her. She's not the one I want to eliminate. All this suppressing and holding her down, keeping her caged, perpetuating this fraud, this sham. I can't do it anymore." He shook his head. "I can't." He raised his chin and looked at me. "It won't go away. No matter how much I wish, or pray, she's always with me. She *is* me. I am *her*. I want to *be* her. I want to be Luna."

"You are," I said. "You can be."

"No." He blinked. "I mean all the time. I want to be free. I want to transition."

Transition? He'd never used that word. Transition meant change. Like, move from one place to another. But how? Where?

He was searching my face, probing my eyes. "You understand, don't you, Re?" he asked.

"Uh, yeah," I lied. He'd talked about coming out before, breaking free. Lots of times. But that's as far as it went, being free.

He continued to stare at me, watch me. It made me uneasy when he did that. I broke off a corner of scone and nibbled it. Stale. "You want this?" I shoved it at him.

He said, "Mom was right, you know. You look like a zombie. A dab of Preparation H under your eyes would shrink those bags."

"Shut up." I smacked his arm. "You're the reason I have bags."

"Hey, did you like the blonde wig I wore this morning?" He brightened a little. "It goes well with red, I think, but the color's a bit brassy. Too platinum. And too bold to wear with casual slacks. I think the brown curly is better for casual wear. Don't you?"

Once she started talking hair and clothes, we'd be here forever. "I need to get back to school, Lia." I checked my watch. Nine forty-five. If we hauled ass I could make my history class. Then I'd only have to repeat half the year.

She sighed. "It's *Luna*. You're so narcissistic and demanding."

"What about you?" What was narcissistic?

She batted her eyelashes and finger-tipped her chest. "Me?"

She was so weird. "Don't you have class?" I asked, swaddling my scone in a napkin for burial.

"Senior Seminar," she replied. "Nonrequired attendance." Gulping down the rest of her latte, she slid off the stool and added, "Will you run into Wal-Mart and buy me some underwear first? Mine are getting a little gray."

I trailed her to the door. "You have to use bleach with your whites."

"So I've been told," she said over her shoulder. "I'm just a girl, not a domestic goddess like yourself."

I ground a knuckle into her shoulder blade. At this rate we might make school by noon. Oh, well. It was bad enough he had to take his girly wash to the Laundromat. There was no way *I* was going to wash it. I didn't mind buying him panties and bras, but handling the dirties . . . ew.

We climbed into the Spyder. Liam dug out his wallet and handed me a twenty. "Get me Maidenform high-cut in beige, if they have it. White if they don't. Size five."

"Size five," I mocked. He grinned as I ripped the money out from between his first two fingers. It irked me that he wore a smaller size than me — and knew it.

Chapter 4

We got back to school around lunchtime. Liam's lunch. Mine was already over. He headed off to find Alyson in the cafeteria while I barreled up the stairs to the science wing. The closer I got to class, the sicker I felt.

I hated high school. It hated me back. All the cliques and clubs and sports and spirit squads going on around me, without me. People joking and laughing with their friends in the hall. High school flaunted it, threw it in my face, all the fun I wasn't having. All because of —

No. Not fair. It wasn't Liam's fault. This was my choice, my way of dealing.

Fifth period was already in progress, so I slithered in the door, head down, praying Mr. Bruchac was his usual talking head. Lecturing, oblivious to bodies dropping like flies from boredom.

No such luck. He was sitting at his desk, and I had to pass by. He peered over his horn-rims, making sure he caught my eye, then ticked a check by my name on his seating chart.

Bastard.

The one class I would've loved to ditch, I couldn't. Not today. Today we were starting labs.

Bruchac had been warning us for a month, since the winter term began, that we should carefully consider who to pair up with for labs. The rest of the semester we'd be living and breathing chemistry with this person, he said, so we should choose someone we could work with closely.

Closely. Close. The word set off an alarm in my head.

Our final grade was contingent on how well we worked together, our total contribution. The contribution part didn't scare me, since my share was going to be one hundred percent. Every day I'd taken a head count. There were twenty-three of us. Divided by two. That left a remainder. Me. I'd volunteer to work alone. No problem. It'd make my life so much easier.

Up front Bruchac droned on about how laboratory reports had to be signed by both partners; problem sets and worksheets were to be individual efforts; anyone caught cheating would receive an automatic zero. "Goose egg." He got up and drew it on the board. "And that, folks, is not the symbol for oxygen."

He was such a dork. He wore a suit and tie every day, which wouldn't be too bad if his outfits matched. His jackets were checkered and his shirts striped, like he'd built his wardrobe from the Barnum & Bailey liquidation sale. Not that I was glam girl of the year or anything, but get a clue. All the other male teachers wore jeans, mostly.

"Quizzes can be retaken once," Bruchac said. "But if you miss a test, it'll take the promise of your firstborn child to persuade me to let you retake it."

Oh ha ha. I was carving an infinity sign into my notebook cover when the moment of doom arrived. Bruchac announced, "With a minimum of ruckus, choose your partners and stake your claim to a lab station."

My stomach lurched. Surreptitiously I glanced around the room. A lot of the people in here I knew. Not well, of course, but I'd grown up in this neighborhood. My only real friends were Alyson and Liam, which was fine. Really. I mean, who had time for a hundred friends? Sometimes I felt as if my brother and I shared one life. His. We were both disembodied hollows.

My eyes landed on a solitary figure in the back who was thundering up the aisle toward me. I swiveled around fast. Please, God, no, I prayed, invoking my invisibility shield. Not Hoyt Doucet. He was evil. Satan incarnate. I despised him so much. He'd been Liam's worst nightmare ever since the Doucets had moved in down the street a few years ago. Moved into Alyson's house, as a matter of fact, when the Walshes upscaled. Liam had had to leave for school half an hour early his whole eighth grade year to avoid being ambushed by Hoyt Doucet.

If Hoyt asked me to be his lab partner, I'd regurgitate my scone all over him. It'd be an honor.

There was a tap on my shoulder. "You want to work together?"

I whirled, prepared to blow chunks. But Hoyt charged past me, the stench of sewer gas in his wake. My eyes refocused. The voice had emanated from lips, which smiled down on me, and a head, which tilted, on a neck, which extended from a body. Nothing hollow about it. Rock solid, top to bottom.

"How 'bout it? We could be the dynamic duo. Make that the dynamite duo — blow up the lab. Kaboom!" He grinned.

This was a dream. Who was this guy, and how had he penetrated the shield?

"You want . . . me?" I croaked, palming my chest.

Bruchac bellowed, "Could we get this done today, people? You have thirty seconds to find a lab rat and a station."

I scooted back my chair and stood. Stunned. This guy, this real-living-person-like guy, motioned me to follow him. Which I would have, into a noxious cloud of carbon monoxide probably. He was like, hot.

"Is this one all right?" he asked, indicating an unclaimed sink area by the periodic table chart.

I was paralyzed. It was all I could do to nod.

"I'm Chris," he said.

"Um, Regan." My voice sounded strained, weak. Same way I felt.

"I'm sorta new here." He looped a leg over the lab stool. "Are you, too? You looked the way I felt when Bruchac said we had to pair up."

I laughed a little. "No, I'm just your basic loser."

He made a face. "Yeah, right." His eyes plumbed my depth, causing my internal temperature to soar. Was he checking me out?

God. What if he was? I'd dribbled mocha down my shirt.

A spike of fear lodged in my spine. For some reason, my vocal cords engaged. "You still have," I looked at my watch, "twelve seconds to change your mind. Find someone else and save your reputation."

One side of his lip cricked up. "I found you. I'll take my chances."

Meltdown. Massive nuclear meltdown. I'd been rehearsing this so often — hiding behind my shield until everyone else had a partner; assuring Bruchac I didn't mind working alone; making the lie sound convincing — that I was having a hard time believing the scenario was playing out differently. Should I pinch myself? Pinch him?

The silence between us grew, like we didn't know what to say next, or do. Incompatible species, crossed my mind. We were. He was human. Chris? Chris, did he say? He was turning on and off the water faucet, running his index finger back and forth under the spigot. Flicking me with water. Grinning. Baiting me.

Maybe I could handle this. I mean, it wasn't like we were dating or anything. Should I act mad? Splash him back?

I didn't even know how to be with a guy. What did you say?

Was it permissible to remark, "Your hair is gorgeous?" Because it was. Black as ink and silky soft. A shock of it fell across his right eye. The left one seemed to gleam, twinkle, tease me.

Get a grip, Regan. I leaned away from him and opened my spiral. Should I comment on his clothes? I mean, he looked cool. He might take it wrong, though. Think I was being facetious. His clothing wasn't new, or nice. His jeans had a rip under the pocket and his long-sleeved tee was frayed at the cuffs. His hands were huge, I noticed. And there was grease under his cuticles. Real grease.

I remembered this time Liam was in tenth grade, I think, and he'd gotten a job at Jiffy Lube. It didn't last long. He'd only done it to appease Dad, that whole macho thing. But Liam said if Dad ever asked about the gunk around his cuticles, he could always claim it was grease.

Pink grease? Right, Liam. Good thing Dad never asked.

As Bruchac began to explain our first assignment, scribbling equations on the board that might as well have been scientific notation in Swahili, Chris seemed enthralled with the way water trickles through a loose fist. This might've hypnotized me all day, too, if Bruchac's voice hadn't sliced through the stupor. "Before we begin," he said, "in the top drawer you'll find a laminated sheet titled, 'Laboratory Safety Guidelines.' Remove this now, if you will, and read along with me."

I pulled on the drawer handle. It stuck. I gave it a good yank. It wouldn't budge. Chris jimmied it. No use. He bent down to check underneath, while I braced against the cabinet leg with my foot and wrenched on the handle. The drawer flew open, smacking Chris in the forehead. He grunted and reeled backward, losing his balance and thudding to the floor on his butt. His stool teetered and fell on top on him. Everyone around us snarkled with laughter.

I died. As I slid off my stool to help him up, he scrabbled to his feet. "Are you okay?" I asked.

"I'm cool," Chris said.

I reached over to brush him off. God, I almost touched him.

"Sorry," I mumbled, as he righted his stool. "I'm sorry. Are you hurt?"

"I'm fine." Chris slammed the drawer back into the slot. He seemed mad.

"I'm sorry."

He resettled on his stool.

"I'm really sorry. Are you okay? I mean it, I'm sorry. I didn't think —"

"I'm fine, Regan." He looked at me, hard. "Regan," he said again and smiled. "I like your name."

My name. It sounded strange coming from his lips. Sounded . . . nice. I never liked my name. It was a last name, not a girl's name. He wasn't mad. Good.

Bruchac was eyeing Chris and me over his glasses. *He* was mad. Oops. Not missing a beat, Bruchac continued his recitation. He was on safety tip number four by the time my brain caught up. "'Report all accidents. No accident is too small to report. Five. Know the location of fire exits.' Mister," Bruchac scanned his class list, "Garazzo. Can you point out the fire exits?"

Chris flinched beside me. He long-armed the two doors. "Front. Rear," he crossed his arms, "and over the wings. Emergency exits must remain clear at all times."

I snorted.

Bruchac sighed wearily. "'Safety glasses,'" he went on, "'i.e., splash-proof goggles, must be worn while working with any chemical that could be harmful to the eyes.'" Bruchac paused and glanced up. "This means at *all* times. Sorry, girls. It's a state law. Chemistry is not a beauty contest."

Oh, brother, I thought. Talk about sexist.

Chris muttered, "Pig."

I was beginning to like this guy. Not Bruchac.

"'In addition, you must confine long hair while working in the laboratory. Keep it away from flames and machinery.' Girls." He widened his eyes at us again. "Got that?"

Hey, come on. There were guys with long hair, too.

My head tingled suddenly. Chris dangled my hair over the Bunsen burner and went, "Pssst." Made me laugh. Too loud.

Bruchac nailed us with a death look. Chris and I ducked our heads, but couldn't suppress the snickering.

As Bruchac wandered around, noting lab partners on his chart and passing out the first lab assignment, Chris surveyed the contents of our cabinets. He located the goggles and handed me a pair. "You must wear these at all times," he mimicked. "It's a state law, girls. Chemistry is not a beauty contest." He snapped the elastic band over his head. I copied him and put mine on.

We looked at each other through the clear plastic, and burst out laughing again. Me, because I was hysterical. Him, because I looked like a geek.

Bruchac stalled in front of our station to glare and tick off our names. Apparently, fun was not an element of chemistry. He handed us the lab paper and moved on.

Chris plastered the single sheet against his goggles. "What are we supposed to do first?" he asked. "I can't read this."

It was a terrible Xerox, like Bruchac couldn't splurge on fresh toner for us. I scanned the sheet and read out loud, "'Inventory the supplies. Familiarize yourselves with the lab equipment. Count the test tubes and pipets —'"

"Who are the Pipettes?" Chris goosenecked the room. "Are they here?"

I went to smack him, but stopped myself in time.

"Is this a good school?" Chris asked suddenly. "I mean, I transferred here to play ball, since Horizon took state last year. Hewitt's, like, a legend. I'd kill to play for him. What's the social life like? I hear it's a big party scene."

He was asking me? My social life consisted of one word: utter void. Okay, that's two words, but you get the gist. "Yeah, it's wild," I said. According to Aly and Liam, who actually got invited to parties. Aly got invited more often, and dragged Liam along when he'd go. Although, Liam was pretty popular himself. With girls, anyway.

I felt Chris staring at me. What? He was just staring, his dark eyes boring holes into the side of my face. I swiveled my head slowly to face him.

His eyes dropped.

Did he blush? I thought only girls blushed. Liam blushed, but he was a girl.

Chris mumbled, "Sorry. You're just . . ."

Melting? Freakish?

"Are you two planning your wedding or what?" Bruchac boomed behind us.

We both jumped.

"You might want to get hopping on this assignment before the honeymoon is over."

I twisted around. Bruchac's tie drew my attention, since it was dangling in my face. Down the entire length, a hundred little Tweety Birds were embroidered in full color. Please. Why not advertise you're Looney Tunes?

"You're Liam O'Neill's sister, aren't you?" Bruchac said.

I turned back.

He added, "I just now made the connection."

Break it, I thought. Every semester I deliberately avoided taking classes taught by the teachers Liam had had, since he was like their wunderkind. Scientists should publish the definitive study that proves genius does *not* run in families. Ever since I started school, I felt like I had this older sister to live up to. She was smarter, nicer, prettier — or would've been if she could dress the part. Liam's footsteps were way too big for me to follow in. I kept tripping on his high heels.

Bruchac circled our lab station and pointed a finger me; actually waggled it in my face, as if to say, "I've got your number now, missy."

Crap. Why was he the only one teaching Chem I?

Bruchac addressed the room, "I have high expectations of everyone in this class." In a lowered voice, he added, "Especially you, Ms. O'Neill, now that I know." He trundled off toward the front.

Chris arched eyebrows at me.

"Don't ask."

He said under his breath, "On the A.B.S, I put Bruchac at ten."

I frowned. "The A.B. what?"

"A.B.S. Asshole Behavior Scale."

I grinned. He got that right.

We busied ourselves with the assignment. We were deep into counting pipets and test tubes when Chris reached over and wrote at the bottom of our inventory sheet:

Sofa

King

Wee

Todd

Did

I blinked up at him. "Huh?"

"Say the words," he told me. "Keep repeating them. Let me know what you come up with." He clinked both sides of a beaker with glass pipets.

I read aloud, "Sofa king wee Todd did." Again. "Sofa king —"

I got it. I burst into laughter. I couldn't stop laughing. My eyes began to tear. I was giggling so hard it got Chris going and we sank to the floor to fly under Bruchac's radar.

The bell saved us. "Turn in your inventory forms and you're dismissed," Bruchac said over the rising din.

Chris stood up and began to scratch out his Sofa King message on the inventory form. I snatched the sheet out from under his pencil. Rushing it to the front, I smacked it atop the stack of assignments on Bruchac's desk and exaggerated a smile. Bruchac smiled back and winked.

Gag.

At the door I turned and sailed a real smile across the room to Chris. He seemed kind of freaked, but I didn't think he had anything to worry about. Bruchac'd never figure out the joke. And if he did, maybe he'd figure out something else — I wasn't Liam.

Chapter 5

*M*y head was still in a helium balloon when I floated into the house after school. Wow, I had a lab partner. I flung open the basement door and the lights flickered. Down the stairwell, I called, "Yo."

Liam had rigged up a silent alarm system years ago — his safeguard against detection, should anyone wander downstairs while he was dressed as Lia Marie. Excuse me — Luna. He'd wired it so the basement lights blinked on and off whenever the door opened. It used to drive Dad crazy. For months he searched the electrical system for a short, and never could find the problem. For times when the lights weren't on, Liam had programmed sound effects to mimic footfalls on the stairs. *Creak, creak, creak.* It felt like you were tripping off to Transylvania.

Liam was careful. Paranoid, actually. He'd never been caught. At least, not by Mom or Dad.

It seemed like a lot of worry for nothing. The parental units pretty much designated the basement as our private space. We had our bedrooms and shared bathroom down there, plus the big room where we could hang out and watch TV. Mom and Dad rarely ventured downstairs, and when they did they always announced themselves. The way I do automatically. Which, if you think about it, is weird behavior for parents. Aren't they usually nosing around, invading your space? Aly's parents were, which is why she hung out here.

As usual, Alyson was in the basement playing video games with Liam. His job — one of them — was a game tester. This company, Games People Play or something stupid like that, downloaded beta versions of all the new games their cyber-heads created, then sicced Liam on them. It was his job to play all the levels, to evaluate them, rate their fun factor, graphics, ease or difficulty of user interaction. Most of what he spent time on was seeing if he could crash the system. And he usually did. It got to where the geeks were asking him to look at the code and fix bugs. The company paid him megabucks to do this. Their kid wizard, they called him.

From the computer speakers mounted overhead, a scream split the air — *Aaah!* It was Alyson's voice. My feet hit the bottom steps running. "Are you okay?" I dropped my pack at her side. "What happened?"

She glanced over, briefly. "He vaporized me." She returned to the monitor, thumb-punching her joystick. "Dammit, Liam. How did you find me?" Aly said.

Liam's voice echoed out of the speakers: *"Ha. Ha. Ha."* A sinister laugh. Spooky.

Liam pressed a series of buttons on his joystick and I crouched beside Aly to study the monitor. The characters in the game were Alyson and Liam, perfect clones, right down to their clothes. "How'd you do that?" I asked.

Neither responded. A fireball shot out of a handheld bazooka that Liam was carting. Alyson pedaled down an alley, but the blazing cannonball hit her square in the back. Her scream made my ears squinch. Blood splattered the screen and dribbled down. The Aly clone dissolved in green goo. "Goddammit, Liam," live Aly shrieked. "Give me a chance, at least."

His laugh echoed overhead: *"Ha. Ha. Ha."* Live Liam smirked at Alyson. "You're toast, baby."

"What is this game?" I asked again.

Alyson flung her joystick to the ground. "Something Liam's writing. He's fixed it so he's the only one who can win." She scrambled to her feet.

"Not true," Liam said, tallying his score and hers. "The characters are able to learn from their mistakes. Unfortunately, you keep making the same one. I told you, Aly, stay out of dark alleys."

She slapped him on the head. "Kill him for me, will you, Re?" She stalked across the room.

I reached for my backpack. "He'll have to do that without my help."

Liam's head shot up and fixed me with a look.

"I didn't mean —" I began. Stupid. Stupid, stupid, stupid.

Liam resumed the tally.

"Did you guys decide what you want yet?" Alyson spoke behind me.

I whirled around and saw we weren't alone in the basement. There were two other girls here who I hadn't noticed in my rush to rescue Aly. They were huddled over the scarred coffee table that doubled as Liam's office. One of them was ordering a computer.

Liam's other job was building PCs for people. Actually taking orders and assembling hardware in the basement. Like I said, brainiac.

Great. He had to have customers today. I really wanted to lock myself in my bedroom and put on my *Carmen* CD. Crank up the volume and lose myself in, "L'amour est un oiseau rebelle." Love is a rebellious bird. Forget that now. Alyson was okay with my opera addiction — though she called it an "unnatural bent," an expression she'd obviously picked up from Liam. But I wouldn't want it to get around.

Like anyone would care what I was into.

"How much if I want a scanner?" One of the girls wound her hair around her index finger. She didn't look familiar. Had an accent, too. German? Russian? Was Liam going global now?

"What kind do you want?" Aly asked. "You can get an all-in-one copier, scanner, fax for about the same price. Right, Liam?"

He grunted. I watched him rekey a line of code in his game.

It made me wonder again if Liam paid Aly to be his business partner. Probably not. He was so cheap.

She wouldn't care. She'd pretty much do whatever he asked.

"Just check off everything you want," Alyson told the girl. "We'll give you the best price." She retrieved her Diet Coke off the top of the TV and went back to Liam. Plopping down beside him, she said, "One more game." She handed him her soda and picked up her joystick. "Start at year one again, with us as babies. Except give me the pink Pampers this time. And let me re-record my baby scream. It sounds too *Rugrats.*"

The lights flickered and Liam's head swiveled automatically, his gaze leveling the stairs. A voice called down, "It's the FBI. You're busted." Dad.

Liam relaxed and resumed loading the game, while I made a beeline for my bedroom. "Regan, Elise called and asked if you could come an hour early tonight," Dad yelled. "She and David want to go out to dinner with friends. I told her you'd be there."

I exhaled in disgust.

"Regan?"

"I heard you." It was fine, but I didn't need Dad making my decisions for me.

He waited, for what I wasn't sure. There was nothing else to say, was there? The basement door closed.

Alyson frantically punched at her joystick, then shrilled, "Dammit, Liam!"

Her baby scream rocked the speakers: *"Waaah!"*
Liam laughed: *"Ha. Ha. Ha."*
I closed my bedroom door to shut out Planet Weird.

⁓

There was an hour before baby-sitting. I could do homework.
Or not. I loaded *Carmen* and remoted to the "oiseau rebelle"
track, then slid to the floor next to the bed and rested my head
against the mattress.

Carmen.

Carmen. My best friend, Carmen.

*"What time is everyone coming?" Carmen asks, dumping her
overnight bag on my bedroom floor and squatting beside it.*

"I told them seven."

*She smiles up at me. "Good. We'll have time to listen to most of
Tristan and Isolde." She hands me the CD from her bag and I slip
it into my player.*

*Carmen's been my best friend for almost a year now, my whole
sixth grade year. When she moved here everyone thought she'd crash-
landed in a time machine. She wears these long flowered skirts and
tie-dye shirts, right out of the sixties, with lots of jangly jewelry. Carmen's mother is a contralto who sings opera in a professional company. She named Carmen after the feisty peasant girl in the opera
Carmen. Carmen was raised around music, theater; they're just a
part of her life. She knows everything about opera, and she teaches me.
She's really turned me on to it.*

*It was friendship at first sight for Carmen and me. I don't know
why. Don't know what she saw in boring old me. She is exotic and in-
teresting and different from all the neighborhood girls I grew up with.
What I like most about Carmen is that she doesn't care what other
people think of her. She's true to herself.*

Carmen punches up the volume and we sit on my floor against the bed, breathing in the "Prelude to Act I." *Glorious. This is a tragic opera, sort of like* Romeo and Juliet, *where lovers are betrayed and die in each other's arms. Carmen and I both swoon along with Isolde.*

People arrive for the slumber party at the worst possible moment — Isolde's dramatic death scene. As Isolde sinks dying upon her lover Tristan's already lifeless form, Carmen grabs the box of Kleenex and passes it to me. We quickly dry our eyes.

Why was I having a slumber party? It wasn't my birthday. Couldn't have been Christmas break because all the girls were wearing shorts. Maybe we were celebrating the end of sixth grade, our continuation. Yeah, that was it.

Shannon Eiber surveys the basement and directs where each girl in her entourage should roll out her sleeping bag. Carmen whispers to me, "Control freak."

Really, I think. But I'm almost grateful Shannon's taking over. I've never hosted a slumber party at my house before. Never had much to do with Shannon Eiber, either.

So why did I invite her to the party?

I didn't, I remembered. She'd invited herself. She had the hots for Liam at the time. All the girls did. If they only knew . . .

Of course Shannon doesn't go anywhere without her groupies. I'm not proud of it, but I long to be one Shannon's chosen few. Just to know what it feels like to be popular. For one day.

"Hi, Re," *Shannon says, rolling her sleeping bag beside me.* "Your house is really nice."

"Thanks," *I reply. Compared to hers, our house is a dump.*

She asks, "Where's Liam?"

My eyes cut to Liam's bedroom door, which is locked, of course. I breathe a little sigh of relief, knowing he's been banished to the guest room upstairs for the night.

Before I can answer, the lights flicker. Footsteps creak on the basement stairs as Alyson calls, "Got room for one more?"

"Sure," I sing, happy to hear her voice. I scoot my sleeping bag over so she can squeeze between me and Shannon. When Aly heard about the party, she asked if she could come. I was surprised. Aly's two years older than us; I'm sure she thinks we're babies. She'd never say it, though. Aly's too good a friend.

"Where's Liam?" she asks as she settles in. She removes her scrunchie and shakes out her ponytail.

"Didn't you see him upstairs?" I answer. The lights flicker again and Dad bellows, "Man overboard. Take cover."

A couple of girls squeal and burrow into their sleeping bags. Oh, brother. We haven't even put on our pj's yet. Dad makes a big production of covering his eyes and acting all embarrassed. He's wearing his cutoff sweatpants, which reveal his white, hairy legs. I'm mortified. Go away.

"Who wants pizza?" he asks.

Hands shoot up. Dad takes our order and disappears. Thank God.

I've been to a couple of sleepovers at Carmen's, but I'm not sure what to do next. If it was just us, we'd play an opera.

I don't have to worry; Shannon's a pro. "Let's play Yes, No, Maybe," she pipes up. "Everyone get in a circle."

Carmen rolls her eyes at me. Really. I hate party games. I should've had a plan.

Shannon's roving eyes take in the current company and zero in on a victim — me. "Regan," she points a lethal-looking fingernail at me. "You're in the hot seat."

"Um, okay. How do you play this game again?" I ask.

Her finger directs me to the middle of the circle. Shannon explains, "Whatever question we ask, you have to answer honestly with yes, no, or maybe."

Carmen huffs and says, "That isn't how you play. You can't answer with yes, no, or maybe." She scorches Shannon with a look.

"Oh yeah, huh?" Shannon grins. "Get it, Regan?" She blinks innocently at me.

"Yes," I say. How dumb.

"You're out." Shannon smirks.

"No fair," Carmen jumps in. "We haven't started yet."

"Just kidding. God, Carmen. Chill."

Carmen and Shannon are not compatible units. Oil and vinegar, as Mom would say. They do not mix. "I'll start." Aly raises her hand. She's curled cross-legged on her sleeping bag. "Is your brother's name Liam?"

I almost say, No, it's Lia Marie, but catch myself. "Yes."

"You're out." Shannon smiles.

"What?"

"You said yes."

I look at Aly. She shrugs and makes a sorry face. Shannon adds, "I didn't think it was that hard a question." Which cracks everyone up. Crap. I hate party games. As I slither back to my bag, Aly informs me, "You get to pick the next victim, Re."

"Okay, you," I tell Aly. I know she won't embarrass me.

She curls a lip, but scrabbles into the middle.

"You get to ask the first question, too," Carmen informs me.

I think. Not very hard. "Is your real name Alyson?"

"That's original," Shannon mutters behind her hand to her best friend of the week, Kylie.

"Mmm hmm," Aly hums.

Shannon asks her, "Are you in love?"

Aly shoots her a dark look. "I might be. Why? Are you?"

Shannon blushes. "You can't answer a question with a question. But since you asked, no. Are you?"

"None of your business." Aly lifts her hair and lets it fall.

"No fair," Shannon whines. "You have to answer. Regan, make her play the game."

Shannon doesn't know Alyson. You don't make Alyson Walsh do anything.

"This is so juvenile." Carmen clucks her tongue. She gets to her feet, adding, "I thought we were celebrating our coming-of-age, not our return to kindergarten. Could we just watch a movie or something, Regan?" She touches my shoulder.

"Yeah," I say, feeling relieved. "That's what I had planned."

The circle unravels. I remote on the TV. While Shannon and Kylie paw through our videotapes and DVDs — which are mostly Liam's classic movies that he records late at night — Alyson heads for the stairs.

"I'm going to check on the pizzas," she says over her shoulder.

I realize suddenly why she's here. To protect her property. Her footsteps creak and the lights flash.

Shannon rejects all the movies. Big surprise. I'm tempted to tell her these are all Liam's favorites, but something stops me. Liam's private world. I'm the only one who knows what goes on in it.

We channel-surf until we find a rerun of Angel. A few minutes into it, the pizzas arrive. Dad carts down the boxes, stacked across his outstretched arms, with exaggerated ceremony. Behind him, Liam and Aly carry plates and napkins and sodas. They set everything on the coffee table.

"Hi, Liam," Shannon purrs. All the other girls greet him, too. He says "Hi" and smiles at everyone.

Alyson sees this exchange and narrows her eyes. She rises to her tiptoes and whispers something in Liam's ear. He doesn't react.

Yes, he does. He lowers himself to the floor and opens the top box of pizza.

"Come on, Liam." Dad motions him to the stairs. "This is a girls-only party."

"I need to taste-test these," he says. "Food safety saves lives."

All the girls giggle.

It wasn't that funny.

Dad scoops the air with a cupped hand. "Let's go."

Liam looks at Aly, then me. Questioning. Almost pleading.

"It's okay, Mr. O'Neill," Aly says. "He can stay and eat. Right, Re?"

I don't want him to stay. I don't know why.

"I don't think so," Dad replies. "You've heard of raging hormones?" He thumbs at Liam.

I want to die. So does Liam. I send him a mental message: Let's murder our father in his sleep.

"Liam!" Dad barks.

Liam sighs and pushes to his feet. He trundles up the stairs after Dad.

We inhale the pizzas, then Shannon retrieves her backpack and upends it. Jars and containers and tubes of cosmetics tumble out and into a pile. The collection rivals Lia Marie's stash. "Have you guys seen this nail polish that glows in the dark?" Shannon digs around for it. "My cousin brought it back from London when she went over on spring break." She finds what she's looking for — three bottles: pink, green, and yellow. She passes them around.

We remove our sandals and start painting our fingernails and toenails. The lights flicker again. Out of the shadowy stairwell, Liam appears. "Sorry," he says. "I need to get a book."

Every eye follows him across the room.

He hesitates at his bedroom door and turns around. I'm the only one not gawking. He's behind me, but I can feel Liam taking in the scene. Aly swivels on her rear and sticks out her foot to show him her multicolored toenails.

"Cool," he breathes.

"Come here." She crooks her index finger at him. "Take off your shoes."

I turn around then. Liam's eyes fix on mine. I know how much he wants to.

What could it hurt? Ten minutes. I shrug okay.

Liam bends to unlace his high-tops and kicks them off. He kneels between me and Aly. Aly tells him, "Move around in front."

He obeys.

She yanks his foot into her lap and begins to spread pink polish on his right toenail.

Liam goes, "Oh God, that tickles." He giggles like a girl.

Aly giggles, too. Shannon glances up from painting Kylie's toes. "Want your fingernails done too, Liam?"

"Sure," he answers. It was a joke, I think. Shannon arches her eyebrows like, Is he serious? Joke or not, now she has to do it.

Alyson isn't happy about Shannon scooting closer and taking Liam's hand. He splays his fingers apart for her. I see Shannon examining his nails. They're perfectly manicured, unlike mine which are all jagged-edged from chewing and picking.

Liam's nails also bear traces of old polish in the cuticles. Please, I pray, don't let Shannon notice.

Next to me, Carmen's watching Liam, an odd expression on her face.

I want him to go — now. Just go.

Shannon finishes with Liam's right hand. He blows on his fingernails like a girl. Like he's done it a million times. God.

"Okay, let's turn out the lights," Kylie says, "and see if we glow."

I get up fast and flick the switch. Our toes and fingers light up. We balance on our tailbones and stick our hands and feet into the air; wiggle them around so the room is swarming with neon fireflies. "Sweet," Liam breathes. His toes are the biggest and brightest.

He says, "Know what? I have some glow-in-the-dark decals that'd look absolutely fabulous over this polish. Hang on a sec." We see his dark shape rise and disappear into his room.

"*Absolutely fabulous?*" Shannon repeats. "How gay."

"Shut up," Aly snaps. "I hate that expression."

"Me, too," Carmen says.

Tension sparks the darkness. Aly adds, "He was just kidding. Obviously, you don't know Liam."

"Obviously," Shannon snipes.

Kylie breaks the tension. "Your brother's really weird, Regan. If I wanted to polish my brother's nails, he'd be like, 'ew, ew. Keep that gunk away from me.'"

"Mine, too," someone says behind me.

My face catches fire. Thank God they can't see it in the dark.

Aly clucks her tongue. "He's not weird. He's probably in there taking it off."

The lights go on and Aly returns from the wall switch. She screws the lid on her bottle of polish and collects the other bottles. As she passes them back to Shannon, she says, "Let's put on some music and dance off this pizza."

Who could argue with that? We're all on diets.

By the time Liam emerges from his room, we've moved the coffee table and cleared the floor. Everyone's forgotten about the nail polish, I hope. Alyson is lingering by Liam's door and she snatches the sheet of decals away from him. I notice they're little butterflies and stars and hearts. "Cute, Liam," she coos under her breath and nudges him. "What else do you have in that secret room of yours? Puffy paint and beads?"

"As a matter of fact . . ." He grins.

She smiles and leans against him. Liam stumbles a little, but balances himself by clenching Aly's arm. This makes her beam. She slides her arms around Liam's waist.

Carmen loads an old Madonna CD into the player and the music floods the basement. I'm thinking, *Why isn't Dad down here dragging* "raging hormones" upstairs? *Kylie and Shannon begin to dance, sort of tentatively, eyeing Liam. Carmen grabs my hand and yanks me to the middle of the floor. I'm not a good dancer. I'm too stiff, too tight.*

Liam isn't tight. He's rocking out with Aly. Wow, he's a great dancer. He has all the same moves Aly does, as if they've been practicing in private. Or he has.

Then it happens. She exposes herself. Lia Marie. The change is visible, noticeable, at least to me. She throws her arms in the air and begins to gyrate her hips in double, triple time to the beat. Wild, out of control, as if she's been holding back for years. Which, I realize, she has. She may not even be aware she's out.

She's singing now, too, in a falsetto to match Madonna. Her eyes are closed and she's obviously off in another world. Her world.

Everybody stops dancing. Even Aly. We all step back to make room for Lia Marie. Her elbows are lethal weapons.

Oh God. Oh God. What should I do?

Carmen leans over and whispers in my ear, "Is he tripping out or something?"

Shannon snickers behind us.

I charge over to the CD player and punch it off. It takes a moment for Lia Marie to acknowledge the silence. React. She lowers her arms and shrinks into herself, morphing back into Liam.

The lights flicker. "Liam, are you down there?" Dad hollers. "Get up here and leave those girls alone."

Liam's eyes cut to me. To my fiery face. "S-sorry," he stammers. "Sorry, Re." He stumbles toward the stairs.

"Liam, you don't have to go," Shannon calls after him. "We were planning on doing your makeup next." She laughs, evilly.

I don't. Neither does Carmen. Or Aly.

Later, after everyone is asleep, I hear in the dark, "Re?"

I'm staring at the ceiling, through it, up into the night. "Yeah?"

"What's with your brother?" Carmen asks quietly.

"What do you mean?"

I feel her eyes boring into me. "You know. Is he like, on drugs?"

"No!" My voice is louder than I mean it to be. I lower it. "Of course not. He hates drugs. He's totally anti-drug."

"He's different, though, isn't he?"

Yeah, I don't say. She's different. I turn my face away from Carmen's penetrating gaze.

"Come on, Re. You can tell me." I feel her hand reach out and grasp my arm. She squeezes. "I'm your best friend."

I close my eyes.

She adds softly, "I don't have any secrets from you."

I pull my arm back, rolling away from her. I can't tell you! I scream inside. I can't ever tell you.

In the morning — more like noon — everyone packs up to leave. They say they had a good time, but what happened last night hangs over us like toxic smog. I'm not sure they know what they witnessed — Lia Marie revealing herself.

I think Carmen suspects. I don't know what she suspects, exactly. Maybe that he's gay. He isn't gay. If he were, I'd probably tell her despite the fact I'm sworn to secrecy. I don't dare tell her the truth.

That was the first — and last — time Liam ever lost control. Why then? Why at my party, with my friends? That next week Carmen began to act cold toward me. I didn't blame her; I don't blame her still. What kind of person keeps secrets from her best friend?

My *Carmen* CD skipped a stanza and I scrambled to my feet to pause the player and remove the CD. With the corner of my sheet, I wiped the disc clean. It was wearing out from overuse.

That was my last slumber party, to host or attend. Along with Carmen, everybody else sort of drifted away. Or I drifted. I heard Carmen's mom got invited to tour in Europe over the summer and Carmen went with her. She didn't even say good-bye. Just went away and never came back.

It wasn't like I'd never had friends before Carmen. I had lots of friends when I was little, in preschool. First grade. Second. Before friendship got complicated. Before it came with expectations.

Chapter 6

Elise and David Matera were the parents I wished I had. I'd been baby-sitting for them since I was twelve, and hoping any day now they'd adopt me. They were a regular family. They loved their kids. Really loved them. They were always hugging and kissing and playing games with them. Cody was currently in his "why" phase. He must've asked David a hundred times now, "Why is the sky blue?" and each time David would patiently explain, "Because every color in the rainbow has a wavelength. Like this." He'd demonstrate on Cody's drawing paper. "When light passes through the atmosphere, the wave gets scattered. It spreads out." He'd squiggle the lines. "The blue we see is actually millions and millions of scattered blue lights. Tiny little pinpricks of light, all streaming into our eyeballs at once."

"Wow," Cody would breathe.

I would, too. I mean, I didn't know that. I doubted my dad did. I know he didn't because when I asked him the same question he said it was because God's a boy. If God were a girl, the sky would be pink.

"What about sunrise and sunset?" I'd asked.

Dad had looked dumbfounded. "You kids. You think too much."

It frightened me how shallow the gene pool was that Liam and I were wading in.

The Materas were my single source of income. A constant

source lately. That was another thing; they were always doing stuff together. Like dating. The last time Mom and Dad went out on a date was . . . I can't even imagine them dating. Mom and Dad?

"I left the number of the Arts House and restaurant by the phone," Elise told me, slipping on the coat David held open for her. "Thank you, darling." She smiled up at him, lovingly. I hadn't seen my parents share a private look like that since . . . Never.

"Tyler has a runny nose, but don't worry about it, Regan." Elise pulled a tissue out of her purse. She bent down and swiped Tyler's snot, adding, "He's getting over a cold. Which he caught at that day care." Her eyes narrowed at David.

"I know, I know." He held up his hands. "We should never have left him there, even for a morning. Those places are breeding grounds for bacteria. That's why we praise Buddha for Regan."

Did they really? Wow.

"Waygon, come watch me dwaw a T-Wex." Cody tugged on my hand.

Mirelle shot to her feet. "Regan's going to play Barbies with me. Right?" She planted herself in front of me, her curly hair springing corkscrews all over her head. "You promised."

"I did." I straightened her bow barrette. "I can't wait, either. I've been thinking about it all day. Why don't you go set up your Barbie village and I'll check out this T-Rex. Just for a sec." I winked at her.

"Thank you, Regan." Elise squeezed my arm. "You're so good with them."

David pulled open the front door. "We'll be home by ten-thirty at the latest. If anything happens, the phone numbers are on the corkboard by the phone."

"I told her that." Elise slapped David's back. "I swear, you're going senile." She turned back to me, rolling her eyes. "The kids have eaten, but I left you a pan of lasagna in the oven in case you hadn't. I really appreciate you coming early. Also," she lowered her voice so the kids wouldn't hear, "I baked brownies for you and hid them in the cupboard. A little study snack."

See? Perfect parents.

As soon as they left, the baby pooped his diaper. Mirelle and Cody plugged their noses and split to opposite ends of the room. While I changed Tyler's Pampers on the dining room rug, Cody drew his dinosaur with green Magic Marker at the table.

"Do you want to be Bride Barbie or Working Woman Barbie?" Mirelle called from the living room.

What a choice. "Bride," I answered.

Cody said, "I got a new G.I. Joe. Want to see him?"

"You bet."

He dropped the marker and motored into his bedroom. As I resnapped Tyler's onesie, it struck me how ordinary these kids were. "They fulfill their gender expectations," Liam would say. Whatever that meant. All I knew was you'd never mistake Mirelle for a boy, or Cody for a girl. Tyler was still a baby, so he didn't count. If you dressed Ty in frilly clothes, people would probably coo over him and call him a "pretty little girl."

Pretty. A word for girls. The way handsome described boys. Liam was right; people did use boy and girl language. They expected different behaviors. When kids acted "out of role," as Liam put it, they were labeled tomboys or sissies.

There were lines you didn't cross, in clothing, behavior, attitude. Like, if I wore lipstick and lace to school, nobody would even notice. Well, they might, since I'd never worn either. I wasn't that girly-girly. People could accept if you moved along your own gender scale — be a princess one day and a slob the next. Same with boys.

To a point.

The gender scales didn't extend equidistant in both directions. For example, if you were a girl you could be off-the-scale feminine and that'd be fine, but if you acted or felt just a little too masculine, you were a dyke.

Same for guys. Mucho macho, fine. Soft and gentle, fag.

What if you happened to be born off both scales, between scales, like Liam? Then you were just a freak.

I know that's how Liam felt. He told me once there was no place for him in the world, that he didn't fit anywhere. He really was off the scale. Boy by day, girl by night. Except, he was a girl all the time, inside. It was hardwired into his brain, he said, the way intelligence or memory is. His body didn't reflect his inner image. His body betrayed him. The way people viewed Liam, as a boy, meant he had to play to their expectations. Dress the part. Act the role. And Liam was good at it, expert. He'd had all those years of practice. It had to be horrible, though, day after day after day, seeing all around him what he wanted so desperately to be and never could.

"Waygon! Look at me!"

I jerked to attention.

Cody emerged from his bedroom, clutching his G.I. Joe, and clunking across the entry in an old pair of Elise's high heels. I had to laugh. So much for gender expectations.

David and Elise never forced Cody and Mirelle to play with boy or girl toys exclusively. Or to dress the role. David even bought Cody a baby doll last summer when he begged for one. Cody's interest in playing with her lasted about two minutes before he was back throwing dirt clods at the neighbor's dog.

The whole gender role expectation thing was too confusing to me. Why couldn't people just be accepted for who they were?

I carted Tyler into the living room and plopped him in his bouncy seat. "Let me see your doll," I said to Cody, extending my hand.

"It's not a doll." He huffed. "It's a action figure."

"Oh, right. Sorry." I smoothed G.I. Joe's camouflage jacket down to cover his exposed and bulging parts. "Where are his pants?"

Cody shrugged.

"He flushed them down the toilet," Mirelle informed me.

"You did?"

Cody smirked.

"Okay, Regan. I have Barbie all dressed for her wedding." Mirelle skipped over and thrust Bride Barbie at me.

"I want to play," Cody whined.

"No," Mirelle snapped. "You wreck my dolls."

"No, I don't."

"Yes, you do. You chew off their feet." Mirelle said to me, "He does, Regan. My Malibu Barbie is crippled now. She can't even stand up."

"She always was a little top-heavy," I said.

"Huh?" Mirelle blinked.

"Forget it. Cody, you can play if you promise not to play Cannibal Barbie."

He just looked at me. So did Mirelle. *I* thought I was funny.

"I don't want him to play," Mirelle said, pouting.

"He'll scream if we don't let him," I told her.

She clucked her tongue and expelled a short breath. "Okay."

Cody kicked off the pumps and scrabbled over to the Barbie village.

I followed him. "Who's this?" I removed another figure from the front seat of Barbie's sports car.

"The Hulk," Mirelle and Cody said together.

The Hulk. Right.

"Okay, Barbie is going to marry G.I. Joe," Mirelle said. "And The Hulk will be their baby."

Barbie, G.I. Joe, and The Hulk. Whoa, I thought, that'll stretch the gender gap.

⤙⤙

"Regan. Re."

Consciousness swam just under the surface, causing my dream to dissolve. It was a happy dream. Glorious, in fact. I was onstage, singing Verdi's *La Traviata* at the Met.

"Re!"

I gulped a breath and lurched up in bed, my hand flying to my heart. "Geez, Liam. Don't do that."

"Luna," she said.

I mumbled a curse. Falling back on my pillow and yanking my comforter up to my chin, I added in a snarl, "Why do you have to keep waking me up? I don't care if you use the mirror —"

"What do you think of this outfit?" She crossed into the moonlight, spreading her arms out from her sides, palms up.

I exhaled wearily. "For what?"

"Everyday wear."

I scanned the length of her. She had on tight blue jeans and a red knit top. The top was short-sleeved, which I noticed right away because Liam always wore long sleeves, even in summer. He shaved his arms. He shaved his legs. He shaved everywhere. He hated the hair.

"It's fine," I said. "A little tight around here." I wiggled fingers across my front. "Do you have a smaller bra?"

"Yeah." Luna turned and examined herself in the mirror. "But I like this one." She posed sideways, arching her back to enhance her figure. She twisted to view the other side.

Hours. She could do this for hours — posing, preening.

Why couldn't she put a mirror in the big room between our bedrooms? I answered my own question: Same reason Liam had shattered the mirror on his dresser. Same reason he avoided every mirror in the house. He might catch a glimpse of himself. As much as Liam despised his looks, Luna couldn't seem to get enough of herself — of the image she longed to project.

"What about shoes?" Luna asked. "The black slip-ons or my ankle boots?"

"Go with the boots. The slip-ons look like guy shoes."

"Oh goddess. You're right. I wish my feet weren't so enormous." She raised one foot behind to view it in the mirror. "They stick out like sore thumbs."

I yawned. "Bind them, like geishas do in Japan. Go to bed."

She blew me off. "Does this wig look real?"

"You look like a freakin' fashion model. Can I go to sleep now?"

"Re?"

I exhaled a long breath. "Luna, if you were walking down the street in that outfit, no one would be able to tell. You look like a regular girl."

Her smile warmed the room. She loved hearing that, that she could pass. Most girls spend hours and hours working on themselves so they'll be striking, eye-catching, desirable. Liam would give everything to live one day as a plain, ordinary girl.

Chapter 7

I was anxious to get to school. That had to be a bad omen. I even brushed my hair and put on a clean shirt.

At breakfast Mom chattered on incessantly about a new account she was bidding on, hoping to land. Some big society affair with horse-drawn carriages and limos. "It'll make or break Weddings by Patrice," she said, shoving aside her half-eaten slice of dry toast.

Liam and I continued doing homework at the table.

Mom sighed deeply. In my peripheral vision, I caught her gazing out the patio door into the gray day, then running her hand down the back of her head. She stopped to grasp her neck, tilt her head to the side, and rest her arm on her breast. Absently, she added, "This one could put me on the map. Not that any of you care."

Dad glanced over the newspaper. "Of course we care." He cleared his morning throat. "We care, Pat. Don't we, kids?"

Sorry, I couldn't even feign interest. Liam, however, seemed enthralled. Not in Mom's career, especially, but in watching her. He was girl gawking, which is what I called it, where he sat mesmerized studying how girls talked and gestured and moved. Absorbing, memorizing, imitating. He had Aly down perfectly. The way she tossed back her head when she laughed. Bit her bottom lip when she was worried, or deep in thought. The way she crossed and uncrossed her legs, tucked them underneath her.

Played with her ponytail. He could sit in front of my mirror and do her for hours.

He could do Mom, too. Trancelike, he reached up and grabbed the back of his neck.

Mom blinked over at him and started. She stood up fast. As she headed for the kitchen to refill her coffee cup, Liam said to her, "I'm really excited for you, Mom. I hope you get it. Is that a new dress, by the way? It looks stunning on you."

I choked on my OJ. My head twisted in either direction to catch Mom's reaction, and Dad's.

Mom didn't blush, the way I expected. The way she would have if Dad had complimented her. Or Andy. Or anyone else. She said curtly, "Thank you. I've had it for a while. Just never found an occasion to wear it."

Dad bobbed his head up from the paper again. He added his obligatory, "You do look nice. Where are you going?"

"We're meeting the Rosenbergs for lunch at the Marriott."

"Who are they?" Dad asked.

Mom stopped dead in the doorway. "Haven't you been listening to a word I've said all morning?"

I could've answered that one.

"The Rosenberg wedding." Mom filled her cup at the coffeemaker. "You're going to be hearing a lot about it. And Regan," she ripped open a packet of sugar sub, "there'll be days when I'll have to meet with the bride and her mother in the evening because they both work. I expect you to take over for me here."

Liam opened his mouth to volunteer services, and got as far as, "I —" before getting hammered by a look from Dad. If Liam and I could shatter gender expectations now, please? Out of the blue Liam said, "Did you get a haircut, Dad? It looks good on you."

Dad blushed. Dad? "No," he said. "But I need one." He scratched the back of his stubbly neck. "And so do you."

Liam didn't implode, the way he normally did when Dad told him to cut his hair. Liam so wanted to wear his hair long. Instead, he nodded. "I know. I'm going this weekend. I already have an appointment."

He did? What was this about? In the last five minutes Liam had initiated more conversation than he had in years. Whatever it was, it was making me extremely uncomfortable. Too much Luna.

"I'm outta here." I scraped back my chair. "Liam, you coming?"

His eyes met mine. "You look nice, too," he said. "What'd you do, hire a stylist?" He smiled like, Seriously, you look nice.

Way too much Luna. I widened my eyes at him. Shut up. Let's go.

He daubed his lips with a napkin and stood. As he intercepted Mom returning from the kitchen with her coffee, he bent down and kissed her cheek. She jerked away like it hurt. "Good luck with the Rosenbergs," Liam said. "I'm sure you'll plan a gorgeous wedding for them. I just wish I could be there."

"You're not invited," Mom snapped.

Liam's spine fused. "I know. I wasn't asking to be."

She set her cup on the table. Her hand was shaking. She picked up her Daytimer. "I'm just saying . . ." She flipped it open.

What was with her? What was with him? All of them. They were psycho. Freaky.

"Oh, Dad." In the front foyer, Liam slipped an arm through the letter jacket he despised and rarely wore. "I talked to Coach Hewitt yesterday, the way you asked. He's going to start me on a weight training program next week."

Dad's eyes bulged. So did mine. A grin creased Dad's face,

ear to ear. "All right!" he cheered, punching the air. "Go get 'em, son."

Liam trailed me out to the porch. "Don't say it," he mumbled under his breath. "That even made me sick."

"What are you doing?" I asked. "You're acting weird." Then, like a high heel to the head, it struck me. Was this transitioning?

"Don't do it, Liam," I told him. "Not yet." Not ever, I was thinking.

Liam looked at me. "Acting. That's all I ever do. I've been doing it so long, that's all I *can* do." Unexpectedly, his eyes welled with tears.

"Liam," I began. "Luna —"

"I know." He hunched in the jacket, squeezing the bridge of his nose. "I know."

We stood on the stoop for a moment, our breath visible in the morning air. "I guess I'm just testing the water," he said. "It's a little chilly."

"Chilly? It's frigid. It's freezing. It's a freaking glacier in there." Why? I wondered. Why test the water? You'll only drown.

A movement caught my eye and I twisted my head. Dad had drawn the curtains and was watching us through the picture window — girl gawking, his version. He was creeping me out. Dad and Liam both.

I bumped Liam's arm with mine. "Let's get out of here."

We hustled to the driveway and climbed into the Spyder. At the end of the block, when Liam swerved in the opposite direction from school, I reached out and clamped a hand over the steering wheel. "I need to go to school today, Liam. Sorry, but I can't play your shrink and nursemaid twenty-four-seven."

He seared me with a look.

I blanched and dropped my arm. "I didn't mean that the way it sounded. It was a joke."

"Yeah, my whole life is a joke."

I started to say . . . What? Life sucks, especially yours? He already knew that.

Change of subject. "What's with Mom lately?" I asked, glancing out the side window.

"What do you mean?" Liam squealed a U-turn and headed back toward Horizon.

"She's so amped up on pills. She's obsessed with this job. Weddings by Patrice," I mocked. "I'm so sure."

Liam blinked at me. "What's wrong with it?"

I blinked at him. "A wedding planner? Liam, our mother is a wedding planner."

"So?" he said. "She makes people happy."

"Other people." I didn't voice the rest: When did she stop making *us* happy?

Liam slowed at a yellow light and added, "She only wants to be fulfilled. As a whole person. She wants her life to count."

"She said that?"

He shrugged. "Not in so many words. You have to read between the lines."

I could barely read the lines as written. Her lines were blurry, even before the drugs. Liam would know about wanting to be a whole person, but what did he see in Mom that I didn't? "Doesn't she think being our mom counts for anything?" I asked.

Liam cast me a withering look.

"What?"

"Mom's smart, in case you hadn't noticed. She has a brain. She could've accomplished something if she'd finished college, chosen a career path instead of full-time motherhood. I think she feels her talents are wasted on perfecting the art of home-making."

"What's wrong with homemaking?" I said. "It's an important job. It's the most important job in the world when you have kids."

Liam gunned the engine at the green light. Pulling up short behind a school bus, he said, "You're not a card-carrying member of the feminist party, are you? With that kind of attitude, you could set the women's movement back a hundred years."

I clucked my tongue. "What attitude? She's a good mom. At least, she was. Before she went all Weddings by Patrice on us."

Liam shook his head.

What? I was right and he knew it.

"It isn't easy for her. Our mother is sensitive, delicate. A little high strung, maybe."

"Strung out, you mean."

He sighed wearily.

We caromed into the parking lot at school, out by the back forty, which meant Liam wasn't coming in. He shifted into park and idled the car. Turning to me, he said, "Mom is reshaping her destiny. Or trying to. We should all be given that opportunity." His eyes glazed over and he added wistfully, "I wonder what my destiny will end up being."

"Nobody knows that," I told him. "You can't change your destiny."

Liam's brow furrowed. "You don't believe we can engineer our own destinies?"

"Of course not. It's destiny. Duh." Mine was predetermined. High school graduate by thirty-five, if I was lucky. Domestic goddess — not.

"If that's true, Re," Liam said, "then I'll never be fulfilled."

Oh God. Here we go. "Don't say that."

Liam stared out the windshield unseeing into the empty football field. "I won't be able to follow my heart."

"You know what? You think too much."

The head stuff, the heart stuff, the hopeless, helpless, hurt stuff. It put a damper on my day. "Maybe you could get a job at Weddings by Patrice," I suggested. "Be a bridesmaid."

That made Liam crack a smile. He had to say it, though: "Always a bridesmaid. Never a bride."

Chapter 8

*C*hris was sitting at our station when I got to Chemistry. Our eyes met across the crowded room, like in the movies, except we didn't share a knowing smile and race into each other's arms. Instead I fell into the trash can. Well, almost. I hit it with my boot and overturned it, which made such a racket everyone stopped talking and turned to gawk.

Great. So much for the invisibility shield.

"Nice entrance," Chris said, pulling out my stool.

I wanted to slug him, but didn't know if that'd be too intimate a gesture.

He handed me my goggles and quipped, "These must be worn at all times. This is not a beauty contest — grrrls." He snapped his on and fluffed his hair.

It made me laugh. He was cute. Beyond cute. Handsome. There was that word again. One time when I was little, Mom took me with her to Sears to pick up Dad after work. Dad was with a customer selling a refrigerator so we waited by his desk. Mom nudged me and said, "Look at your father. Isn't he the most handsome man you've ever seen?" I remember thinking, He's my dad. Duh.

Had she really said that? Maybe they had dated.

Relatively speaking, Dad was better looking than most geezers his age.

Bruchac boomed, "As I gaze around the room, I see that only

a few of you have a memory span longer than a sitcom. I realize yesterday was long, long ago, but you might recall my mentioning that when you come to class from now on, the first thing you should do is retrieve your lab assignment from the basket on the back counter. The basket is labeled Chem I, Lab Assignments. Ring a bell?"

I turned my head to check out the basket and Chris said in my ear, "Bruchac better watch it today. My A.T.Q. is on low battery."

I must've looked clueless, as usual.

"Asshole Tolerance Quotient," he explained. Chris slid off his stool to join the others who were straggling to the rear of the room.

He got that right. I glanced up to see Bruchac staring at me. What?

Oh my God. Sofa king. I hid my face under my hand.

Chris returned and slapped the paper on the counter. "Would you mind reading this? I forgot my 3-D glasses."

The copy was clearer than yesterday's, but not much. It was a stupid experiment. Heat up an ice cube until it reached the boiling point, recording the temperature in Fahrenheit and centigrade at various stages of meltdown. There was an additional exercise about converting Celsius to Fahrenheit and calculating absolute zero. I think I did this in fourth grade.

It was hard to concentrate with Chris sitting so close, brushing shoulders with me every once in a while. I noticed how he held his stubby pencil between his thumb and index finger. How he printed the measurements in perfectly square, block numbers. How his fingernails were jagged, like mine, as if he chewed them, like me. Maybe we could compare blood loss.

"What?" Chris said.

I flinched. "Huh?"

"You're smiling. Am I doing something wrong?" His face fell. "Are you laughing at me?"

"No. Of course not."

"You sure?" He looked worried.

"You're doing it right. I just . . ." I shrugged. "It's kind of a wee-Todd-did experiment."

He reeled backward, jaw dangling. "You don't think knowing how fast an ice cube melts is important? My God, woman. This is vital science. What if I wanted you to bring me a frosty brew with a piping hot plate of nachos? Do you know how much time you'd have to get it to me before the beer got warm?"

I knuckle-fisted his chest. "Pig."

He snorted like one.

"Hey, Chris."

We both jerked around. The thermometer I was holding slipped through my fingers and clinked on the counter. Chris managed to capture it between cupped hands before it hit the floor and infected us all with mercury poisoning.

The person behind us winced an apology: "Sorry." The person: Shannon Eiber. It'd barely registered that she was in this class. She'd changed a lot since sixth grade. Physically, anyway. Who hadn't? Me. I lived in a state of eternal stasis.

"Aren't you guys done yet?" Shannon asked. "That experiment took us three minutes."

I curled a lip at her, which she missed because her eyes were glommed onto Chris.

"There's a rave Saturday night in Genesee." She wedged herself between us, speaking directly, and only, to him. "You want to go? We could drive together — you and me and Morgan and Tay." She thumbed across the room where Her People, the Chosen Ones, had staked out the choice lab stations. No doubt they'd put them on reserve a year ago.

Chris smiled at her. "Maybe," he said. "Can I let you know?"

He radiated heat. Or was that me?

"Sure," Shannon said. "Call me." She grabbed his hand and flipped it over. Wrote her number on his palm in red ink. "Later." She strutted off.

A bubble burst — the one that had sucked me up in its helium high. "I thought you were new here," I said, taking the thermometer and repositioning it in the beaker of boiling water. "Didn't know anyone."

"Yeah, well," his lip cricked, "that was last month."

A shroud of darkness descended over me. I don't know why I thought it'd be different. He'd be different. Someone as cool as him? All he had to do was cross the threshold of Horizon High to be instantly absorbed by Them. The ones with shape, form, matter. They Who Mattered.

Reality check, Regan. How dare you wish he was yours.

Shannon cast him a little finger wave as she wriggled back onto her stool. Her lab partner was Hoyt Doucet. No wonder she was stealing mine.

When had Hoyt become a member of TWM? Shannon's standards had taken a plunge.

The bell rang, jolting me back to my destiny. "Are we done?" Chris asked.

"I am." I filled in the solution to the absolute zero equation and thrust the lab report at him. "All you have to do is sign it."

He scribbled his name next to mine. Regan O'Neill. Chris Garazzo. I imagined a plus sign between them. Which confirmed my unstable state of emotional delirium. As Chris rushed around to clean up our station, I hustled to the front to turn in our paper.

On the way out I made a mental deposit in the hazardous waste receptacle. Disposed of any dreams I might've had of us hooking up.

When I got home, Liam's bedroom door was closed. I wondered how he'd spent the day, if he'd even bothered with school. Considering how my day went, I should've blown it off, too.

A wave of music washed up from under Liam's door. Then singing. My heart stopped. Dana International. Oh my God.

Pounding the door. "Liam."

He can't hear because he's got his CD amped up to earsplitting volume. Dana International, this Israeli singer I can't stand. Liam idolizes her.

I knock again. "Liam!"

When he doesn't answer, I do the unthinkable. I barge in.

First thing I see are the pill bottles. A row lined up neatly along the edge of his bookshelf. They're Mom's; they have to be. I'm thirteen and I already know my mom's a popper.

But that's not what freaks me. The bottles are all empty.

"Liam?" I punch off the music. "Liam!"

"What?"

His voice is faint, but it's a voice. I run toward it, to the closet. He's huddled in the corner dressed in his football uniform. I rush over and grab his arm; try to wrench him to his feet.

He resists. He buries his head between his kneepads and mumbles, "Leave me alone."

"No."

"Go away."

"Come on." The panic registers in my voice. "You have to throw up."

He goes limp. He doesn't budge. My first impulse is to kick him, so I do.

"Ow!" He scoots further into the closet. "Why'd you do that?"

I fall to my knees and clench his shoulders; start to shake him. "You have to throw up, Liam. I won't let you die!" This comes out a screech, which makes him raise his head and look at me. His eyes are already dead.

"Liam. Lia Marie. Please." My eyes well with tears. "Please."

His left hand reaches out and snags the football helmet beside him. He holds it up to me by the faceguard. Inside is a mound of pills. Blue, purple, orange, white.

"I can't do it," Liam says. "I can't even do it. I can't do anything right. I'm wrong. All wrong."

"No, you're not." I feel so relieved I throw my arms around him.

"Please, Re." He clasps my wrists and pulls me away. "I wasn't meant to be born." He transfers the helmet to my right hand. "Help me die. Pour these down my throat, okay?" He pleads urgently, "Please?"

My fingers grip the faceguard. I straighten up and charge for the bathroom. I flush all the pills down the toilet. I flush it over and over and over until all the pills have dissolved, disappeared. Then I crumple to the floor and rest my forehead against the toilet bowl. And cry. Just cry. For my brother. Liam. God, Liam.

After a few minutes, I leave the helmet in the bathroom and return to Liam. He's perched on the edge of his bare mattress, the shoulder pads heaped on the floor at his feet. He's already kicked off the cleats.

"You don't have to play football," I inform him. "Just because Dad's coaching doesn't mean you have to play. Why did you tell him you wanted to? You hate football."

Liam's eyes bore holes through the blank wall.

"Liam —"

"You wouldn't understand." His eyelashes glisten. He blinks and a tear overflows the rim. I reach to wipe it away; wipe all the tears away.

He beats me to it and swipes his eye with a knuckle. Then sniffles, and heaves.

I gather the jersey and shoulder pads and cleats off the floor. "I'll take care of it," I tell him. "You don't have to do this." I'm mad, seething mad.

At the bottom of the stairs, I stop. I drop the bundle of gear. There's something else I want to say.

"Lia Marie?" I stand in the doorway. "You can wear my new nightgown to bed. You can have it. And you can use my room to dress in from now on, whenever you want."

Liam glances over his shoulder and meets my eyes. Slowly, the color in his face returns. He comes to life. I see him physically morph into Lia Marie. "Okay." She smiles. "Thanks, Re."

I breathe a sigh of relief.

Liam's door swung open in my face and Dana International assaulted me. "Hey, Re. Come here, look at this." Liam motioned me inside.

I breathed a sigh of relief — the same one I've breathed every day since that Liam's been too chicken to do it.

If he'd considered suicide again, Liam hadn't discussed it with me. Not that he'd give me the date and time. But I watched him pretty close. I think he'd gotten to a new place, a better place. Having the freedom to dress in my room had cured him — I thought.

His room still creeped me out. It was stark. Cold. Abandoned. He never used sheets on his bed, or even a comforter. Just this scratchy wool blanket he'd bought at army surplus or something. During the day he kept it wadded up at the top of the mattress where most people have pillows. The walls were bare, too, except for the books and paperbacks and notebooks and computer manuals that were stacked to the ceiling. The room always felt vacant to me, unoccupied.

Liam was speaking, but I could barely hear him. I de-amped the volume on Dana.

". . . and I found all kinds of history on TG's. For instance, did you know in ancient Greece and Rome, Philo writes about men transforming into women?"

TG's. Transgenders. "Well, yeah. Everyone reads Philo."

He ignored the sarcasm. He was sitting on the floor, sur-rounded by all these piles of printouts. "And King Henry the Third of France was referred to as *sa majesté*. *Her* majesty. Abbé de Choisy in the seventeenth century actually wrote, 'I thought myself really and truly a woman.' Then there's Joan of Arc."

"Joan of Arc was a man?" My eyes bulged.

Liam tilted his head. "In her mind," he said. "There's enough evidence to suggest it."

Wow. I never considered that girls could be transgender. I dropped my backpack on his bed and slid down beside him. I wondered, too, what his sudden interest in history was all about. "Why are you researching TG's?" I asked. "I mean, why now?"

"Why not now? One day I'm going to be a part of history."

My heart sped up. Did he mean he was going to *be* history?

"Lots of Native American tribes pass down stories about trans people," Liam babbled on, "the Mohave, Navaho, Pueblo. They accept, even embrace, females who are men, and vice versa. 'Two-spirit' people, they call them. Did you know in the Yuman Indians there were groups of people called Elxa who ac-tually underwent a 'change of spirit'? Isn't that cool?"

My mind was reeling. I glanced at the page of text Liam was reciting from. He'd highlighted sections, starred names of fa-mous people. Dana International. Oh. She was trans. I never un-derstood why he liked her so much.

"Mick Jagger says he cross-dresses at home."

I frowned at Liam. "Does that make him trans?"

Liam shrugged. "You never know. It's not either or. There are shades of gray to people's gender."

"I know that."

"Ru Paul," he said.

"Ru Paul? I thought he was a drag queen."

"Maybe. Probably. But she is beautiful."

"Is that what you want to be, a drag queen?" God, was Luna going to be on stage? Performing?

Liam said, "We're not all so gifted. I just want to blend in. And look." Liam got all excited. "I found these testimonials from TG's who're transitioning. What they're going through. It's me, exactly me, same as me." He grabbed another stack of printouts that he'd set aside on his treasure chest. That's what he called it — the locked steamer trunk that contained his life. His desired life. The girl clothes. The makeup. He'd even wired the trunk with an alarm system.

"There's this one T-girl, Teri Lynn, who transitioned a couple of years ago. She calls it 'remaking herself.' She's following the Harry Benjamin standards to the letter so she can have her SRS next year."

"Her what? Wait. Who's Harry Benjamin?" He was addressing me as if I was on his level, his plane.

"Harry Benjamin," Liam repeated. "The Benjamin standards. You know, the steps you have to go through before you can get your SRS."

"Slow down, Liam. You lost me. SRS?" I picked up a Web page and skimmed over it. "Welcome to the Gender Identity Center," it said at the top.

Liam touched my shoulder. "Sorry. I should keep you filled in on the lingo. SRS: Sex Reassignment Surgery."

I dropped the page. My brain engaged. "You mean a sex change operation?"

His smile extended across his face. Her face. Luna's eyes grew dreamy. "Oh, Re. It's all I've ever wanted my whole life. You know that."

No, I didn't know that. How could I know that? My eyes fell from her face and grazed the floor, unseeing. I couldn't look at her. Why did this shock me? Because I never allowed myself to go there.

Transition. Is that what it meant? An actual, physical transition? A sex change operation?

Liam gathered the printouts together. On the fingerpad he'd installed atop his treasure chest, he pressed a series of numbers and letters. The latch released and he lifted the lid. He set the stack of papers inside, dug out a leather purse and a tapestry bag. The tapestry bag looked familiar. Wasn't that Mom's?

Liam said, "Which of these look more everyday?"

A wave of nausea washed over me. I pushed to my feet.

"Re?"

"Neither. Both. They're fine," I mumbled, lurching for the door.

He called to my back, "What's the matter?"

"Nothing." Don't desert him, my brain screamed. Don't do this. Don't let him down. Don't let him know.

He asked more softly, "You understand, don't you?"

I stopped in the threshold, my eyes squeezing shut. I took a deep breath and let it out slowly. Holding my stomach, I opened my eyes and forced a smile over my shoulder. "Well, yeah," I lied. "Of course."

Chapter 9

"*T*his experiment involves two potentially dangerous chemicals. The first is potassium permanganate, a strong oxidizing agent that will react quickly with skin and clothing. The second is sulfuric acid, which is caustic and corrosive. Wash off spills of either solution with *large* amounts of water. Goggles must be worn at all times. Any questions?" Bruchac cleaned his nerd glasses with his Tweety Bird tie.

Chris handed me my goggles. "You should probably leave the handling of all dangerous chemicals to me," he intoned in a deep voice. "Since I'm the man."

Yesterday I might've smacked him. Or laughed. Today? What difference did it make? The world was all wrong, skewed, out of natural orbit. We could never be close. Not that he'd want to be.

"Fill a Beral pipet with commercial hydrogen peroxide and label it," I read from the lab instructions.

"Hey, Garazzo. You coming to tryouts after school?" a voice sounded beside Chris. This senior I didn't know had stalled at our station on his way in. Ten minutes late. Bruchac was scorching the back of his letter jacket with a glare.

Chris said, "You know it, man. Think Hewitt will let me start? Or am I going to be warming the bench this year?"

"Mr. Atchinson, you're late," Bruchac announced to the universe. "This is the second time. Three strikes and you're out."

Atchinson's eyes slit. Against his chest, he flipped Bruchac the bird.

"Mr. Atchinson —"

"Got it, Coach," he gave Bruchac a thumbs up, and took off for his station.

I resumed reading the instructions.

Chris said, "Isn't this the stuff you use to bleach your hair?" He unscrewed the lid on the hydrogen peroxide bottle and sniffed it. "I could streak you." He clamped a hand down over my head like a helmet. "One long strip, right down the back. Skunky."

I wrenched away.

He looked hurt. "Just messing with you, Regan."

My name, from his lips. It still made my heart leap. "I know. I'm sorry." I smiled. Relaxed a little. Let down my invisibility shield. It was probably good we'd never get together. He'd never have to know.

As we set up the experiment to prove or disprove the percentage of hydrogen peroxide claimed by the manufacturer on the bottle, Chris counted out loud the drops he was adding to the beaker, "Fourteen, fifteen . . . so, you want to go?"

I uncapped the sulfuric acid. "Where?" Tipped the bottle.

"To the rave."

I had a grand mal seizure. The muscle spasm in my head caused my hand to jerk the acid bottle and sulfuric acid splashed all over my arm.

Like a silent movie, Chris's face registered horror. My mouth opened and a gasp escaped. It didn't hurt, at first. Then the intensity grew and my arm began to burn. I felt myself slipping into a catatonic state — shock.

I gaped at my skin as it bleached white and started to bubble. Did I scream?

"Mr. Bruchac!" Chris bellowed. "Come here, quick." Chris

grabbed my wrist and screeched on the faucet, shoving my hand under the gushing cold water.

Bruchac arrived just in time to witness my resurrection from the dead. The scream was real this time. Eardrums shattered. A torrent of tears gushed from my eyes as I whimpered and gulped for air.

"Take it easy. You're going to live," Bruchac said. He had to raise his voice to get through to me. Chris held my arm under the cold water. "For heaven's sake, calm yourself." Bruchac clamped a claw around my upper arm.

After a couple of minutes, my hand went numb. The crying ebbed and I managed to regain my composure, sort of. Bruchac examined my wrist, where most of the damage was done. "I have an antibiotic cream in the cabinet. Hold on." His voice sounded far away, in a beaker. Was I fainting?

"Regan, you okay?"

I blinked at the voice. Chris had my arm in a vise grip, his face as green as I felt.

I nodded. Loosening his fingers, I wiggled mine, trying to return circulation to my limb.

He laid my hand in his, examining my arm. My wrist. Then he did a weird thing. He lifted my hand to his lips and kissed my palm.

I died. That was like the sweetest thing.

The damage was minimal. No skin grafts or wrappings required. For the rest of the day, though, I cradled my hand to my heart. Protective, like. Not because it hurt; just to cherish the feel of Chris's soft lips against my skin.

⁓

I dreamed about him that night. We were in a canoe floating down a river. The weather was warm, balmy, and we both wore white. Chris had on a white shirt, white pants, white shoes. I wore an alabaster gown. Moonlight shimmered the glassy surface of the water, reflecting off our clothes, our faces, giving us an aura, a glow. Chris held one oar, I the other, and we were rowing in perfect harmony. Strains of *La Bohème* drifted out from the wooded shore. We rowed and sang, rowed and sang —

The music cut out.

"Re, help me."

My eyes flew open. Beside my bed, Luna burst into tears.

It took a minute to 1) wake up fully because I didn't want my dream to end, and 2) calm Luna down. She was crying so hard, she was hyperventilating.

"What happened?" She seemed fine earlier. Liam was no different at breakfast — total boy role — except he had gone to school. I'd seen him entering the media center on my way to History. "Luna?"

She sniffled. Slumping at the edge of my mattress, she sobbed, "He made me do it. I-I didn't want to do it, but he made me." Heaving uncontrollably, she cried into her hands.

"Who made you?" I asked, scrambling out of my twisted sheet to sit up beside her. "Who made you do what?"

Luna's shoulders shook. "Dad," she whimpered.

Dad. I looped an arm around her waist. "What'd he do now?"

"He m-made me try out." Luna gulped a breath and straightened. "He actually came to school and met me after class. I didn't think he even knew my schedule." She wiped her nose. "I suppose he could've gotten it from the office."

What was she talking about? "Try out for what?"

She blinked at me, eyelashes glommed with tears. "Baseball."

Oh God.

"He forced me to go out there and pitch," she said flatly. "And he sat in the bleachers the whole time, so I couldn't leave."

Silently I cursed Dad. Not so silently.

"Oh, Re," Luna breathed audibly, holding my eyes. "I have to transition. I don't care how much it costs. I have to transition now."

I dropped my arm behind her back. "How much does it cost?"

She shook her head. "I don't mean money."

What other costs were there?

"You have to help me," she said; pleaded.

"Help? How?" Did she expect me to perform the surgery? I'm sure.

"I'll start slow, start presenting myself. Dress in public. How do you think I should go about it?"

"Why are you asking me?" My chest constricted. I didn't know anything. Don't do this.

Luna shifted so she'd be more balanced on the bed, more direct, one knee bent underneath her. She took my hands in hers and rested them on her thighs. "Because I trust you, Re. I trust you with my life."

Don't! I screamed inside. All these years I'd been her confidante, I'd kept the secret. But that was no reason to trust me so completely.

She was gazing at me, hard. I couldn't look at her.

"You just want to dress in public?" I asked, trying to sound nonchalant, inching away from her.

"Yes. I want to be me."

If that was all . . . I pulled my hands from hers and pushed off the bed. Slogging through the crap on my floor, I trudged to my desk, which was now Luna's little corner of heaven, and picked up a tube of lipstick. "Well, I think it'd be easier if you dressed for strangers." I pulled off the top. Maroon. Not my color. What was my color? "I mean, you wouldn't be risking so much.

Like, if they couldn't accept that you were trans, so what? You wouldn't have to deal with them knowing who you are — were. Before. You know, being Liam."

"The actor," she said. "The hologram."

"Whatever. They wouldn't have to get past that."

"It'd give me a chance to feel comfortable in public, too. In the daylight."

The daylight? My head whipped around. Could she sense my panic? She seemed to emit a glow as she smiled and added, "You are so smart, Re. So. Smart."

"Oh, right." I turned back. Compared to Liam I was a stem cell.

"Where shall we go?" Luna asked. "And when?"

"I don't know." I set the lipstick down. Did she need all these colors? "We could hang out at the mall, maybe. Not our mall," I added quickly. "Another one, waaay across town." My arm flew out to the side to indicate distance. Lots of distance. "We could go shopping."

"Shopping," Luna repeated. "Do you know how long I've dreamed of going shopping with you?"

She had? I didn't know that. I didn't go shopping all that often. Only when Aly needed something and none of her friends was available. Aly had other friends besides me. Seniors, of course. People her age, her people. Shopping seemed such a small dream to have.

"When?" Luna asked.

"Huh?" I'd checked out. I was so tired. I wanted my own dream back, the one with Chris and the canoe.

"Tomorrow," Luna said.

"No, I have school. You've heard of it. People go there to learn? To engineer their own destinies?"

She didn't smile. "After school?"

What was tomorrow? Thursday? Was it already tomorrow? "I have to work," I told her. David and Elise were starting this yoga class together, thank Buddha. They needed me.

"When, Re? When can we go?" The desperation in Luna's voice hurt my heart.

"Saturday," I said. "No, wait. I have to work then, too."

I caught a glimpse of her face in the mirror. Total devastation. But I couldn't help it. David and Elise had asked if I could sit while they went skiing. It was an all-day gig. I didn't need the money so much as . . . I wanted to go. I needed my "real" family fix.

"What about Saturday night?" Luna asked. "How late are the malls open?"

Like I knew. "Probably nine, at least."

She waited.

Saturday night would work for me. It'd give me a couple of days to prepare. For what, I wasn't sure. "I won't get home until six, probably, depending on where David and Elise decide to go skiing."

Luna jumped to her feet and sailed across the room. She lifted me bodily from the chair and hugged me. She held me so close her joy rippled through my bones.

Okay, this wouldn't be so bad. Bunch of strangers. Saturday night. Who went to the mall on Saturday night? Besides every girl in the world looking to pick up guys. This according to Aly.

I quelled my rising terror. We'd just be two girls out shopping. Who would notice? Who would care? Who would even look at us twice?

⌒

"Ms. O'Neill, will you please come to the front of the room?" Bruchac crooked a finger at me. Chris was just looping a leg over his stool, having rushed in at the late bell on the heels of

Atchinson. I hadn't even had time to say, "Hi. Do you know where we can rent a canoe?"

"Ms. O'Neill?"

Did Bruchac want me to come up there, or what?

"Today would be good." He tapped his watch.

I backed off my stool, almost toppling it. Chris caught the seat. He frowned a little, like, What's going on?

Like I knew. Everyone stopped what they were doing to gawk at me. Stare at me. Follow me with their eyes.

I felt naked as I weaved through the lab stations, my pulse racing. What was Bruchac plotting?

He motioned me up beside him. "If you would please show the class your arm, Ms. O'Neill. Enlighten them about the consequences of unfortunate mishaps such as spilling sulfuric acid on yourself."

Unfortunate mishaps? I was considering giving my other arm an acid bath today. My wrist was still a little red, the skin splotchy white and bubbly in spots, but it didn't hurt.

"Ms. O'Neill, if you please. Your audience awaits." Bruchac swept a dramatic arm out to the side.

Jerk. Ten on the A.B.S. Screw you, I thought. I crossed my arms over my chest self-consciously. Take the hint.

"*I* spilled the acid," Chris's voice echoed from the back.

"No, you didn't," I said.

"Yes, I did."

"No, you didn't."

"Continue the lover's spat outside of class," Bruchac sniped. "This is the kind of accident I've warned you about. This is what can happen when you're not paying attention. These are toxic chemicals, girls. Play with fire and you will get burned."

I almost made a crack about getting *him* burned for sexual discrimination. Add jail time for violating my personal right to suffer in silence. Speaking would only prolong my agony up here, though. I started back to my seat.

Bruchac stepped in front of me. "Show everyone what happens when acid makes contact with human skin, Ms. O'Neill."

I huffed a little. Was he serious?

Apparently. He wouldn't let me pass.

Unfolding my arms, I held up the left wrist. People in the front row leaned forward over their stations. Those behind goosenecked a view. I wanted to tell them there was nothing to see besides me incinerating up here.

"Tell us how it feels," Bruchac said.

"Pretty good," I quipped. "Great, if you're into self-mutilation."

People chuckled. Did they?

Bruchac snarled, "I cannot stress *enough* that safety is our number one concern. Be careful. Be focused. Be vigilant."

"Be all that you can be," I added.

That raised a chorus of sniggers. Beside me, I felt Bruchac bristle. His quills could've drawn blood. I skittered down the aisle, like the scared rabbit I was. People were smiling at me. Not in a mocking way. More . . . amused, entertained.

Bruchac said, "Everyone take out a clean sheet of paper. You've just earned yourselves a quiz."

Communal groaning. As I slid onto my stool, Chris muttered, "Off the A.B.S."

No kidding. Thank God the quiz wasn't hard or I'd be off everyone's A.B.S. There were two questions about the freezing and boiling points from our earlier lab. The chemical formula for sulfuric acid, H_2SO_4. Now etched permanently in my brain.

As I finished up, I caught a glimpse of Chris's paper. It was mostly blank. I think he answered number one, then bailed mentally.

"Hey, Regan." He caught up with me in the hall after class. "What about Saturday night?"

I stopped dead. Saturday night? How could he know about Saturday night?

Chris must've interpreted my slack jaw as cluelessness. Which it was. "The rave?" he said.

The rave. Oh my God. It wasn't a hallucination. He had asked me, right before I tripped out on acid.

Someone barreled into us from behind and Chris steered me over to the wall. He brushed the hair back from his face, looking deeply into my eyes with both of his. "So?"

"So." I licked my dry lips. Opened my mouth. Closed it. Saturday night. Why did it have to be on Saturday night? Luna was so psyched about shopping. She'd stayed in my room until dawn trying on outfits appropriate for a mall crawl. She couldn't stop talking about shopping. If that didn't prove she was a girl, what did?

No, this meant too much to Luna. To Liam. He'd been waiting his whole life to go shopping with me.

"I can't Saturday night," I told Chris. "I'm going shopping with my . . . um, sister."

His face changed. Fell? "Okay." His eyes drifted back over his shoulder. Was he disappointed? Mad?

He said coolly, "Guess I'll see you around, then."

What did that mean? I'd see him tomorrow. He retreated and vanished into the crowd.

"Damn you, Liam." I wheeled around and kicked the wall. Then cursed myself because I think I broke a toe.

Chapter 10

*C*hris never showed in chemistry the next day. Bruchac said he had our quizzes graded and would hand them out during lab, adding, "They are way below my expectations."

Expectations. Why was everything about expectations?

Bruchac paused in front of my station. "How's your arm?" he asked.

"It'll live," I muttered. "I mean, I will."

"Good." He smiled and slid my quiz across the countertop. "I guess experience is the best teacher. Too bad some teaching moments have to be painful."

I glanced down at my paper. One hundred percent.

"I see your partner in crime isn't with us today," Bruchac said. "Would you tell him to come see me after school?" He slipped Chris's quiz to the bottom of the stack, but not before I saw his score. Zero. Zero percent.

In all my life I'd never gotten a zero percent. How did that feel?

As Bruchac trundled away, I debated whether or not to deliver his message to Chris. Not, I decided. Today was Friday. By Monday it'd be ancient history.

For some reason I felt responsible for Chris's failure. I *was* responsible. He wouldn't have had to take the freaking quiz if I hadn't spilled acid all over myself. By the storm raging around me, everyone else had figured this out, too. I was going to need new batteries for that invisibility shield.

⁓

Saturday morning as I was leaving for the Materas', Alyson clomped down the basement stairs. "It's snowing. It's gorgeous out," she said to Liam, who was bent over a printout, studying code. "Let's drive to the mountains and go tubing." She yanked back his head by his hair and stared upside down into his eyes. "Please? We never go anywhere."

"I can't," he told her in a strangled voice. "I have to finish this, then assemble two systems today."

Yeah, right. The only thing he'd be assembling was an outfit for tonight.

"You want to go, Regan?" she asked.

"I have to work."

"Shit." Aly flopped onto the sofa. "Another boring Saturday down under in Geeksville. My life is one serious drag."

Get a job, I thought. Go shopping. Take Liam out for a hair weave. That was pretty funny. I wish I could've said that to Aly. Instead, I mumbled, "Sorry."

My day at the Materas' was anything but dull. Between playing games with the kids and watching movies and entertaining Tyler and fixing lunch and letting Mirelle style my hair with scrunchies and barrettes, it was six before I'd even looked at the clock.

And almost seven by the time I got home.

Liam ambushed me at the front door. "You're late," he said. "You were supposed to be here by six."

"Give me a break." I peeled his claws off my arm. "I said six, maybe. David and Elise got stuck behind a jackknifed semi on their way back from the slopes. It's blizzarding, in case you hadn't noticed."

Liam lifted his canvas duffel off the foyer floor and jingled his keys.

"Can I go to the bathroom first?" Brushing by him, I hurried down the hall. The bathroom door was closed, apparently in use. As I made a U-turn for the basement, the toilet flushed and Dad emerged.

He glanced from me to Liam in the foyer, Liam's hand on the doorknob. "You're not going out in this weather, are you?" Dad said.

"It's not that bad," I answered, slipping in behind Dad and shutting the door. I gagged at having to put the toilet seat down. It made me thankful for Liam's restroom etiquette — not that I knew the personal and private details of what he did on the toilet, or ever wanted to.

When I exited the bathroom, Dad was in the kitchen hanging up the phone. Liam shot me eye daggers and mouthed, Come on.

"Your mother is working late again with Handy Andy," Dad grumbled. Handy Andy. Good one, Dad. If he meant it as a joke, it wasn't evident in his face. Dad whirled on us. "You kids are staying home."

"Dad —" Liam and I protested in unison. Liam looked to me to finish.

"We're just going to the Y," I lied. "It'll be less crowded tonight."

Dad arched his eyebrows. "Yeah? I'll come with you."

Crap. That was not the intended response.

Liam jumped in. "I need to do this alone, Dad. You understand."

Dad opened his mouth, then shut it. You understand? Liam

had never spoken those two words to Dad before. Dad looked shell-shocked. "All right," he said. "Just be careful out there."

"Will do." Liam hitched his chin at me toward the door.

Before Dad figured out what it was he apparently under-stood — because I sure had no clue — we bailed.

~

Liam chose the West Meadows Mall about half an hour from our house — on a good day. With the streets paved in black ice and gale force winds impeding every inch of progress, it took us close to an hour to get there. We were lucky to arrive alive.

"Not too many people out tonight," Liam noted as he cre-ated a parking space in the deepening snow near the pillared mall entrance.

"Yeah, well, they lock the dangerously insane up at night," I muttered. The lot was practically empty. I opened my door and got blasted with pellets of sleet. As I stood and twisted to slam the door behind me, I noticed Liam hadn't budged. He was just sitting, staring out the frosted window.

I blew back inside. "What?"

"I can't do this."

"Liam."

Mechanically, his head shook from side to side. "I can't."

Damn him! I smacked the dash with the palm of my hand. Ow. Add a broken wrist to the toe and acid burn. What were we doing here in the middle of a blizzard on a Saturday night when I could be out with Chris, rowing down the river of love?

"Come on, Liam. It won't be that bad."

He just looked at me.

Okay, I couldn't know.

A thin smile parted his lips. "Teri Lynn likes the name I chose — Luna. She thinks it sounds mystical and mysterious."

"And Teri Lynn is . . . ?"

"The T-girl I met online."

T-girl. Trans girl. Right.

"She's nice," Liam said. "She told me all about her first time being out, trying to pass. She was seventeen, too, but she didn't have a car. She had to ride the bus. So she takes this bus to the library because she knows there's a unisex bathroom there where she can change. She lives in Seattle." Liam paused and blinked at me. "Washington?"

"I've heard of it. This is really fascinating." I stifled a yawn. "But what does it have to do —"

"She chose this sundress with a jacket," Liam went on, "and open-toe sandals. All she owned at the time was a really bad Halloween wig, like Elvira, Mistress of the Dark."

"Oh God." I winced. "You're kidding."

Liam chuckled a little. "So she walks across the park to a City Market and the first people she encounters are a mom and her two kids. Teri Lynn knows they're looking at her. Staring. She almost chickens out. But she keeps on walking, holding her head high. She thinks she's done it, that she's past them, when one of the kids goes, 'Mommy, why is that man wearing a dress?'"

My eyes closed involuntarily.

"I know," Liam said. "Teri Lynn just about had a coronary. Before her electrolysis, her beard was really dark. All the foundation in the world wasn't going to cover it." Liam smiled to himself and dropped his head.

I exhaled a long breath. "So what happened next?"

He traced an index finger across the lower arc of the steering wheel. "The mom was sympathetic. Extremely kind. She apologized to Teri Lynn and scolded her little girl. Teri Lynn was pretty traumatized, she said, but it'd taken her so long to get to this point, to build up the courage to dress as herself, that she wasn't going back. She said she'd die if she ever had to go back." Liam's chest rose and fell.

"So . . . ," I cocked my head at him, "I guess she lived."

His eyes found mine.

"You can do this," I told him. "You can."

A long moment passed. Then an expression I'd never seen before seized Liam's face. Determination? Resolve? His jaw set. He nodded once and opened his door.

Chapter 11

I stood guard outside the women's restroom on the second floor of Sears. Sears. Why did it have to be Sears? I didn't expect to see any of Dad's old cronies, since this was a new store, but it was Dad's territory. He didn't work the store floors much after Corporate transferred him to Human Resources, where he'd had to issue his own pink slip.

It felt creepy being here. I shivered in my parka. The door inched open and Luna's hand extended, yanking me inside.

"Okay, how do I look?" She posed in front of me, trembling.

"Not bad."

Her face collapsed.

"No, I mean good. Really good." Surprisingly good. She'd chosen a pair of Levi hipsters, a little tighter than I would've worn, and a cornflower blue sweater with a pale yellow blouse underneath. Black ankle boots. Stylish. "You look . . . ordinary."

She beamed. She must've scoured all the thrift shops in town for stuff this good. Next time she was taking me with her. "And your wig definitely does not scream Mistress of the Dark."

Luna smiled. She feathered her auburn bangs in the mirror. It was a flattering color for her pale skin and freckles. What was I saying? This wasn't *Cosmo* girl.

"You think anyone will read me?" Her eyes met mine in the mirror. "Tell me the truth."

The truth was, I thought she'd stand out. Not because she

looked like a guy. She was tall, and more attractive than most GG's our age. GG's — Genetic Girls. That's what Liam called us, as opposed to TG's or T-girls. "You look gorgeous, Luna," I told her, repositioning the collar on the blouse to mask her Adam's apple.

"Teri Lynn had hers shaved." Luna stretched her neck in the mirror. "She says you can hardly see it now."

"Can we go?" The thought of her throat under a knife made me queasy. Not to mention, once Luna began preening in the mirror we'd be here for days.

She exhaled a shallow breath. Looping her purse strap over her shoulder, she hefted her duffel off the counter and said, "They have lockers down this hall where I can stash my bag."

How'd she know that? Had she been here to scope out the territory? Probably. It'd be like Liam. Paranoid, prepared.

There was one last, tense moment when my fingers curled around the handle and Luna pressed the restroom door shut. She's going to chicken out, I thought. She can't do it.

She dropped her hand, licked her lips, and pronounced, "I'm ready."

~⁓

The first person we ran into was an appliance salesman. He barreled down on us like he was on a search-and-destroy mission. Luna clamped a tourniquet over my arm with her hand and whimpered.

"Just keep walking," I said.

A few feet away the salesman called, "Hey, Ralph. Did you get my overtime report for January?" He rushed by us like we were display racks.

Luna steadied herself against a refrigerator. She pressed a hand to her chest and wheezed, "Oh goddess. I'm having a seizure."

"No, you're not." *I* was. My heart was breaking ribs. "He didn't even see us," I told her. "Luna. You passed."

She blinked down on me. A slow smile radiated across her face. "I did, didn't I?" Her eyes illuminated. "I did."

The aisles were devoid of humanoids tonight — thank the weather goddess. One cashier eyed us suspiciously, but I think she saw us as juvie d's out to lift a little merch. After every encounter, I found myself glancing back over my shoulder to check out people's reactions. Only one person did a double take, a bored clerk at the camera counter, and it appeared to me he was checking Luna out.

"Nobody's reading me," Luna said as we crossed the Sears entrance into the main mall corridor. "This is such a rush."

Yeah, I was flush with excitement. Quit it, Regan, I chided myself. This is hard for her.

We sauntered past the Hallmark and the Williams Sonoma, Luna clutching her purse so tightly against her side I thought she'd rupture her spleen. "Don't do that." I loosened her grip. "You look like a terrorist."

"Okay, thanks." She cast me a nervous smile.

She was stiff, taut, and wired. She kept walking faster and faster. "Slow down." I caught up with her at The Gap. "Look, we're just two sisters out slumming the mall on a Saturday night. Losers," I added, "or why else would we be here?"

"Speak for yourself," Luna said. "We're here to hit on guys."

I snorted. Yeah, right. "You're kidding, right?"

She was kidding. She wasn't kidding!

"Relax." She bumped my shoulder. "It seems early in the season to have all the spring fashions out. Does it to you? What do you think of that mock-neck shirt?" Her finger grazed my nose as it rose to point through the open entrance to The Gap.

"I don't know. Let's go look."

She grabbed my arm. "You mean, inside?"

"No, out here in the mall. You did bring binoculars, didn't you?"

She didn't respond.

I added, "Unless you want to come back in August when the shirts go on sale."

She swallowed hard, gazing into the depths of the store. The belly of the monster.

Maybe it was too soon. "We don't have to —"

"No," she cut in, dropping her hand. "We do. We do have to." She took the first step, but I still had to practically prod her over the threshold. The saleslady was helping the only other deranged person to be out on a night like this, so it gave us freedom to browse. I sensed Luna relaxing a little.

"Is this me?" She unfolded a pink tee and held it up to her.

"It's all over you," I said.

"Hi."

We both jumped. Oh, great. Another clerk had been lying in wait. "Can I help you?"

Luna looked from me to her. "Do you have this in teal?" she asked.

I died.

The clerk said, "No, just what you see here."

"Darn."

The saleslady shrugged at Luna. Then it happened. Her eyes expanded, took Luna in. She stepped back, away, and began to blink real fast.

I felt Luna shrinking in place, shriveling. I reached for her hand. It was trembling, cold.

"They don't have your color," I said. "Let's go." I tugged her out into the mall.

Hurtling away from The Gap, my heart in my throat, I croaked, "Have you had enough? Can we go home now?"

No answer. I turned to her.

"Not yet," she said. "We just got here."

Yeah, a year ago. I'd had enough. That clerk's reaction made me feel like crawling into a hole. "Dad's going to kill us. Or ground us for life. He'll probably call the Y and figure out you were bullshitting him. We should go. Have you seen a phone? I better call him and check in. Breathe heavy in the background so it sounds like you're working up a sweat."

"Hey, Blockbuster." Luna pointed. "I want to get the sound-track for *Hedwig and the Angry Inch*." She hurried away.

Without me to protect her.

I raced to catch up.

Inside the music store Luna headed directly to the movie soundtracks in back, while I shadowed close behind, cursing under my breath. I just wanted out of here. As she passed the Pop and Rock section, this trio of guys appeared out of nowhere. One of them jostled his friend on the left and whispered under his hand.

They sniggered.

Thirteen, I figured. Going on six. Insignia jackets with matching baggy jeans. Oh God. They were following Luna.

I sped up and wedged between them. Closing in on Luna, I shoved her from behind around the end of the CD racks and back toward the entrance.

"What are you doing?" She tried to slap me off.

"Saving you."

That's when she saw them, over the median of CDs between us. "Fag."

My ears burned. Luna's spine fused.

"Hey, fag!"

A girl in the rock section, reading liner notes on a CD, raised her head. She caught my eye. Did I know her? Keep moving, I thought.

"Yo. Fag."

Move!

The lights flicker and the door to the basement slams shut. Liam pounds down the stairs. He flings his backpack over the sofa, where I'm sprawled out doing my homework. The backpack smacks the coffee table and knocks off my cup of soup.

"Liam! Nice going." I retrieve the mug but not before the contents have bled all over my map assignment. "Look what you did!"

He throws himself into the overstuffed chair across from me, hugging his knees. I don't catch whatever he's muttering because I'm trying to salvage my homework. Shaking off the chunks of chicken and noodle and daubing the broth with my T-shirt, which is smearing the Magic Marker on the poster board where I'd just spent an hour delineating all the countries of Africa. "Dammit, Liam!"

"I am not," Liam swears under his breath. "Don't you call me that. You ignorant pissant."

He's talking to himself again. Conducting a conversation with an invisible being — someone other than me. He's such a head case. I'm not sure when he started talking to himself, but I think it was the beginning of eighth grade. Last year. He seemed to recede more and more into himself all year.

Dad noticed. He asked me about it. I told Dad that was just Liam. He said he didn't understand that kid. But then, he never had.

Then Aly noticed. She'd be having a conversation with Liam, or they'd be doing homework together, and he'd disappear. Mentally. Physically. He'd simply fade away.

"It isn't you," I informed Aly. She seemed so worried. "He does it to everyone."

"Where does he go, Re?" she wanted to know. "He goes somewhere. In his head. I don't know. He gets so . . . lost."

I wish I could tell her. I want to tell her.

"Cannot put up with that. I won't. I am not a fag."

"Liam, what are you saying? Who's a fag?"

He snaps to attention, as if he just crash-landed to Earth. His eyes slowly focus on my face and he says, "I'm not a fag. I'm not gay. Tell him that."

"Tell who?"

Liam shakes his head, looking straight at me. "I'm not gay. I'm trans."

"I know that. Who says you're gay?"

His eyes darken. He doesn't have to say who. Hoyt Doucet. Was he on Liam's case again?

"Hoyt's a pus pocket," I remind Liam.

He jumps to his feet and storms off to his room. Funny thing is, I think, if anyone's gay it's Hoyt Doucet. He just won't admit it. He even dates girls. I don't care if he lies to himself; hates himself for being gay. He has no right making Liam's life a living hell. Liam hasn't done anything to Hoyt. He sure isn't interested, if that's what Hoyt's afraid of, or wants. Hoyt's not his type. Not even his species.

Liam returns a minute later with a slab of poster board, which he fwaps down on the coffee table. "We did the same assignment in Trumbo's class."

It's my map. Beautifully colored in with pastel pencils, all the countries outlined in black pen. An A+ circled at the top.

"I'm not gay." Liam spins away. "It's not the same. I'm a girl."

"Whoo hoo. Faggy boy."

They were coming after us.

Luna forged ahead of me, almost knocking over this gorilla dude in a blue suit. A blue suit?

"Hey." I wheeled around, snagging the suit. "Those guys back there? They won't leave us alone." I pointed. "I think they're stalking us. Luna!" I called for her to wait.

All the security guard had to do was evil-eye the wastoids and they bolted. Punks.

"Thanks," I mumbled to the guard before tearing off after Luna. She'd ducked into an alcove between a cigar kiosk and a frame shop, where she was doubled over, hyperventilating.

"It's okay. They're gone." I rubbed her back trying to calm her. Calm myself. I scanned to get our bearings. "There's a girls' restroom down the hall by that shoe store." I showed Luna. "Wait for me. I'll go get your stuff so you can change and we can leave. Give me the locker key."

She unlatched her purse with a shaky hand and dropped the key into my palm. Any second now she was going to disintegrate, implode, disembody. "Oh God. Luna." I squeezed her hand. "I'm sorry." What else could I say? What could anyone say?

Chapter 12

Dad grounded us for life. Until he decided we could be trusted, he said, which might be longer than life. He'd waited up. Probably called the Y. In addition to the prison sentence, he impounded Liam's car — took away the keys and didn't say for how long. Like that was going to work. Liam had that car wired with a fingerpad remote so that anyone who tried to break in would get electrocuted. At least, that's what he'd told me. For years, though, Dad had been aching for any excuse to separate Liam from his beloved car. On Liam's sixteenth birthday Dad had towed home this junk heap of a VW and said, "Hey, son. We're going to rebuild this baby together. Won't that be fun? I know it isn't much to look at now, but wait'll we get it running and do the body work. . . ."

Liam let him know how involved he was going to be in that little father/son project by going out and buying himself a Mitsubishi Eclipse Spyder. Brand new. Sterling Silver Metallic. Convertible.

He must've been saving up for years to buy that car, same way I've been for my own car. Except the current dollar amount in my savings account would finance, oh, a pair of Dad's retreads?

Dad had never forgiven Liam.

Get over it, I thought. Who wants to drive around in a junk heap?

As Liam relinquished his keys to Dad, he didn't even put up

a fight. In his current state, Liam probably would've handed over his entire Dana International collection.

We shouldn't have gone to the mall. It was a stupid idea. Dangerous. Liam must've realized it. I know he regretted it. The rest of the weekend he moped around the basement, incommunicado. I didn't know what to do for him. Step up the suicide watch? I did, actually. I cleared the room of all sharp objects, which was dumb. If Liam was determined to do it, he'd find a way. Not without me, though. Never without me.

$\sim$

Monday morning Liam was back to his old self — hollow boy. I could deal with that. So could he. Hopefully he was over this whole transition phase.

Chris wasn't in chemistry again, which should've been a relief. There was *way* too much chemistry between us and it took a lot of energy to keep my distance. The one bright spot in an otherwise dismal day was that Bruchac was off attending some teacher in-service, so we were treated to a sub. Which meant everyone screwed around. Which meant I sat in a corner by myself, pretending I loved to be alone.

Aly was hanging out in the basement after school, curled in the corner of the sofa watching *Judge Judy*. She motioned me over to her and I flopped down. "What's with Liam?" she said.

Where was he? Nowhere to be seen. His bedroom door was closed.

"I know he's in there," Aly said. "I can hear movement."

"Did you knock?" I asked.

"Yeah. Twice. He wouldn't answer. That was a while ago."

At that moment his door opened and he emerged. Without a word, he walked over, retrieved his PDA from atop the TV, and returned to his crypt.

"Hel-loo," Aly sang, widening her eyes at his retreating back and closing door. "God. He hasn't been this weird for a long time. What happened?"

He was born, I thought. "I have no idea," I lied.

"Guys." She shook her head. "They're so moody."

Were they? I wouldn't know.

Aly returned to feigning interest in *Judge Judy*, concentrating more on the show and less on me. The TV screen suddenly became a mirror. I imagined the three of us reflected in it — our eyes, wide open, gazing into the unknown. Searching, seeking, longing.

What did each of us long for? Liam, of course, longed to be free. To be Luna; to be loved and accepted for the person she was inside. Good luck.

Aly? She longed to be with Liam. She wanted him to be something he never could be. A boy. The man of her dreams. Good luck.

Me? I had no dreams. No longings. Dreams only set you up for disappointment. Plus, you had to have a life to have dreams of a better life. I saw Liam and Aly and me, peering deeper into our futures. This terrible sense of foreboding seeped up through my core. One of us, or all of us, was going to take a fall.

⌒

Mirelle and Cody both rushed me at the door, throwing their arms around my legs and cheering, "Regan, Regan." A wave of love washed over me. My body took form, shape. A life materialized in front of me — mine. At times I felt guilty for taking money from the Materas. They were my lifeline, my only connection to a world outside my brother. A world I could only imagine.

Thank God Dad hadn't grounded me from working.

Mirelle laced her tiny fingers in mine and said, "Come see my mural, Regan."

"Come see mine first." Cody grabbed my other hand and they yanked in opposite directions.

I laughed. So did David and Elise. "Okay, okay. Let me get Ty first. Is it okay?" I queried Elise, motioning to Tyler in his baby swing.

"Of course," she said, continuing to rub in hand cream. It smelled good. Sweet. Same as her.

I retrieved the baby and trailed the kids to their rooms. In her spare time — when she wasn't working at her *important* job of being a mother — Elise freelanced as a graphic artist. She was really good. She'd been working for months on these bedroom murals for the kids. Cody's mural was a baseball player winding up for a pitch. Number four, his jersey read. If that was someone famous, I wouldn't know. Liam would hate this wall. Mirelle's wall was a magic castle with a knight stationed beside his trusty steed, bowing to a fairy princess. The princess's outfit resembled a costume I'd worn for Halloween one year. Or was that Liam? It was more him than me. I think he tried it on when we got back from trick-or-treating. After Mom and Dad had gone to bed, of course. I never did see that costume again. It was probably at the bottom of his treasure chest.

David and Elise left for their dinner date — they actually called it a dinner date — and the four of us watched the last half hour of *Spy Kids II* on *Nick at Nite*. I put Tyler to bed, then Mirelle and Cody coerced me into a game of *Chutes and Ladders*. It didn't take much coaxing. Around the fifth time I fell down a chute, my mind began to wander. I couldn't stop thinking about Liam and what had happened Saturday night.

He hadn't said a word about it. As if it never happened. No doubt he was traumatized and blocking it out. He'd resumed his midnight forays into Luna land, playing dress-up in my room. Nice and safe.

I wished I could forget. Those punks. The clerk. The punks' reaction could almost be expected. It didn't prey on my mind so much as the clerk. The moment she saw what Luna was, when she physically repelled away from her, that feeling seared a scar on my soul. She was actually repulsed.

Luna saw it. She felt it.

I couldn't bear for my brother to be viewed as a freak. It hurt him; I know it did. He didn't deserve that. Nobody deserved that kind of pain. If he decided to live the rest of his life as Moon Girl, he could trust me to keep his secret. He could trust me to keep him safe.

⁓

"Seems your lab partner jumped ship," Bruchac informed me the next day as he handed back last week's problem sets.

I glanced up at him. "What?"

"He dropped the class."

My heart plunged through the sink.

"Since Mr. Doucet's partner doesn't feel the need to make it here most days, why don't you team up with him?"

I glanced over at Hoyt, who flared nostrils at me. No way. Never. Where was the leftover person, the twenty-third? Everybody had partners. Had another person dropped? Atchinson, where was he?

"I'll just work alone," I told Bruchac.

"You could," he said. "But you really should spread some of that cerebral cortex around."

If he only knew how little I had. I looked at Hoyt again and shuddered. "I'll work alone."

"Okay, but I can't give you extra time to finish the labs. No special treatment; I don't play favorites."

Did I ask for extra time? Did I request special treatment? "I can handle it," I said, seething.

"I know you can," Bruchac said. "That's not my concern." In a conspiratorial voice, he added, "It's everyone else in here I'm worried about."

Heat fried my face. He couldn't mean that. As Bruchac returned to his desk, I stared down at the lab assignment for today. Neutralization, normality, titration. Could I handle it? Did I have a choice? Did I ever have a choice? I sighed and X'd out the second name slot.

⁓

"I ran into Skip at the gym today," Dad said at breakfast on Wednesday.

My eyes rose slowly from the problem set I was struggling with. I couldn't extrapolate the equation; I wasn't understanding the logic. Bruchac had me all rattled now with his show of confidence. I think I preferred him as a sexist pig.

If Liam heard Dad, he wasn't acknowledging.

"I asked him about your conditioning program, what I could do to help." Dad folded the newspaper closed. "He told me you've never shown up for practice."

I fixed on Liam. He feigned absolute absorption in his Wheat Chex. At the end of the table, Mom continued to scribble notes in her Daytimer. Her cell rang and broke the tension. Or heightened it. Dad got all tight-lipped and shifted his attention to her.

"Oh, hi, Andy. What? What!" The crescendo in Mom's voice prickled my ears. "We got it?" She exploded, "We got it!"

Covering the mouthpiece, she said to us, "We got the Sorensen wedding!"

Liam's head raised. "Congratulations." He smiled at Mom. He turned to Dad and said, "I lied to you."

Mom stood and headed for the living room, jabbering away at Andy. Dad blinked at Liam. "I figured. What I want to know is, why."

Liam shook his head at the floor. Exhaling a long breath, he answered, "No, Dad, you don't. You really don't want to know." He scraped back his chair and rose. When Liam met my gaze across the table, all I could see was the terror.

"Can I get a ride?" I shot to my feet.

Dad barked, "Sit down, Regan. Both of you. Sit!" I collapsed in my chair. Liam kept walking. "Liam, come back here. I'm not done talking to you."

"Yes, you are," he said under his breath. That one even took Dad by surprise. Before he could react, Mom laughed hysterically and wheezed, "She can't be serious. Feed five hundred people for two thousand dollars? Is she out of her mind? I tell you, rich people can be so *cheap*."

The front door whooshed open and closed behind Liam.

"I really have to go, Dad," I said. To chase down Liam, yeah, but that wasn't the only reason I wanted to fly today. There was an assembly before school that I'd been psyched about for months. An opera performance. In the *Horizon High Notes* before Christmas break an article had run on the last page about the Santa Fe Opera touring schools, trying to promote more interest in the arts. They didn't have to sell me. With all the distractions lately the assembly had slipped my mind. Yesterday, as Aly was channel-surfing, I caught a snippet of Maria Callas singing *Madama Butterfly* on PBS and it triggered my memory.

I needed opera, especially this morning. The music would help me relax and figure out this stupid problem set.

"Do you know what this is all about?" Dad's eyes bore down on me.

"What?"

Dad hitched his chin toward the door.

Oh, that. I opened my mouth, then shut it.

"If you know, tell me, because he's not going to. I don't know what's going on with him anymore. He never says boo to me. We used to talk. We used to be able to communicate. Didn't we?"

Clueless, Dad. You are so not with the program.

Dad's focus shifted to the living room, where Mom was laughing on the phone still, and scribbling in her Daytimer. "He's never lied to me before."

My jaw might've unhinged. His whole life has been a lie, Dad, I wanted to say. Open your eyes.

Dad added, "What did I do? What did I ever do to turn him against me?"

"He isn't against you. It's just —" I stalled. I blew out a breath. "You expect things."

"What things?" Dad snapped. "All I ever wanted was for him to be like every other kid. To be like me. I was a normal, happy kid. My dad wasn't perfect either. Far from it, but I idolized the old man." He stopped suddenly and swiveled his head to gaze out the patio doors. "Okay, maybe that's too much to ask. The kid's a friggin' genius, I know that. I wouldn't want him to lower himself to my level, or believe for one second that his doddering old dad might have a pearl or two of wisdom to share. I just think a little exercise would do him good. Sports builds character, teamwork. He'll need that in life."

"Jack —" Mom appeared suddenly, her cell dangling at the

end of a limp arm. She exhaled wearily. "Why don't you give it up?"

Yeah, I agreed. Thank you, Mom, for once.

"What?" Dad asked. "Is it so much to ask? You tell me." Dad met my eyes. Mine!

Why are you asking me? I wanted to scream.

"Do I expect too much of you, too?" Dad said to me. He waited.

"No, Dad," I answered honestly. It's the rest of the world that expects too much of me.

⟋⟍

I got to school late, even though Dad dropped me off on his way to the Home Depot. The assembly was already in progress. My breath caught. They were doing *La Traviata*. Strains from Violetta's aria, "E strano to sempre libera" wafted down the hall. "Ever free my heart must be," I translated in a whisper. It was my favorite aria. I could sing that aria in my sleep, and did whenever I *got* a full night's sleep.

The double doors nearest me were closed, but one on the opposite end was propped open with a doorstop. I tiptoed in. Adjusting my eyes to the dark, I slipped into the back row. As I curled into a seat hugging my knees to my chest, my eyes closed automatically to soak up the gloriousness of the music.

The soprano's voice sent shivers down my spine. Such clarity and range. I opened my eyes and squinted to see her. Wow. She was young. Younger than I expected. I'd never seen an opera performed live on stage. When had she started singing? She'd obviously had years of voice training to reach this level, and acting experience, and language classes.

The only language I'd ever taken was Spanish, in eighth grade. There aren't too many Spanish operas. I'd always planned to audition for choir, but never took the initiative. Never had the courage. I thought I had an okay voice. It resonated in the shower, anyway.

The aria ended abruptly. The show was over. Already? I checked my watch. I could've stayed to listen for a year, a lifetime. As the stage cleared and the few people who'd attended straggled out, I lingered in the auditorium, absorbing every moment. The feeling, the sense of floating, the transference to another time and place.

The first bell rang for class. Reluctantly, I got up. As I wandered down the hall to my locker, still humming "Sempre libera," a sharp object poked my back.

"Keep walking."

Every muscle in my body seized. We had metal detectors at the doors of the school. How could a knife get through?

"Your lunch money or your life."

"Liam!" I whirled on him. "God." I restarted my heart.

He clicked his mechanical pencil in and grinned.

"Don't do that. You'll make me paranoid."

"Gee." He cocked his head. "I can't imagine how *that* feels."

I sneered at him. He held my eyes, boring into my soul. It scared me to have him look so deep. He accompanied me to my locker. Five or six girls said hi to him on the way. Satisfied customers. Or girlfriend wannabes.

I spun my combination lock and Liam said, "Can we go again Saturday?"

"What?" I rocked back on my heels. "You really want to?"

"It isn't a matter of wanting to, Re. Do you have to baby-sit again? I was hoping we could go earlier. Maybe around noon."

Stunned, I opened my locker and retrieved my English book. "You're going to let Luna emerge in the light of day?"

"She has to, eventually."

Why? I wondered. Why can't you just give this up? Leave it the way it is, the way it's always been? I turned to say it, but the vibes emanating from Liam made me swallow the words. His need, the longing, they were palpable, physical, flowing back and forth between us as if we shared one vascular system. One heart.

"Are you buying me lunch?" I asked instead. "Lunch at a really nice restaurant. That's what this will cost you."

Liam just looked at me.

What?

"Oh, all right." He huffed like it was a big sacrifice.

"Good. Because if the Materas ask me to sit and I can't because of you, it'll cost me like thirty dollars."

Liam frowned. "I'll pay you back." He sounded hurt. Making me feel guilty for caring about the money. It was just a joke, sort of.

The late bell clamored overhead and Liam added, "I better get going."

He didn't leave, though. Just stood there blocking my way. "Did Dad say anything after I left?" he asked.

I gulped a lemon. "Not really."

Liam surveyed the empty hallway behind me. "Did he say he was disappointed in me?"

"No."

Liam nailed me with a look.

"I'm not lying," I lied. "He said — get this — he said he's worried that you don't idolize him." I snorted.

Liam's face welded shut. He lowered his head and let out a ragged breath. For a prolonged moment he didn't move a muscle. Then he lifted his head and said the weirdest thing: "Dad is my hero. Doesn't he know that? I feel like I spend my whole life trying to prove it."

Chapter 13

We arrive at the mortuary a few minutes before the service. Grandma's there greeting everyone, getting consoled. When she sees us, she breaks away from the crowd and bustles over.

"Pat." She embraces Mom.

Mom says, "I'm so sorry, Virginia."

Grandma smiles down on me. "Hello, Regan."

I burst into tears. All the holding back finally catches up.

"Oh, sweetheart." Grandma hugs me hard. At least she's not crying. We'd all be basketcases if she were.

"Liam, don't you look handsome." Grandma squeezes him around the waist.

He barely flinches. He's wearing the new black suit he and Dad went out to buy yesterday. The suit is stiff and so is Liam. He resembles a mannequin. I bet if I kicked him he'd crack and split in two.

A mortuary guy in a dark suit approaches Grandma and says softly, "We're ready to begin, Mrs. O'Neill."

Grandma nods and we trail her solemnly into the chapel. There's a pew reserved for our family. Mom slides in first, then me, Grandma, Liam. I catch a whiff of some old lady's perfume behind us and sneeze. It smells like moldy weeds. When I plug my nose, Mom hands me a Kleenex.

The service for Grandpa O'Neill begins with a song. "Nearer My

God to Thee." It's nice, and I close my eyes to feel the music. A minister leads us in prayer and quotes a Bible passage. Then he turns around and sits down.

Uncle Phil rises from a side pew and heads for the lectern. Dad and Uncle Joel remain in the pew, their heads bowed. Uncle Phil clears his throat and says, "Let me tell you about my pop."

I see Dad's shoulders begin to shake. Uncle Joel loops an arm around Dad as Uncle Phil launches into a story about Grandpa taking them all hunting for elk, the way he did every fall.

Grandma snarls something under her breath.

"What?" Mom whispers, leaning across me.

Grandma twists her head toward Mom. "Phillip hated to hunt. Every time they came home with a kill, he'd lock himself in his room and cry his eyes out. I guess he forgot about that."

I glance up at Uncle Phil, who's chuckling over the time Grandpa got chased up a tree by a skunk. He swore it was a bear.

"Jack never enjoyed it either." Grandma seethes, "Look at them, all three of them. It just makes me sick."

My eyes widen. I've never heard Grandma talk like this. She's always so sweet and kind. Reserved, like Liam.

His part finished, Uncle Phil shuffles back to their pew. He, Dad, and Uncle Joel all blow their noses. Tears stream down Dad's face. He's next up to speak, but waves Uncle Joel ahead.

Grandma leans across my lap and says to Mom, "He beat them, you know. He used to drag those boys to the basement and belt them till they bled. He was a mean son of a bitch." She straightens her spine and adds, "But they worshipped him."

Mom shifts uncomfortably. If she's as shocked as me, she doesn't show it. Grandpa was always nice to us. To me, anyway. He used to tease Liam about being a sissy. Spar with him; punch him in the stomach. There was an argument once. Loud. Grandpa hit Liam so hard he fell down and Dad charged across the living room, spinning Grandpa around and threatening him with a fist. "Keep your hands off him," Dad said. "Don't you ever touch my son again."

I try to meet Liam's eyes, but he's got a weird look on his face. He's staring up at Dad, transfixed.

I guess Mom feels she has to defend Dad because she bends over and whispers to Grandma, "Jack said they deserved it. That they were pretty wild kids."

"Deserved it?" Grandma's voice carries. Across the aisle, I see heads turn, eyes lock on us. Grandma lowers her chin. She takes my hand and whispers, "What child deserves a beating? You tell me that, Patrice. What child?"

Mom doesn't answer. At least, not right away. I'm thinking, Thank God Dad never hit us. He never even spanked us.

A tear slides down Grandma's cheek and she digs in her purse for a hankie. After blowing her nose, she murmurs to herself, "They were boys, Pat. They were just being boys."

Did that make Dad a hero in Liam's eyes? There was another time, too. With Hoyt. I don't know how Dad found out Hoyt was harassing Liam, but he stormed down the block to the Doucets' house. A few minutes later he returned, red-faced and swearing. I think he almost got into a fight with Mr. Doucet.

Nothing changed with Hoyt; I'd see him lying in wait for Liam. What changed was, the whole rest of the year, Liam's eighth grade year, Dad had driven Liam to school and picked him up afterward.

Liam worked so hard to please Dad, to earn his respect. Liam was right; it'd never be enough. The weird thing was, Liam didn't emulate Dad; he didn't want to be like him. He wanted to be Mom. If Dad was Liam's hero, why was he so scared of him?

"Where are we going for lunch?" I turned to Liam as he exited the on ramp and merged into traffic.

"Taco Bell," he answered. He swerved the Spyder to miss a chunk of ice that flew off the rear end of a garbage truck.

"Taco Bell? I got all dressed up for Taco Bell?"

Liam's eyes flickered over me. "That's dressed up? You're lucky I want to be seen with you in public."

I reached over and slugged him.

We were feeling proud of ourselves for slipping out under Dad's nose. He was comatose on the couch, lulled asleep by a hockey game, comforted in the knowledge, no doubt, that Liam and I were safely locked away in our holding cells. Wake up, Dad.

It didn't surprise me that Liam had an extra set of keys to the Spyder. What did shock me was that he'd so openly defy Dad by taking the car out after Dad had expressly forbidden him to drive it.

"I brought the fuchsia sweater and my black jeans," Liam said. "How do you think that'll look?"

"You wouldn't catch me dead in fuchsia. But hey, that's me."

Liam said, "It wouldn't hurt you to add a little color to your wardrobe, you know. Everything you own is so drab."

"I had my colors done," I informed him. "Drab matches my personality perfectly. Gray is so ultra, über me."

He shook his head.

What? It was true.

We'd driven a mile or so in silence when the mood in the car changed. Liam's face muscles clenched and he gripped the steering wheel so hard his knuckles turned white.

"Which wig are you going to wear?" I asked, trying to distract him, engage Luna.

"The brunette pageboy," he answered automatically.

"Good choice," I said, even though I thought the pageboy made him look like a throwback to the twenties. Maybe that was the look he was going for. I remember staggering out of bed one night to go to the bathroom and finding Liam glued to the TV watching this silent movie: *Diary of a Lost Girl.* He'd seen it a hundred times. Still, he'd smiled dreamily at the screen, totally engrossed. He adored old movies, don't ask me why. I thought they were hokey.

We exited at Washington Street and headed downtown. Downtown? I almost said what I was thinking: Why so public? We could find a Taco Bell at a strip mall. Minimize the risk; eat in the car. He seemed to know what he was doing, though. Typical Liam — he always measured every angle.

We pulled into an upscale Taco Bell beside a Virgin Records music store. The place was packed, people streaming in and out the door. Liam turned off the ignition and froze, his hands in a death grip on the steering wheel. If I had to talk him into it again, forget it.

"Okay," he said. "Here's the plan."

I flinched at the command in his voice.

He reached over the seat back and retrieved a yellow placard with a link of chain attached. "You go in and check out the girls' restroom. Make sure it's empty, then give me a signal. Once I'm in, hang this sign on the door."

It was a custodian's warning notice: Temporarily Out of Order.

"Where'd you steal this?"

He grinned sheepishly.

I took the placard and opened my door. Liam grabbed his duffel and followed me as far as the front bumper. "Stay in the hall and guard the restroom until I'm done," he said.

"Duh." I widened my eyes at him. "Do you want me to wear this around my neck, too?"

He sneered. His expression sobered. "Thanks, Re. I know I owe you. I owe you so much I'll never be able to pay it all back."

My eyes dropped. "Just hurry," I told him. "I'm starving."

There were only six or eight tables free. It was noisy, chaotic. People were too busy eating to register a guy slipping into the girls' restroom, I hoped. Nobody seemed suspicious of this drab queen either, loitering around the toilets for a day and a half. The smell of spicy hamburger made my stomach growl. I loved Taco Bell. Liam knew that.

I checked my watch. What was taking so long? If she was posing —

"Re. Hi. What are you doing here?"

I jettisoned through the ceiling.

Chris smiled at me. Chris? My bones disintegrated. "Uh, fine," I said.

He made a face.

"Wait. What was the question?"

He laughed. "I never expected to see you clear down here." He dumped his trash in the bin beside me and stacked his tray on top.

"Well, here I am." My voice sounded wobbly. Same as my knees. "So. How are you? Traitor."

He grimaced. "Yeah, I meant to talk to you about that."

I shot him my best killer look. It was a half-hearted effort, since I was thrilled to see him. Or would've been if —

My eyes darted to the restroom door. No movement. I willed Chris to leave. No, stay. Leave.

He propped himself against the opposite wall, shoving his hands into his front pockets. "I didn't mean to bail on you, Regan. But . . . um . . ." He seemed uncertain, ready to bolt.

"That's okay," I said quickly. Don't go.

"No, it's not okay." He held my eyes. "After that quiz, which

I knew I bombed, I had to get out of there. I only took chemistry because I needed a science credit and figured, Hey, how hard can chemistry be? Mix A and B. Pour in C. Heat and serve."

I snorted.

Chris cricked a lip at me. "Yeah, no one told me you had to be a math jock." He crossed his eyes.

It made me laugh. He had a knack. He was cute.

"I suck at math. And I couldn't fail the class. I've got to keep a C average to play ball. You know?"

I nodded, like I did.

Someone wrenched open the entrance door and stuck his head in. "What are ya doin', man? We're ready to go."

"I'm coming. Don't get your balls in a sling."

The guy glanced over at me, then back at Chris. He rolled his eyes. "One minute, man." The door swung shut behind him.

"I would've helped you with the math," I told him. "You didn't have to drop."

"Yeah, I did, Regan."

My name again. It made my stomach flutter.

"I knew the only way to pass that class would be to use you, and . . . okay." He ground his shoe into a chunk of taco shell on the floor. "I confess that was sort of my plan. At first." He raised his head and met my eyes. "I noticed you got A's on the tests when we were memorizing elements and stuff the first couple weeks in class. But I just couldn't do it. You were too cool. I liked you."

My heart raced. What did that mean, he liked me?

"Oh, shit," someone said in my face. A woman with a screaming toddler. She twisted around and whined to her friend, "It's out of order."

Shit was right. I checked my watch. What was Luna doing in

there? It'd been forty minutes. The bigger question was, what if she made her grand entrance at this very moment? A horn honked out front, snagging Chris's attention. "You better go," I told him. I willed him away. Far away.

"They can wait." Chris raked his fingers through his hair. Nice fingers, not slender and shaved like Liam's. Guy fingers. "You never told me what you were doing here. Do you come downtown a lot? Because my sister has a loft right around the corner." He thumbed over his shoulder. "We could maybe meet there. I could stay downtown today if —"

"No!" My bark echoed in the hallway. "I mean, I never come here. I'm just waiting for someone."

He followed my eyes down the corridor. I felt his whole demeanor alter, shift. Same way it had before. A horn blared and, out of the passenger side window, Chris's friend flipped him the bird. "You really should go," I said.

Chris pushed off the wall. "I guess so."

His tone of voice suggested . . .

The door slammed shut behind him. Out of order on the girls' room. Me waiting for someone. Someone in the men's room? Is that what he thought?

"No, Chris. Wait!"

I'd taken two steps toward the door when car tires squealed out of the lot and, at the same moment, Luna emerged from the restroom.

⁓

"What a rush. What a total rush." She kept repeating it on the way home. "What a rush. A total rush." She was like Mom on the phone with Handy Andy — yammering away a hundred miles a minute, faster than anyone could listen or respond. "No one read me. They didn't know. They didn't even blink."

Luna was wrong. Several people did more than blink. After we got our orders at Taco Bell, the cashier grabbed one of the assembly goons and whispered to him, pointing at Luna. They both snickered, then alerted the other employees. Every hair on my body stood at attention, afraid one or more of them might come over to our table and make a scene. A guy in a jumpsuit across the room had spotted Luna and glommed onto her. He gawked at her the whole time we ate. When he finished his meal, he made a point of meandering through the aisles, taking the long route to the exit, deliberately passing our table. He slowed and stood for a moment, staring. The expression on his face — God. Disgust, loathing, I don't know what it was, but it made me cower in fear.

I prayed he'd go away and he finally left.

Thank God Luna hadn't noticed. She just kept eating her tostada and sipping from her straw. How could she not have noticed? She had to have noticed. She wasn't blind.

After lunch we'd wandered around the renovated area of lower downtown. Luna was bolder this time out, leading me into Banana Republic, the Sharper Image, a leather store to look at purses. She bought a purse on sale for fifty-eight dollars. Last purse I got was a Wal-Mart special — $4.76, marked down from $5.53. The whole time we were out it felt as if people's eyes were on us. Undressing us. Exposing her, and me. How could she not feel it? How could she miss the stares?

It was bizarre. Unreal. As if she knew what was happening and didn't even care.

Liam's whole life was caring what other people saw when they looked at him. What if, after he'd done his best to appear as Luna — to *be* her, the girl he pictured inside — all people saw was a boy in girls' clothes?

When Liam talked about the cost of transitioning, is this what he meant? Because this was more than I could bear. This was costing him his dignity.

Chapter 14

*L*una didn't wake me at two A.M. I was already awake. I couldn't sleep. The scene with Chris in the hallway played out in my head like a tragic opera. The soprano and the baritone. She wins him. She loses him. She longs for him. At last they reunite, then she dies in his arms. In my opera, though, I wasn't in his arms. I was alone at the end, a dying swan.

I must've made Chris think I was putting him off. The other time, too, when he asked me to the rave. Shopping with my sister — I'm sure. It had to make Chris feel diminished, rejected, unwanted. I couldn't stand that. I had to talk to him. As soon as possible. Monday. I'd find him, explain how I was waiting for my brother at Taco Bell. The other time, too. My brother again.

It's always about my brother.

My brother was a black hole in my universe. He was sucking the life right out of me. It seemed as if I was being pulled into this crater by a force I couldn't fight. Liam was already down there. We were together at the bottom. The crater was deep and dark and closing in on us. We couldn't move, couldn't rise, couldn't see to find our way out.

Chris had to know it wasn't about him. It was me, and my duty to Liam. Chris didn't have to know about Liam. I was interested, available. That's all the information he was required to have.

Third period, during study hall, I set up surveillance at the gym. I figured Chris had to show up there eventually.

Bingo. Right after lunch he jogged past my stakeout behind the open door. Through the wired security window, I saw him drop his backpack on the floor and lope over to a couple of guys who were shooting hoops. He asked if he could join them.

Damn. I sank to the floor again. I couldn't barge in there now like I was some love-starved groupie, stalking him. Which, in actuality, I was.

I cursed myself for not revising Act II of my tragic opera. It needed a climactic moment where the conniving diva figures out a way to lure the unsuspecting baritone into her lair.

Liam's goddess must've been smiling down on me — for once. The bell for fifth period rang and the other two guys hustled off to class, leaving Chris alone, dribbling around the foul line and under the basket. He layed one up. *Whoosh.*

The shot was beautiful, and so was he. Not in a movie star way, or a jockster way, or even a tall, dark, and hot kind of way. He wasn't as tall as Liam, or even perfectly proportioned. His parts were all in place, for sure. But he needed a shave. His nose was crooked, like it'd been broken. He wore faded jeans and a crewneck sweater that he'd chopped off above the elbows. Sloppy, shabby even. But cool. I don't know what it was about him. He was a regular guy. Nice. Ordinary. Maybe that was the attraction.

"Do it now," I heard myself say.

My feet didn't obey.

"Now!"

"Okay, don't get your balls in a sling." Was that me? Who was I talking to? There was no me. I was without matter, without form. I stood, walked around the open door, and took one step inside the gym. Then pivoted and skittered off down the hall like the spineless chicken I am and always will be because I'm such a coward and disgust myself for being so scared of everything and everyone that I'll never have a life, ordinary or otherwise.

~

Dad's crusty VW — the one he'd rebuilt himself — was parked in the driveway at home. He's home early, I thought. Or did they change his schedule again at the Home Depot? His boss, who was like eighteen, was always doing that to him. Forcing him to work the graveyard shift so he could inventory the nails and wood screws. Or transferring him to Interior Design and Window Coverings, which Dad dreaded. He said he came off looking like a numbskull every time a customer had a question about how to measure miniblinds. For about a year after he got tanked at Sears, Dad had babbled on and on about how no one is indispensable and that loyalty means nothing anymore.

Must've been one of those pearls of wisdom.

It was pathetic, really, to see what my father had been reduced to. I always thought he was King of the World, Lord of the Rings. Guess Liam did, too.

Dad wasn't glued to the TV the way I expected, although there was a bottle of beer on the coffee table, half empty. He was probably in the john. I made my own pit stop at the fridge for a Coke before heading to the basement.

My breath caught. The basement door was open.

The door was never left open.

It couldn't be Liam. The Spyder was gone. It wasn't Mom. She said this morning she'd be working late. It could only be . . .

"Dad?" I called from the top of the stairs.

No answer.

I stomped down, flatfooted, the creaking sound effects

ricocheting in the stairwell. Across the row of PC's at Liam's long workstation, screensavers built skyscrapers in silent unison. Which wasn't unusual. He had a habit of leaving his computers on all day. What freaked me out was seeing Liam's bedroom door open. He never left it unlocked when he wasn't home. Never.

Maybe he *was* home. "Liam?" I called.

"Regan, is that you?" Dad.

My feet paved a path through the computer components spread out on the floor. "What are you doing?" I drew up at Liam's door, eyes sweeping the interior of the room. Everything seemed in order. Liam was too careful to leave evidence out in the open. Except, he had. There was a purse on top of his treasure chest, that tapestry bag. "How did you get in here?" I said.

"The door was unlocked," Dad replied.

Liar.

"What are you doing home from school early?"

My face flared. "I, uh . . . ditched." Actually I'd sped out the nearest exit from the gym and just kept running.

A smile snaked across Dad's lips. "At least you're honest." His smile faded. "You're grounded. You don't ditch."

"Am I grounded again? Or still?"

Dad fixed on me. "Oh, forget it." He waved a paw in my direction. "You're ungrounded. Both of you. I don't want you staying home because you're forced to. I want you here because your old man's such a stud you can't wait to show him off to your friends."

I snorted. Right, Dad. Sick. Suddenly my backpack weighed a ton. I let it slip off my shoulder and thunk to the floor. I had the strongest urge to run to Dad and hug him, the way I used to. To hold onto him, feel him lift me in the air and make me fly;

spin me around until we were both giddy with glee. Daddy's girly whirligig.

Instead, I took a glug of Coke.

"Let me ask you a question, Re. Come here." Dad motioned me inside.

I didn't like the sound of this. "Liam doesn't want people in his room, Dad. Especially me." You even more.

"Why? What's in here? There's nothing to take. I can't even find his drug money."

"Dad!"

"I'm kidding — I hope. I wasn't going to steal anything. I was just —" He stopped. "What's in that box?" He pointed to Liam's treasure chest.

My blood froze. "How should I know?"

Dad looked at me, through me. "Because he tells you things. He talks to you. Which is more than he does with me or your mother." Dad charged out the door, forcing me to jump aside or get trampled. "What is all this crap?" He waved an arm over the computer parts stacked along the wall, some still in shrink wrap. "Is he stealing this stuff? Selling it?"

"No." I screwed up my face. "He builds PCs for people. You knew that." What did Dad think Liam was? A stoner? A dealer? He was so *not* what Dad imagined.

Dad grunted. Surveying the components, all meticulously arranged and sorted, Dad said, "Well, at least he didn't lie about that."

As I reached over to close Liam's door, Dad shocked me by saying, "Tell me this, Re. Is he gay?"

My hand melded to the doorknob.

"I need to know. Is he?"

Slowly I turned. "No."

Dad's eyes narrowed; burrowed into me. "You're lying," he said. He lumbered over to the sofa and perched at the edge, covering his face with his hands. "I'm not stupid, you know." His voice muffled.

"Dad, I'm not lying." I felt this sudden surge of sympathy for my father. Or empathy. I went and sat beside him, setting my Coke on the coffee table. "Believe me. He isn't gay."

Dad raised his head and twisted to face me. He blew out a shudder, the way you do after you've had a bad scare. "I don't know. All this time, with Aly and everything. He's always got girls down here so I figured he was all right. It's just that lately —"

"He is all right," I snapped.

Dad studied my face. "Does he date? You know, take girls out? Buy them meals? Go to the drive-in?"

"We don't have drive-ins anymore. We have cineplexes."

Dad widened his eyes. "Don't be a smart-ass. Answer the question."

I stood and crossed the room; switched on the TV. "He doesn't tell me everything." Which was the truth, at least. "Probably he doesn't bring dates home because his father's such a studly guy and he's worried about the competition." I smirked over my shoulder.

Dad rested an arm along the back of the sofa. "But he does like girls."

Drop it, Dad, I thought. Grabbing the remote off the top of the TV, I surfed through the channels, hoping he'd take the hint.

"Regan?"

I wanted to scream in his face, No! He's not into girls, okay? He likes guys. We both do. That doesn't make him gay. It makes him as straight as me because inside he's a girl, Dad. Just like me. You have two daughters, okay?

I settled on *Scooby Doo*. The remote control dangled at my side.

"Well." Dad pushed to his feet. "I guess I'm satisfied."

Like Liam, Dad saw what he wanted to see. Heard what he wanted to hear. A genetic defect.

Dad approached from behind and looped both arms around my shoulders. "Tell him I promise to behave myself. Tell him if he brings a girl home and introduces her, I might let him borrow the VW." He gave my lifeless body a quick squeeze.

I forced a smile, but my heart ached. Liam could never tell him. Never.

At the top of the stairs Dad called down, "Tell your brother to lay off the cologne, too, will you? It smells like a brothel in that bedroom."

~

Liam got home around ten-thirty that night. From the middle of my bed, where I was doing homework, I heard him sit in the desk chair and start clicking away. My body begged sleep, but I had to get through these chemistry problems. I was two days behind on worksheets and late with a lab assignment. Bruchac dropped our grade a notch for every day late, and he wasn't giving anyone a break. Especially me, it seemed. He'd waggled a fat finger in my face as I'd slithered past him after class today.

I thought about asking Liam for help, but he had enough on his plate. Now he had to worry about Dad breaking into his room. I'd better warn him. Why did Chris have to drop? I would've helped him. We could've flunked chem together. Which is probably what would've happened if he'd stayed. My interest in the class would've hovered somewhere around absolute zero, since I'd have spent the whole hour making goo-goo eyes at Chris. Better not to have the distraction. For some reason, this inexplicable desire to live up to Bruchac's expectations consumed me. Like it was my big opportunity to glorify the sisterhood or something. Glorify myself.

My bedroom door flew open. "Look at this." Liam rushed in.

"Don't you knock anymore? Doesn't anyone around here respect people's privacy?"

He slid to a stop. With exaggerated steps, he tiptoed backward and closed the door behind him. He rapped twice.

What a dork. "Go away," I muttered.

He rapped again.

"Liam, I'm busy."

"I just want to show you something." The door cracked. "Please? It won't take long."

I exhaled exasperation and remoted off my *Carmen* CD. "You have thirty seconds," I informed him. "Twenty-nine."

He bounced up onto my bed and curled cross-legged opposite me. "What are you working on?" he asked, his gaze skimming over the comforter, where all my papers were strewn.

"Chemistry," I droned.

He picked up my half-finished worksheet from yesterday and said, "You got brutal Bruchac?"

"How'd you guess?"

"Looks familiar. Speaking of looks . . ." He bit his lip. Whatever he was hiding behind his back, he whipped out and slapped on the bed between us. "Check this out."

I eyed the printout. Lifting it, I brought it closer to my face and scanned the page. It was a blurry picture of a guy — a pimply guy with glasses. It appeared to be a blow-up of a bad driver's license. "Yeah, so?" I set down the page.

"Now look at this." Liam placed another printed photo on top of it.

My eyebrows raised. "Wow. Who's this?" I picked it up. It was a girl. A beautiful girl with long black hair and blue eyes. She was posed like a model or something, for a studio sitting. I glanced up from the photo to find Liam grinning at me. "That's Teri Lynn."

"Really?" I examined the photo. "Wow."

"They're both Teri Lynn."

"What? No way." I snatched up the nerd picture for closer scrutiny. Studied both side by side. There was no resemblance at all. "You're kidding."

"I'm not." Liam let out a little laugh. "She's amazing, isn't she?" He picked up the female photo. Gazing into it, his eyes caught fire.

A wave of fatigue flooded over me. I yawned and said, "Tell her to share her makeup secrets, okay?" I stretched my arms over my head and heard the cartilage cracking in my shoulder blades. Stiff, achy.

"It's not all makeup. She's had surgery. A chin implant and nose reduction. But she says the hormones made the difference."

"So take the hormones." I handed him the boy picture so I could get back to work.

"I am." He scooted off the bed, leaving the boy picture behind. Cradling the view of Teri Lynn's new face like it was a sheet of gold leaf, he padded out, leaving the door open behind him.

An alarm sounded in my head. Liam's taking hormones? What hormones? Those were serious drugs. Where was he getting them? Off the Internet? That had to be illegal. I clambered to the end of the bed, then stopped. Did I really want to know about this?

Yes. But not tonight. It was too late to get into a deep discussion about hormones and surgery and transitioning. My mind needed to focus. On *my* life, for once.

I shut the door and resumed my homework. We had to calculate the molecules of acid rain yielded by copper ore conversion — big thrill. My concentration lagged. My eyes came to rest on the picture Liam had left behind.

Teri Lynn's other face. Her false face. It wasn't the difference between the male and female that struck me so much as the change in demeanor, the attitude, the confidence. Teri Lynn, the male, seemed to be another person altogether. A dead person, the way Liam appeared sometimes. Sad, vacant. The other Teri Lynn, the real one, had blossomed and sprung to life. The way Liam broke free when he morphed into Luna.

Like a butterfly emerging from a chrysalis, I thought. An exquisite and delicate creature, unfolding her wings and flying away. Except in Luna's case, the butterfly is forced to rein in her wings and reinsert herself into the cocoon every day. Every single day, she has to become this shell of a person.

Tears stung my eyes. It wasn't fair. Why him? Why her? She was such a good person, Luna. Liam. The best brother ever. I remember, after I got my tonsils out, Liam had put on a puppet show for me. He'd built a stage and dressed up sock puppets. In skirts, of course. My throat hurt so bad, I can still feel the rawness sometimes when I swallow. Every night at bedtime he'd read to me, before I learned how. He'd try to teach me . . .

Once, in first grade, when this bully on the playground kept chasing me and pulling my hair, Liam came over and socked him in the face. That was the only time he ever hit another person in his life.

No, it wasn't.

There was that time at the mall with Mom. She was looking at purses. Liam was, too.

He loops a purse over his arm, copying Mom. I get bored and wander off. Behind me I hear Mom say, "Put that back, and go watch your sister."

"Let me try it," I say to Liam, grabbing for the hat.

"Okay, here. I'll put it on you." He places a felt hat on my head and adjusts it so the feather sticks up in front. I hold my neck stiff because the hat feels like it's going to slide off. It's way too big. Liam tries on a green hat with a silk bow in back and netting on top. He delicately draws the netting down over his eyes.

We model the hats in the mirror. Liam puts a hand on his hip and prances around like a model. It makes me giggle. I mimic him. When Liam returns to the counter for another pair of hats, something happens.

I'm on the escalator and this man is holding my hand. I hear Liam's voice behind me call out, "Regan?"

I glance behind and catch Liam's eye. "Regan!"

I suddenly realize I don't know this man. I scream. I try to twist away, but can't. He's got me tight. Liam comes charging down the escalator steps, falling and picking himself up. We're almost at the bottom before Liam catches up. He lunges and tries to wrench my hand out of the man's. "Let her go. Let her go!" He pounds on the man's back. He fists the man's arms and side and stomach.

Liam's yelling and kicking this man and I'm falling and someone is lifting me up and Liam's hugging me hard and I'm crying and he's saying, "It's okay, Re. I've got you now. It's okay."

Mom lunges off the escalator and yanks me out of Liam's arms. She hoists me up and clutches me to her chest. She yells at Liam, "Why did you let her out of your sight? I can't trust you for a minute!"

She makes him cry.

Mom, it wasn't his fault. It happens to kids all the time, even when their parents are right there. It happened to Cody at the playground. Elise said she turned her back for a minute and a man approached Cody out of nowhere. If Liam hadn't saved me . . . If he hadn't been there for me . . . I shudder to think.

Liam's so needy now, I thought, I'm forgetting all the times I needed him. He's always been there for me. Always.

The sound of Liam's humming filtered under my door. Low, sultry strains of an unfamiliar tune. He only hummed when he was happy. Would he ever really be happy? Maybe if he got to the place Teri Lynn was now he'd be okay. No one would even suspect she was a T-girl. Could Luna change her body chemistry, her physical appearance, enough to convince the world that she was the person she knew herself to be?

The image of Chris flooded back into my brain. Why him? Why now?

Chemistry. That was it. The tears in my eyes overflowed the rims. Why did it have to be about chemistry?

Chapter 15

As I was retrieving a box of Cocoa Puffs from the pantry to take to the breakfast table, I heard Mom on the wall phone in the kitchen. "Will you please have Dr. Rosell call me?" she said. "I need an early refill on my estrogen."

I rolled my eyes and slugged down my own daily fix of OJ at the fridge.

Dad said, "Morning, honey" to me as I flopped into my seat.

I grunted, but it took effort. These all-nighters were frying my brain. I think I preferred mindlessly watching Luna put on mascara for three or four hours than shorting out synapses with chemistry.

As soon as Mom hung up, the phone rang. She leaped on it like she was expecting the call from Powerball. "It's for you, Regan. Elise." She sounded irritated. Mom didn't like Elise much. Another reason I did. She told me once she felt Elise and David took advantage of me, always calling at the last minute, expecting me to drop everything. Like I had anything to drop. "Don't be over there all weekend," Mom said. "I need you here." To do her job. Handing me the receiver, she asked, "Where's Liam?"

"She was still in the shower when I came up."

A surge of electricity charged the air. It wasn't until Elise burbled, "Hey, Regan," in my ear, "can I ask you a favor?" that it hit me. What I'd just said. Maybe it was because Luna had been in my room sometime during the night and left a cloud of perfume behind, or my dream at dawn had deposited a strong visual. Before and after. Liam/Luna. The difference between them was beginning to blur.

"Regan?"

"Huh? Oh," I snapped out of it, "yeah, sure, Elise. Whatever."

"David and I finally got tickets to this play we've been dying to see. It's called, *I Love You, You're Perfect, Now Change.* Have you seen it?"

"No."

She laughed a little. "Of course not. You're too young to even appreciate the title."

No, I wasn't.

"Anyway," she went on, "we waited too long to get tickets and now this is the last weekend it's playing, so we were wondering if you could baby-sit Saturday night?" Her voice rose in a hopeful wince. "I know it's short notice and I try not to ask you on Friday or Saturday nights, since you undoubtedly have a busy social life . . ."

Yeah. Me and Titration. "No problem," I said.

"Really? Regan, you're a doll. What would we do without you?"

Why wonder? I almost asked. Adopt me. Give me a regular life, a happy childhood. Oops, too late.

Elise asked me to be there by six-thirty and we disconnected. When I dragged back into the dining room, Liam had materialized. Dad lowered his newspaper and said, "A blind man and his guide dog go into a restaurant."

Liam and I groaned.

"After ordering and sitting there a while, the blind guy yells to the waiter, 'Hey, you wanna hear a blonde joke?'"

I tried to snag Liam's attention for a dual eye roll, but he was immersed in one of his tattered manga comic books. *Call Me Princess*, if that wasn't telling.

"The restaurant becomes absolutely quiet," Dad continued. "In a husky, deep voice, the woman next to the blind guy goes, 'Before you tell that joke, you should know something. The waiter is blonde, the cook is blonde, and I'm a six-foot-tall, two-hundred-pound blonde with a black belt in karate. What's more, the woman sitting next to me is blonde and she's a weight lifter. The lady to your right is a blonde and she's a pro wrestler. Think about it seriously, Mister. You still wanna tell that joke?'"

Dad paused for effect. I popped a mouthful of Cocoa Puffs. Mom lifted her coffee cup. Liam flipped a page. "The blind guy says, 'Nah, not if I'm gonna have to explain it five times.'"

Liam laughed. I sprayed the table with cereal. Even Mom smiled.

"Good one, eh?" Dad winked at us.

"Good one," Liam said.

While I wiped up my mess with a napkin, Dad added, "I was down in the dungeon yesterday. Regan tell you?"

Uh-oh. Brain warp. Bracing for Liam's reaction, I hid my head behind the cereal box. When I peeked over, he was still reading his book. At least Dad hadn't found anything. He hadn't even seen the purse.

"The place is a dump," Dad said. "The stuffing's coming out of that sofa and the carpet looks like a herd of buffalo tramped through. It stinks down there, too. Like moldy pizza. I don't know how you two can stand to live in such squalor."

"We'll clean it up," Liam murmured.

"That's not my point. I was thinking we should give the place an overhaul. You know, paint and recarpet. I could use my store discount. We'll get some shelving units for all your computer parts and get them up off the floor. Once we clear out the room, we can set up a pool table or an entertainment center. Something we could all use."

Liam smiled wanly at Dad. "That's okay. I like it the way it is. We both do. Don't we, Re?"

Dad's fist hit the table. "No, it's *not* okay. We're going to make this a family project. All three of us. We start this weekend." Dad rose to stomp into the kitchen. He yanked open the dishwasher and noisily stacked his coffee cup in the rack.

Liam called to him, "I've got a project to finish at the library on Saturday. And Sunday I promised Aly I'd take her to the movies. It's sort of a date."

Dad reappeared in the doorway, eyebrows arched. "Yeah?"

The thud of my jaw hitting the table almost betrayed Liam. I put in, "Yeah, and I have to work Saturday night. Plus, I have this paper due on Monday for English that I haven't even started." Which was true. I'd neglected all my other subjects to concentrate on chemistry. "Unless you want me to flunk out of school, I was planning to spend all day Saturday surfing the Internet for an essay to download."

Liam got the joke, but the parental units were a little slow. Mom said, "We don't have the money right now, Jack. Not for carpet. And especially not for a pool table or an entertainment center." She continued to work on invoices for her clients, the way she'd been doing all morning. Then her cell rang.

That was our cue. Liam and I stood to go.

Dad charged through the dining room. "Hold it, you two."

We slumped in unison.

"Liam, the walls in your room are a mess. What are all those holes?"

The holes. I'd forgotten about the holes. Every year Mom would buy a complete set of school pictures to send to relatives and friends. She'd frame and display our 8 x 10's on the buffet in the dining room. By the end of the week, Liam's picture would be turned face down and the extra pictures in the pack — the smaller ones and the wallet-sized — would mysteriously go missing. Only I knew where they went: to his room. He tacked them on his wall as a dartboard collage.

Every day Mom used to right Liam's picture on the buffet, but I guess after a while she gave up the battle. She stopped buying school pictures when we got to middle school.

"Termites," Liam mumbled, heading for the foyer.

Dad said, "And Regan, your room is a pig sty."

He'd been in my room, too? How dare he! If he touched anything . . . I had my crap arranged just the way I liked it. "Stay out of my room, Dad," I ordered him. "Stay out of both our rooms." I riddled Dad with eye bullets before barreling out the door after Liam. I had to sprint to catch up. "Don't ask me how he got in there," I wheezed at Liam's back. "You need a better lock."

He didn't respond. He punched his secret code into the car's keypad and unlocked the door.

"Can I get a ride?"

The door lock on the passenger side popped open and I circled around.

As Liam turned on the ignition, he said, "Did he even see the purse? Did he open the treasure chest?"

"No, thank God. I got there in time." I fastened my seat belt.

Liam expelled a short breath. Like he was annoyed with me.

"What? Did you want me to let him try on your wigs?"

Liam's jaw clenched.

Weird. He was sending out some signal I wasn't picking up.

At the corner, slowing for the stop sign, he punched the button to retract the convertible top. It was a hundred below today, easy.

He dropped me off at school and peeled out of the lot. The signal arrived as I was trudging into the building, teeth chattering. He left his bedroom door unlocked on purpose. He meant for Dad to find his secret stash.

Was Liam crazy? Dad would never get it. He'd never understand. Liam was playing with fire, and he was going to get burned.

~

My lunch money was still sitting on the kitchen counter, which I figured out at noon as I approached my locker, plunging my hand into my purse and not connecting with a billfold. Crap. It was bad enough I had to slink into the cafeteria to buy a sandwich and chips from the vending machines so it wouldn't be obvious I was standing alone in the hot lunch line. The machines were closer to my table — the smallest, darkest one in the forbidden corner of the cafeteria. Next to the nerds.

Maybe I could sit at Shannon Eiber's table and share her lunch. She and her Chosen Ones crammed into the center table every day to compare sex lives. What else could be that funny? They laughed maniacally for the whole freaking hour.

The edge of a headache sawed at my eye socket and I wished I'd stayed home sick. I liked it better when mom made my lunch. Bologna roll-ups.

Wow, I hadn't thought of bologna roll-ups in ages. I hated bologna roll-ups. At the moment, though, I'd sell my soul for a bologna roll-up.

In front of my locker I sank to the floor and buried my head in my knees. When did Mom stop making our lunches? In middle school? Same time she stopped buying our pictures? No, before that. Right after Christmas. I'd just turned ten.

"I have a lunch meeting today with sales and marketing," Dad

says, coming out of the hall buttoning his cuffs. "No need to pack me a lunch, Pat."

A crash sounds in the kitchen and Liam and I both jump. We're in the living room, where Liam is fixing my new CD player. Dad tried to program it last night and now it's all screwed up.

Mom shrieks, "Why didn't you tell me? You know I've been in here for the last hour making lunches. I'm always in here at the same time every day making lunches. That's all I ever do. Cook for you, clean for you, take care of the kids . . ."

Dad blanches. "I'm sorry, hon. I forgot."

"You forgot?" Mom shrills.

At times like this Liam and I play a game: Invisible shrinking dolls.

Dad quips, "It takes an hour to make bologna roll-ups? What do you have to do, slaughter the bologna?" He winks at us.

Liam sniggers. There's another crash in the kitchen and Mom snipes, "Make jokes, Jack. That's all you know how to do. Everything's a joke to you."

I sense Dad opening his mouth to make a joke, but he squelches it fast.

Mom goes on, "In the future, will you please have consideration enough to let me know in advance when you won't be needing my services?" She storms out of the kitchen carting Liam's and my thermal lunch bags. She practically throws them at us. "Get ready for school," she snaps. "You're going to be late."

As Dad slips on his suit jacket, looking peevish, Mom stomps down the hall and slams the bedroom door.

I say, more to myself than anyone, "I don't have school today. It's teacher-in-service." I forgot to tell Mom. She should know, though. Why does she make me remind her? She's always spacing important stuff like that.

Mom returns from the back hallway, shoving Dad's wallet at him. "I suppose you'll be late for dinner again." She continues through the dining room and into the kitchen.

Dad pockets his wallet. "I might. I try to get out of there on time, but the big boss is in this week and nobody dares leave before he does. You know how that goes."

I hear the refrigerator door open. Liam's the one who is brave enough to do it. He takes my lunch from me, gets up, and pads into the kitchen. "Re doesn't have school today, Mom," he says nicely. "But I'll take her lunch. I'll take Dad's, too. I get pretty hungry during the day."

"So, what? I don't pack you enough to eat?" There's a clunk in the sink, like a frozen turkey just fell from the sky. "I don't know why I even bother," Mom says. "If I did go to work, none of you would even notice I was gone."

"You know that's not true," Dad says sharply. Liam hurries back to the living room. "What is it with you lately?" Dad snipes at Mom. "Nothing we do around here is ever enough."

"You don't do anything!" Mom yells. "I do it all. You don't even know what I do all day. You can't even appreciate the drudgery of cooking and cleaning and catering to you and the kids. It's mindless. It's stifling."

Dad's barks, "Well, I'm sorry if we bore you. You keep talking about going to work, so go." Dad throws up his hands. "We're not forcing you to stay. Heaven forbid me and the kids should hold you down for one minute." Dad's mad. Madder than I've ever seen him.

Liam and I cower together in the living room. Be over, I think. Just be over.

Dad says, "Did you take a Valium today? Maybe you need to increase your dosage again."

Mom charges out of the kitchen. I think she's going to hit Dad, but *instead, she stops and grabs the nearest object to her hand. It's Liam's picture off the buffet. She smashes it to the floor and the glass shatters.*

Dad grips her wrist. "That's enough. I've had it with you." The way he'd say to us, to a child.

"No, Jack," Mom shoots back. "I've had it with you. *I've had it with you and these kids and my life. It* isn't *enough. I keep telling you that, but you won't listen. I'm dying inside. I just want* out!*" She wrenches free of him and storms to the bedroom.*

I lifted my head, the argument still ringing in my ears. Dying inside. She felt trapped, just like Liam. But opposite of him. She found her escape by looking outside herself, while Liam escaped within.

"Re, hi." A presence loomed over me. "Are you okay?"

I scrambled to my feet. How long had Aly been standing there? "Yeah. I . . . forgot my lunch money."

"Here, I'll give you some," she said. Aly dug in her shoulder bag for her billfold and handed me a five.

"Thanks." My brain was on delayed reaction. "I'll pay you back."

"You don't have to." Aly dropped her billfold back into her bag and pulled out something else. "If you see Liam, would you give him this?" She thrust a book at me, another graphic novel of Liam's. *Love Hina.* "Tell him not to forget about Saturday, my art project, going to that sculptor's studio. He should come by and get me around one."

I nodded, making a mental note. All the mental reminders and memories were jamming up in my brain.

Aly bit her lip and added, "Has Liam said anything to you about prom?"

Prom. A switch tripped in my head. Luna. The flapper dress.

"Because I'd really like to go this year. I know he thinks it's phony and pretentious, but it's our senior year, you know? I even have a dress picked out."

Will it fit Liam? I almost asked. Liam wasn't anti-prom; he just wanted to be Queen. "He hasn't said anything to me."

Aly didn't look convinced. Or satisfied.

Change of subject. "Could I borrow a couple Tylenol?" I said. My headache was carving a canyon in my skull.

"Sure." She clawed through her bag again. "Is Excedrin okay?"

Excedrin. Ecstasy. Anything to dull the pain, blunt the memories.

She emptied two caplets into my palm.

"I'll walk you to the cafeteria," Aly said.

She waited at the drinking fountain while I knocked back the pills. As we started down the hall, Aly continued, "Maybe you could mention it to him. Drop a hint. Plant a subliminal suggestion in that thick skull of his."

"Like it would penetrate," I muttered.

"I know. Tie it to a brick."

At the turnoff to the cafeteria Aly slowed and stopped. She hesitated a long moment. "He isn't taking someone else, is he?"

"What?"

"Hel-loo." Aly angled her head, like, tune in, Re. "He seems distracted lately, even more than usual. Like he's withdrawing from me, from everyone. Keeping his distance. I don't know. He's done this before, but now it's . . . it's different." She trailed off, her gaze drifting over my shoulder. "Like he's involved with someone else?"

Yeah, himself, I didn't say. "There isn't anyone else."

Aly bit her lip again.

"Aly, I swear."

"You'd tell me if there was, wouldn't you, Re? You wouldn't

keep something like that from me. I mean, I'd want to know. Even if it hurt."

"I wouldn't keep anything from you." That lie tripped off my tongue too easily. I'd never hurt her, not on purpose. Why didn't she ask Liam? Why didn't she talk to him? They were best friends.

Her face relaxed a little and she gave me a hug. "What would I do without you?" She smiled. Squeezing my arm, she flitted away.

Who'd said that to me earlier? Elise? Liam? I couldn't remember. Anyone else would be honored to receive a double dose of trust in one day. So why did I just feel used?

Chapter 16

A voice echoed in my ears. Chris's voice, coming from Chris's body, which was sending out sound waves and heat waves next to me. "Hey," he said. Whole language abandoned me. Fortunately, my English book chose that moment to streak off the top shelf of my locker and crash to the floor. As I bent to pick it up, Chris did too, and we cracked skulls.

"Ow!" we yelped in unison.

"Spaz," Chris added under his breath.

"I know," I said. "I'm sorry."

"Not you. Me." His hand reached for my forehead. "You okay?"

I flinched. Reflex, I guess, but he looked offended. Hurt. Like I thought he had AIDS or something.

"Sorry." What was it about him? Whenever he was near, I turned into a biohazard.

"I've been waiting for you," he said. "Hoping you had to stop at your locker after your Skills for Living class. I wanted to talk to you."

Okay, this was weird. Right out of *Tales of the Unbelievable.* How did he know this was my locker? How did he know I took Skills for Living? Did he also know I'd been obsessing about him, that he'd been showing up in my dreams at night? That canoe was getting waterlogged. "Talk about what?" I asked, digging through my locker for . . . I don't know what. A life vest?

Chris moved around to my other side, the side where my frontal lobe wasn't protruding over my eye. "I've been asking around about you and nobody seems to know who you are."

I snorted. Big surprise.

"Except Shannon Eiber."

I tensed. "What did she say?"

Chris gulped.

My eyes slit. "What?"

"She just said you're a little . . . stuck up."

"Stuck up!" My voice shrilled. Is that what everyone thought, that I was stuck up? A snob? A bitch?

"Personally, I don't see it," Chris put in quickly. "It takes one to know one, right?"

All I could do was shake my head. It made me feel like crying, though. That wasn't why I didn't talk to people. I wasn't stuck up.

Chris leaned in closer and cooed suggestively, "You're like a mystery."

My face fried — literally, you could smell the smoke. "Oh yeah. That's me. A mystery, even unto to herself." Oh how lame.

He smiled. His arm snaked behind my head and came to rest on the frame of my locker door, the space around us closing in. Intimate like. He added, "I've had to follow you around to get my real question answered."

Huh? "What question?"

"Are you going with anyone?"

I might've laughed if he hadn't looked serious. "Serious?"

"That guy who drives you to school in the jazzed car. The

one who lets you off in the back of the parking lot. Is he your boyfriend?"

This time I did laugh. Hysterically. I doubled over in laughter, like a donkey with asthma. I couldn't stop laughing; I couldn't catch my breath.

Chris strummed his fingers over the vent on my locker door. "I didn't think it was that funny," he said.

"I'm sorry." I gasped for air, reaching up to steady myself on his chest. I withdrew my hand fast.

"If he is, tell me and I'll back off. I just thought maybe, you know —"

"You thought what?" I sobered fast.

"I thought I'd take the chance. Ask you out. But if you're with someone, that's cool."

"The guy who drops me off is my brother."

His eyebrows shot up. "No shit?"

"None whatsoever."

We both grinned and dropped our eyes. I tried to glance up at him coyly, the way Shannon Eiber does. Would have. Without warning the locker door swung open and crushed Chris's hand between it and the wall.

Bone crunched and Chris went, "Geeawd!"

"Oh my God." I reached for his arm.

He lurched away. He shook off the pain, dancing around, while I stood there bouncing fists off my thighs, apologizing, dying inside.

He rubbed his hand against his chest and said, "So would you go out with me?"

Unbelievable. "Are you a masochist?" I asked. He had to be. He was crazy. Did he mean it?

Through apparent agony, his eyes answered the question. He meant it.

"No," I said, "but thanks anyway. I'm too dangerous. Not allowed to make human contact." That's what my brain said. What came out of my mouth was, "Okay. When?"

"Um . . ." He hesitated. "Saturday night?" He gave his hand a final shake. "There's this party up in Creighton. Sort of a rave, but underground. You know the kind."

"Sure," I lied. "Oh, wait." My heart sank. "I can't Saturday. I have to baby — work. I have to work."

His face changed.

Not again. This might be my last chance, my only chance. "I could find someone to fill in for me, though. I really do have to work. Or did. I mean, I can go. I'll figure something out."

"Yeah?" His eyes lit up. "Cool. Okay. So I'll pick you up around, what? Like seven?"

Six, seven. Could we leave now? "Let me give you my address." I fished in my purse for a pen.

"I know where you live. I've been following you, remember?" He jabbed my arm with his good hand. Then swaggered off.

I drooled all over myself. This was insane, agreeing to go out with him. Scary. What if —

What if what? What could it hurt? One date. How close could we get? Only as close as I allowed.

The minute I got home I called Aly. "Could you baby-sit for me Saturday night? For the Materas?"

"The Materas?" She let out a short laugh. "You've got to be kidding. Don't you remember what happened the last time I sat for them?"

Oh yeah. Aly used to be their regular sitter until she got bored one night and asked a few friends over. David and Elise walked in on them watching Pay Per View on their big screen TV. It's not like she was having a wild party or anything, but Aly was now officially blacklisted by the Materas'. Her loss had been my gain. After that night I'd become their exclusive sitter.

How could I have forgotten? Because my brain wasn't operating on all cylinders.

"I couldn't do it anyway," Aly said. "I promised my mom I'd go to this designer trunk show with her Saturday night. Whoo hoo."

"Do you know anyone else?" I asked; pleaded.

She thought a minute. "What about Brit? No, forget that. One look at her piercings and tats and Elise would freak. C.J.? I could ask, but she's probably going out. She's hot for this senior over at Lincoln."

Aly was silent for a moment. "Wow, I can't think of anyone."

This sense of hopelessness seeped into my soul. There went my first — and last — date.

Aly added, "Did you remind Liam about Saturday?"

"No. I just got home." Where'd I'd be rotting in solitary the rest of my life.

⁓

Thursday night while Elise and David were off exploring their yin and yang at yoga, I was rediscovering sleep. The Materas came home to find me curled in a fetal position in front of their big screen TV. David had to shake me awake. How humiliating. Mirelle and Cody were still up watching TV, not even changed into their pajamas. Some sitter I was. The house could crumble around me and I wouldn't choke on the dust.

I kept apologizing, but Elise said it was all right, she understood. There was an undertone to her voice, though. A note of disapproval.

I tried to refuse the money, but David forced it on me. It

wasn't as much as I usually got, but even so, a dollar less an hour was still more than I deserved.

By the time I got home, I'd decided rather than deposit the money in my car fund, I'd buy toys for the kids. Pay for my guilt trip. I opened my bedroom door and Luna attacked me. "You'll never guess what's going on." She yanked me down to the bed.

"I'm guessing you broke into my room while I wasn't here. You're as bad as Dad." I kicked off my boots. It was early for Luna to be in evening wear; the moon hadn't even waxed poetic.

She tossed her hair over her shoulder. "Teri Lynn's coming here."

"To the house?" My eyes bulged.

"No. Into town." Luna's coral-colored lips curved in a wide arc. "There's a sales convention over the weekend and she's giving a presentation on Monday, so she thought we might get together afterward. Have dinner." She bounded to her feet and flounced toward the mirror.

"How old is this Teri Lynn? What does she do exactly? How do you know she's legit?" I sounded like a parental unit.

Luna slid into my desk chair in front of her lighted mirror. Uncapping a tube of mascara, she answered, "She's twenty-seven. She owns her own consulting company. They do diversity training for law enforcement agencies. I've talked to her on the phone."

On the phone? I spread-eagled backward on the bed. "Wow. So, what's she like?"

"Like a person."

I scoffed. "No, I mean is she independently wealthy or something?"

"Mmm." A smile infused Luna's voice. She turned to me and

added, "I have to go shopping. I'm not about to wear Goodwill rags the first time I meet her. What time are we going Saturday?"

Saturday. Saturday night. I stared up at the blank ceiling. "I have a date Saturday night. Or I did."

"What!" Luna gasped. She rushed over and flopped down next to me. "Who with? Someone I know? Tell me everything."

The joy I'd been confining to mini bursts finally broke through the clouds. "You don't know him, I don't think. Chris Garazzo?"

"Doesn't sound familiar."

"He's new." Brand new.

"What does he look like?" she asked, eyes sparkling.

"Like a person." We sneered at each other. I sighed wistfully. "Make that a god."

Luna squealed.

"There's a problem, though." I sat up and hugged my knees. "Major setback. I'm supposed to baby-sit Saturday night and I can't find anyone to fill in."

"You just did." Luna pushed to her feet. "I owe you. What time is Chris picking me up?" She twisted her head to grin over her shoulder. "Just kidding. When do I have to be at the Materas'?"

I hesitated. I don't know why. I'd just call Elise and tell her I had other plans. My busy social life. I'd found a replacement sitter.

She'd ask who.

I'd say my brother.

She'd say fine.

No, she wouldn't. Elise would never let a stranger in her house. She'd never leave her kids alone with a person she didn't know, especially a guy.

A glint of moonlight reflected off Luna's shining face. Her eager face.

Liam did owe me. It'd only be the one time. Maybe I could work it so Elise and David wouldn't know. Why not? Anyone else in my position would go. "You're on," I said. My brain amped up. I suddenly felt excited. "I don't want you to arrive at the Materas' until after they leave, though. I'll only be gone for a couple of hours. You'll be out of there before Elise and David get home. Wait. You can't come until I put the kids to bed. Otherwise, they'll rat me out."

"Sounds like a plan." Luna resumed her seat at the mirror.

"And I'll tell Chris to pick me up at the Materas'. That way he won't come here and risk having an encounter-of-the-freakazoid-kind with you-know-who." Studly unit. "I'll put the kids to bed early; ask Chris to pick me up at eight-thirty."

"It's settled." Luna slapped her thighs and twirled on the desk chair. "What time are we going shopping Saturday? You're going to need new clothes."

Saturday. Lunch. Prom. Sculptor. "Aly said to remind you about Saturday. Some art project at a studio? You're supposed to pick her up at one?"

"Is that *this* Saturday?" Luna's eyes met mine through the mirror. Her face sagged and she sighed heavily. "Sorry, Re. How about Sunday? We could go shopping on Sunday, for me anyway. What time do the stores open? Eleven? Twelve?"

I was stuck on Aly. "Are you thinking about asking Aly to the prom this year? Because she really wants to go. She already has a dress picked out."

"A dress," Luna repeated flatly. She crossed her legs and hunched over, holding her stomach. "Know what I'd really like, Re? What I'd *love* is to go to the prom as me. In my own dress. Get my hair and nails done. Rent a limo. Rent a date." She lifted her head. "Chris doesn't have a brother, does he?"

I must've looked freaked.

"Just kidding." Luna straightened. She lifted a brush and ran it slowly down her wig, staring vacantly at her image in the mirror.

Luna. Liam. Liam at the Materas'. A knot of fear twisted in my stomach. Why? I'd be fine.

I cast it off. This was the first time I'd ever felt such happiness, such hopefulness about my life. About me. My future.

What could happen? One night. What could possibly go wrong?

Chapter 17

I arrived at the Materas' fifteen minutes early, as usual. Elise said, "Wow, you look nice." She ushered me inside, scanning me from head to toe. "You've done something different. What is it? Your hair?"

"Yeah, I got it cut. Just the ends."

"Where do you go? I need a trim. Last time I went to the Mane Event, they butchered me."

"Um . . . ," I stalled. What could I say? Chez Luna? "A friend did it."

"Really? She's good." Elise turned me around in a circle. "Tell her if she wants to expand her client base, I'd be happy to pay."

"I will." Like that'd ever happen.

Elise said, "David has a pager now, so I added that number to the speed dial." David appeared behind her, proffering her coat, and she slipped it on. "We'll be back by eleven-thirty, at the latest. I bought you some NoDoz. They're on top of the refrigerator." Elise smiled. "That was a joke."

She didn't sound like she was joking. "I won't fall asleep. I promise."

"Make sure you lock the door," David said.

I always locked the door. They knew that.

Elise rattled off the particulars: Where they'd be, what there was to eat, blah, blah, blah. It took forever. Just go! I screamed inside. Get out of here.

Finally, through my peephole in the window blinds, I watched their Ford Explorer back down the driveway. "Can we watch *Monsters, Inc.*?" Cody shoved the DVD at me.

"Sure." I followed Cody and Mirelle to the TV and sat cross-legged between them, which wasn't easy in the tight jeans Luna had forced me to wear. They were white, the only white thing I owned. Why did she insist I wear white?

The movie dragged on interminably. I kept looking at my wrist, which was dumb because I'd forgotten to wear my watch. I did brush my teeth, I think. Finally, the outtakes at the end.

I scrabbled to my feet. "Okay, time for bed."

"Already?" Cody and Mirelle whined. Mirelle added, "We didn't even get our snack."

"You can eat it in bed," I said.

They widened eyes at each other. "All right!" Cody cheered.

Elise would kill me for letting them have food in bed. Oh, well. I might not live through this night, anyway. Mirelle and Cody hustled to their rooms. The baby was out cold in my arms, sleeping like a lamb. I put him down first. As I was digging out a couple of Rice Krispie treats from the pan in the kitchen, the front doorbell rang.

"Shit," I hissed. The oven clock read eight-twenty. I was running late.

"I'll get it," Cody's voice echoed from the back.

"No!" I hollered.

He flew past me, his footsteps thundering down the hall. I caught up as Cody flung open the front door.

"Uh, hi," Liam greeted him. His eyes raised to meet mine.

"You're early," I said.

"I am?" Liam checked his watch.

Cody asked, "Who are you?"

Liam answered, "The tooth fairy. You can't tell anybody you saw me because no one knows what I look like. And if you don't get back to bed right now, I can never come back here and leave you money under your pillow. Fairy rules."

Cody gasped. He blinked once, then pivoted and raced back down the hall. His bedroom door slammed.

I snorted. "Where'd you come up with that one?"

"I read it in your fairy handbook."

I smacked his chest. Back in the kitchen, I resumed dishing up treats and delivering them to the kids; tucking them in; kissing them goodnight. Mirelle wanted me to read her a story. I told her not tonight. I told her she could wear her earplugs and listen to music. Which was also against the rules. Oh well. Tonight I was playing by fairy rules.

When I returned to the living room, Liam was curled on the sofa, reading a paperback. I said, "If they get up, just . . . I don't know. Tell them you're the boogeyman."

Liam made a face. "I'll hypnotize them. Erase their memories. They'll never know I was here."

"Sometimes Tyler wakes up if he gets too hot. Check on him occasionally, okay? His diapers and stuff are on his bureau in the bedroom. If you can do it without waking her up, take out Mirelle's earplugs. The emergency numbers are on the speed dial and to use it, you just punch —"

"I think I can figure out the phone," Liam cut in.

"I borrowed Aly's cell for tonight, so if anything happens —"

"Nothing's going to happen."

Through the window slats, car lights illuminated the living room. "There he is."

Liam dogeared the page in his book and stood.

"I'm going to hurl."

"No, you're not."

"Yes, I am." My stomach twisted and growled. "I can't do this. I'm sick. Really."

"Calm down." Liam clenched my shoulders. "You'll be fine." He bent down to kiss my cheek. "Have a good time, Re."

The doorbell buzzed and I bolted. Or would have if Liam hadn't secured me with a stronghold to the hardwood floor. He steered me to the foyer. My arms were paralyzed at my sides, so he had to reach around me to open the front door.

"Hi," he said to Chris.

"Hey, I know you." Chris waggled a finger at him. "Tryouts, right?"

Liam stiffened.

I freaked. They knew each other?

"Right," Liam said in his deepest voice. He shoved me across the threshold.

"Did you make the team?" Chris asked, goosenecking over my head.

"No."

"Oh. Sorry, man."

I turned and glared at Liam. He shrugged like, Hey, I didn't know. "I'll be home by eleven at the latest," I said between clenched teeth. "The very latest."

Liam smiled. "Just have fun." Leaning closer so Chris wouldn't hear, he added, "He is a hottie." Liam shut the door in my face.

Chris said, "You got your brother to baby-sit? What did you have to do, bribe him?"

"Totally. I sold my soul," I said.

Chris grimaced.

"No, it's okay. It'll be worth it." Why'd I say that? I was saying too much.

A slow smile spread across his face. Checking me out under the porch light, he said, "You look awesome."

My brain sent the signal to act cool, but the nervous system was experiencing widespread shutdown.

"This party's like halfway to Montana." Chris reached for my hand. "We better get going."

I took one step off the porch and plunged to my death — literally. My foot hit a patch of ice and sent me flying. Unfortunately, Chris was attached to my hand and came with me. His momentum carried him past my stooped-over butt to a shoveled pile of slush on the lawn, where he took a header.

Chris's rear arced in the air and he staggered to his feet. Brushing himself off, he cursed under his breath. The entire length of his front was soaked.

"Oh my God." My hands flew to my face. Standing there like a defective CD, I kept repeating it: "OhmyGodohmyGodohmyGod." I prayed a sinkhole would open up and suck me whole.

"Crap," Chris muttered, shaking slush off his pants.

My fingers were fused to my face. "I'm sorry," I whimpered. "I'm so sorry."

"What are you sorry about? I'm the spaz." He examined his wet shirt. "We'll have to make a pit stop so I can change. Do you mind?"

Couldn't he see I was mindless? I skittered behind him to his car in the driveway.

His car closely resembled the VW Dad had thought Liam would treasure forever. It was a rebuilt junker — a mishmash of doors and fenders and hoods — only bigger. Tanklike.

I was reminded again of the day Liam drove home his brand-spanking new Spyder convertible. Dad's resentment had extended to me. He wouldn't even consider buying me a car when I turned sixteen. He told Liam to share. Get real. I'd had my driver's license a month already and Liam had let me drive around the block, once.

Chris opened the door for me, and I was hit with a gust of fire wind. The car was idling, the heater on extreme high. Chris slid in on his side and said, "If I turn the car off, I'll never get it started again. I'm charging the battery."

I nodded like, naturally. I'd dressed in layers on top, about six of them, mostly because I couldn't decide. None of the outfits Luna picked out were me. As in drab glam. I mean, what went with white? I figured, Wear everything that isn't stained, smelly, or holey. At the rave I'd check out the appropriate garb and strip down. "Good heater." I turned to Chris, panting.

"Yeah, it's about the only thing that works in this heap." He ground into gear and the car lurched backward. "Something's funky with the fan, though." He smacked the dashboard. "I think it's stuck."

Stuck on category five hurricane. Globules of sweat beaded on my forehead. Luna had spent an hour on my makeup and now my skin was melting wax. "Mind if I crack a window?" I asked.

I didn't wait for an answer, just grabbed the handle and cranked. The window glass dropped like lead, disappearing inside the door frame.

Chris stopped fighting with the gear stick and twisted his head slowly. "Wow," he said. "That never happened before."

Melt, I ordered my whole entire body. Melt away.

Chris popped the clutch and backfired down the street.

As we drove, frigid air blasted me through the open window. One side of my face was frozen solid, while the other side fried eggs. Chris merged onto the highway, and since he had to com-

154

pete with the whole outdoors now, shouted at me, "What kind of music do you like?"

"Opera," I shouted back.

He threw back his head and howled. "You really are a scream," he said.

I smiled weakly.

"Here, play whatever you want." He reached into the back seat and retrieved a CD case.

Make that a suitcase. It must've contained every CD ever recorded. Plus, it had a trick lock — a weird contraption you either had to press or pull or bite off with your teeth. I wrestled with it for like, ten minutes. When I glanced over, Chris was looking at me. Smirking.

"If you say one word about how unmechanical girls are ..."

His eyes gleamed. "Try the button."

"The button." Duh. I pressed it and the latch popped open. About eight hundred CDs sprang into the air.

He should drive off a cliff and put me out of his misery, I thought. "Sorry," I mumbled as I crouched to the floor to scoop all the CDs back into the case. I was going to mention the invention of plastic sleeves to organize his collection, but decided now was not the time to reveal my nagging mother instinct. On my way up, the crack of skull carried over the wind as my head crunched the dash.

Chris must've heard my yelp because he screeched to a stop. The car fishtailed over the curb, jerking me fully upright and impaling my head against the headrest. Add whiplash to my concussion.

"You okay?" He gaped at me.

"This is going well, don't you think?" I said.

He didn't laugh. Neither did I. I felt like crying. If I did, though, my mascara would run and stain my white jeans.

At some point, probably while I was crawling around on the floor stacking CDs, we'd exited the highway. The curb we straddled was in a war zone: boarded-up windows along an entire block of charred row houses. I bent to retrieve a couple of CDs I'd missed, which were now crushed under my foot.

"Sorry." I winced an apology at Chris.

"We'll just sing," he said.

Was that a joke? Did he smirk? How could he laugh at a time like this? Unless he was laughing at me. Which he had to be. I was a joke. A study in slapstick.

"Don't worry about it." Chris reached over, took the CDs from my hand, and flung them out the window. Then he clipped my jaw with a knuckled fist. A sweet gesture, like he knew how I was feeling.

"If you take me back now, you might still get out of this alive," I told him.

He laughed. Really laughed. It made me laugh, and feel better. He popped the clutch and we hurtled the median.

A few minutes later we pulled up in front of a house. A fourplex. There was a truck parked ahead of us, one of those eighteen-wheeler cabs. "Shit," Chris hissed under his breath. "Denny's back. He wasn't supposed to get home until tomorrow." He explained, "My mom's boyfriend. He's a jerk. He thinks he owns me or something." Chris drummed the steering wheel. "Okay, here's the plan. You stay here. I'll run in and grab a pair of jeans; hope him and Mom are too busy getting reacquainted to notice me. If you hear a shot, call 911."

My eyes bulged. He was kidding, right?

He eased open the car door and climbed out, then sprinted up the gravel driveway and in through a side door. It was dead quiet except for a dog barking down the block. No shots rang out. Suddenly, all hell broke loose. Chris tore out the door with this hulk of a guy chasing him, bellowing, "Come back here, you twerp. Who do you think you are? I'm talking to you, punk."

Chris yanked open his door and threw a wad of denim at me. We pulled away from the curb just as The Hulk reached us, smashing a fist down on the trunk. It made me yelp, and shrivel in fear.

"Your ass is grass, boy," the guy threatened, loud and clear through my open window.

"What a dick," Chris said as he caromed around a corner. "I hate him. A ten on the A.B.S. I don't know why my mom ever hooked up with that creep. They're getting married in a couple of weeks, if you can believe that." Chris vented his anger on the accelerator and we warped back onto the highway.

A familiar sight loomed into view. The Taco Bell downtown.

Chris exited and swerved into the parking lot. He removed the jeans from my lap, which I was only vaguely aware were there, and said, "Be right back." I nodded okay. My brain was stuck on The Hulk shaking his fist in my sideview mirror. "You want to come in and wait for me to change? Your lips are blue."

I had lips? "No. That's okay," I mumbled. "Blue's my natural color." Which was the dorkiest thing in the world to say.

As Chris sauntered into the glassed-in entryway, this revelation came to me. I knew now what my life was about: Waiting for guys to change their clothes.

It didn't take him long — not the hour and a half required for Luna's transformation. Chris sprinted out the door and hurled himself into the driver's seat, then ground the gear into reverse.

I relaxed, figuring, Okay, the worst is over. What else could happen? From here on in it's clear sailing.

On a calm lake in a moonlit dream. But all my dreams had died somewhere around the end of sixth grade.

Chapter 18

We barreled down the highway until it petered out at the edge of North America. Really. We drove by neighborhoods and lakes and landscapes I never knew existed. "I think I missed the turnoff," Chris said, squinting at this corner of notebook paper with hieroglyphics scribbled all over it.

By the time we finally arrived at the rave, the party was in full throttle. We cruised by a string of idling cars to check out the scene. Noise assaulted my ears: horns blaring, people shouting, music blasting out the door every time someone opened it. The rave wasn't in a house exactly. More like a barn. Far enough out in the country that neighbors wouldn't get all bent out of shape, because there were no neighbors.

Chris located a place to park about three miles away. As he wedged the car between a pair of SUVs, I saw from my window the barn door swing open. A hundred thousand writhing bodies were crammed inside. It totally freaked me out. What was a rave, anyway? Like an orgy? Nobody was naked, that I could tell. Naked, the way I suddenly felt. Exposed and small and scared. I'd never even been to a dance at school. Never been asked. I'd sworn off dancing.

Chris looked as lost as me, if that was possible. We just sat in the car, watching the action. He inhaled a deep breath and said, "What are we waiting for?"

I shrugged. "An invitation?"

"Got that." He waved the scrap of paper in the air.

He jumped out and circled around front to open my door. Chris took my hand to help me out. And he didn't let go. As we started toward the barn, he laced his fingers through mine like it was a natural thing to do. If I could've freeze-framed that moment everything would've been perfect. His warm hand sending shocks of electricity up my arm; the happiness of being with someone; someone who wanted me there with him. Me — a shape, a form, a person who mattered. I knew I was giving in to the feeling, but for one night I wanted to live dangerously.

As we neared the building it was obvious drugs were everywhere. The air reeked, and the second we stepped inside some guy tried to deal Chris. "Thanks anyway, man," Chris yelled over the music. "Not into it. " He added in my ear, "If I get caught, I'm off the team. If you want something, though —"

I shook my head no. No, no, no. I wanted to experience every moment of this night with full awareness.

The DJ cranked up the volume and the bass about splintered my bones. Chris hollered, "Let's see what they have to drink."

A few people were dancing, but most just milled around, smoking, drinking, getting high. We arrived at the makeshift bar and Chris bellowed at the bartender, "What do you got?" One speaker hung from the rafters directly overhead, so I couldn't hear the bartender's reply. Chris relayed in my ear, "They have Coke or beer."

"Coke's good." I hoped it was the fizzy kind.

It was. Chris handed me a red plastic cup.

We blended into the crowd surrounding the dance floor, listening to the band and watching the dancers. It was too loud to talk without shouting. Chris sipped his Coke. I mimicked him. He stuck an index finger in his ear, like, Deafening, huh? I nodded.

A familiar form materialized off the dance floor. Shannon

Eiber. She had on this tube top that was held up by hope. Her legs had been dipped into liquid leather. She looked twenty-five, at least. Made me feel twelve.

She spotted Chris and waggled her fingers at him. Dancing over to us, she wiggled close to him and mouthed, Wanna dance? She jutted her hip into his. My invisibility shield must've been set on maximum power.

Chris said something in her ear, then slid an arm around my waist.

Shannon actually met my eyes. Her face registered . . . what? Disbelief? Shock? "Hey, Regan," she yelled.

"Hey," I yelled back.

She wheeled around and danced herself out of our scene.

Our scene. Chris and me, standing there with his arm around me. It was the longest song in history and I prayed it'd never end.

He leaned down and said in my ear, "You bored? You want to dance?"

"No," I replied. "I don't dance."

His head rolled back on his neck. "Thank you, God," he spoke to the rafters. "Thank you, thank you, thank you." He said to me, "I hate to dance. I'm so bad."

"Me, too." I hadn't tried lately, not since the slumber party.

It was hot. We finished our Cokes in record time. Chris took my empty cup, slid it under his, and set both atop a five-foot-high floor speaker, then hitched his chin and said, "Let's go outside."

We wedged through the fleshy mass to the rear exit. A group of people, five or six, were huddled near the door, exchanging baggies for cash. They split when we cut through.

Behind the barn was a pasture with a wooden rail fence extending along the perimeter. The last snowfall had made the ground mushy and our feet squished in unison. The night air was chilly. I was grateful for all my layers. Beside me, Chris shivered.

"You cold? You want one of my sweaters?" I asked him.

"Sure. I'll take the one off the bottom."

"Shut up." I smacked him.

He grinned. We slogged all the way to the fence. Chris stepped onto the bottom railing, swung a leg over the top, and reached back to help me up.

My purse weighed a ton. It was my gigantic Wal-Mart bag, which I'd chosen specifically so I could stuff in all my extra clothes after I changed. I never got that far. As we balanced on the fence, my purse felt awkward in my lap, like a stomach tumor. I looped it around the fence post next to me.

"Cows," Chris said.

"Excuse me?"

He pointed. "There're cows out there."

I had to squint to see that far in the dark. "Oh yeah."

"My sister and I used to play this game," Chris raked a hand through his hair, "where you take turns describing an object. Whatever you say about it has to start with the next letter in the object. You want to play?"

Oh boy. Party games. "Sure," I said.

He shifted to face me. "You go first."

"What's the object?" I asked.

"Cows," he answered. "You come up with a 'c' word that has to do with cows."

Cows. "Okay. Cud."

"Huh?"

"Cows chew their cud."

"What's a cud?" he said.

Was he kidding? He didn't sound it. "Regurgitated stomach contents."

Chris frowned and curled a lip. "You're making that up."

"Totally serious."

"Cud. Huh. I'll have to remember that one. Okay, 'o.'" He thought a minute. "I pass."

You can pass? I racked my brain. O. Ordinary? Odd? Oxygen, which I might need if he was really sliding his arm around my shoulders and moving in closer. He was. "I can't think of anything with 'o', either," I said. Can't think at all.

"It's a stupid game." He drew me into him.

"Ow."

He loosened his hold. "What?"

"I got a splinter in my butt."

"Yeah? Want me to get it out?"

I jabbed him with an elbow. After I dug it out myself, we resumed with the arm around my shoulders experience. Even through my layers, I could feel his body heat. He was still shivering, though. "Really, do you want a sweater?"

"Nah. You're warming me up."

Ditto, I thought.

I let my feet dangle. Breathed in the air. Mine, his. I felt comfortable with him, like this was meant to be. Natural. "Let's play again," I said. "We'll pick something easier." I scanned the pasture. Too dark. The sky? Stars. There were billions of them, and they were all visible tonight. Had they always been this brilliant? "Stars," I said.

"Okay, you start."

"S. Stars are in space."

"T. They twinkle."

"A." I paused. "They . . . um . . ." What starts with A? Astronomy?

"Did I mention you get to sucker punch the person who gets stuck?" He slugged me with his free hand in the thigh.

"Ow. You might've mentioned that earlier." I slugged him back. He had hard, muscular thighs. "Wait, I've got an *A* word. Absent. Stars are absent during the day."

Chris gave me an odd look. "I think we're going to need an official ruling on that." He called over his shoulder. "Skippy?" Cupping a hand around his ear, he went, "Acceptable? Rats."

"Rats doesn't count for your R," I told him.

"Rats."

"Still doesn't count."

"Silence, woman. Let me think." He pursed his lips. "R."

I hummed the *Jeopardy* theme.

He sliced a finger across his throat.

I grinned.

"They're radiant."

"Ooh, nice." Back to S. "S," I said. "They . . . stop shining eventually."

He dropped his arm. "They do? When?"

I met Chris's eyes. "When they die."

His eyes widened. "Stars die? I didn't know that."

"They burn out and leave behind black holes," I informed him.

He blinked a couple of times. He had the longest lashes. "Do your wishes die with them?" he asked.

Was he serious? He sounded totally serious. More sad. Like a little kid who just found out the truth about Santa Claus. "No. The wishes last forever."

He let out a long sigh of relief.

I could never tell when he was joking. I kicked his shin, testing. He caught my ankle in his foot and wrapped it around his leg. Which initiated a leg wrestling match. Shoving. Giggling. We almost fell off the fence. He clamped a hand around my arm to steady me and said, "Did you ever wish upon a star, Regan?"

My name. It made me tingle every time. "Probably. I don't remember. Liam used to. When we were sleeping out back in the summer once, we tried to count the stars. Liam got to a thousand. I couldn't even count that high. Liam said, 'Know what I wished for, Re? I wished God would fix me.'" My breath caught. Did I just say all that out loud?

"What was wrong with him?" Chris asked.

"Nothing," I murmured. "He was just . . . nothing." I hadn't thought about Liam all evening. Now here he was again, intruding.

Chris nudged my shoulder with his. "Where are you? You left."

"No, I didn't. I'm here." I smiled up at him. "Everything's fine."

"Yeah. It is." He gazed into my eyes. Intensely, deeply.

Too deep. I had to look away.

"Do you have other brothers or sisters?" he asked.

"No, just the one brother." One's enough, especially mine, I didn't say.

Chris didn't speak for a long moment. When I glanced over, he was staring at me.

"What?"

"I thought you had a sister."

How did he know . . . ? That day in the hall when I told him I was going shopping with my sister. "I do," I said quickly. "A half sister." Half brother, half sister. "What about you? I know you have a sister with a loft."

"Yeah, she's cool. Pam. When I need to get away, she lets me crash at her place. And I need to get away a *lot* from Denny, the dickhead."

"What happened to your dad? Are you parents divorced or something?"

"No." Chris exhaled a visible breath. "My dad died when I

was two. I don't remember him. Mom doesn't even have a picture. It's like he never existed. Sometimes I think about how different it might've been if I'd grown up with a father, instead of this steady stream of Mom's loser boyfriends." He shook his head at the ground. "I can't believe she's marrying Denny. God. I'm moving out. Are your parents divorced?" He twisted to face me.

"No. I still have the original set."

"Lucky."

"Oh yeah."

Chris caught the sarcasm. "What, they're jerks?"

"No. Yes." I stared off into the middle distance. "I don't know. They don't seem all that happy together. Sometimes I wonder how they even got together. I wonder if they should've gotten divorced. Maybe they would have if . . ." I stopped and swallowed hard.

"If what? You think they stayed together for you guys?"

"No." I tried to focus on the cows, anything solid. "I think they felt stuck with each other. Then they got stuck with us. They wasted their lives, both of them." I looked at Chris briefly, then looked away. The majority of Mom's life apparently didn't count, and Dad's was on a downhill skid. "I don't think the American dream quite lived up to their expectations." There was that word again — expectations. "I don't know," I went on. "They seem . . . disillusioned. Like they're just going through the motions, you know?" I glanced up at him again.

"Do I ever," Chris said. "My mom always wanted to be a model, or an actress. She could've been, too. I never want that to happen to me. To look back on my life, say, ten, twenty years later and think, 'Man, I could've been something. If only I hadn't given up my dream.'"

"Exactly." He nailed it. I had a dream once. I couldn't even remember what it was. "What *is* your dream?" I asked him.

He hesitated. "You really want to know?"

"Yeah. Unless it's private. Or personal."

"No. No, it's just that nobody's ever asked before. Nobody's ever cared." He held my eyes. His gaze was so intense, it almost hurt. He swung one leg over the railing to ride it like a horse and gripped the railing with both hands. "Okay, here it is. I want to be a sportscaster. Like on ESPN, not the flunky local station. On national TV." He raised a fist to his mouth to mime a microphone. "This is Chris Garazzo, coming to you live from Coors Field, where the Rockies have rocked the world with their upset win in the World Series, blowing out the Red Sox in an unprecedented four-oh sweep. We'll be following all the action down in the locker room with Regan O'Neill. But first, back to you in the studio, Al."

I smiled. "You're good. You should go to college and major in communications or something."

"Sure." He rolled his eyes. "Like I'll ever make it out of high school."

"You will."

"Not if I don't pass Chemistry." Chris made a face. Then he leaned forward, his face coming closer to mine. Closer, closer . . . He licked his lips. My heart stopped beating. What do I do?

Suddenly, sirens split the air. Flashing red lights illuminated the night as a fleet of cop cars surrounded the barn. Where'd they come from?

"Shit." Chris launched off the fence. "If I get busted, I'm off the team."

"Shit!" I cried, grabbing Chris's wrist. "Look what time it is." His watch read 10:50. By the time we got back to the Materas' it'd be way past eleven.

He vise-gripped my hand and we tore off across the property toward the car. My feet slid and stuck in the mud, and so did his. We hit a gulley and sank to our ankles in sludge. We had to scrabble up a muddy incline on our hands and knees. It wasn't until I was leaping into the passenger seat that I realized I'd lost my shoe.

"It must've come off in the mud," Chris said. "I'll go back."

"Forget it." Two cops were about to raid the rave, while two others were erecting a barricade on the street. "Let's go."

"You sure?"

A chorus of girls screamed as the cops burst through the doors. "I'm sure. Just go."

We roared out of there. The clock on Chris's stereo flashed 11:02. Panic rose in my chest. "Go fast," I urged him. Warp speed. Break the sound barrier.

Oh, please, God, please, I prayed. Don't let them be home early. I reached for my purse to retrieve Aly's cell and call Liam to check —

"My purse!" I cried. "I left it on the fence."

Chris muttered a curse. "I'll get off at the next exit and turn around."

"No. I have to get back to the Materas'. I was supposed to be back by eleven."

"Yikes," Chris said. "Why didn't you tell me?"

Hadn't I? I thought I'd mentioned it. Before we fell off the porch. Or after. On the way to the rave. Inside. On the fence where he almost, almost kissed me. "Just hurry!"

We hit Mach I. The world flew by in a blur. The night was a blur, too, until flashing red lights lit up Chris's rearview mirror.

"Shit," we cursed in unison. Chris swerved to the shoulder and stopped.

It took twenty minutes for the state patrol to issue Chris a ticket. Of course, the officer had to question him about where we'd been, had we been drinking, were we on anything. He gave

Chris a sobriety test. He lectured him about speeding. We were both filthy from crawling around in the mud, so I could imagine what he thought.

At last, he let us go.

As we squealed to a stop in front of the Materas', I was trying to figure out if we'd had a good time.

"Well, this sucked," Chris said, answering my question. "I'm sorry about your shoe. Your purse, too. Your pants. I'm sorry about everything."

I swallowed a sob. "I'm sorry about the speeding ticket." And *your* wet pants — both pairs, and your run-in with Denny, and the whole sucky evening. Sorry, sorry, sorry.

All the lights were on inside. I couldn't see through the dark garage windows to tell whether the Jeep Cherokee was there. Please, let it not be there. "I have to go." I opened my door.

Chris hopped out his side.

"I have to go!" I fairly screeched at him.

"Okay." He stopped in his tracks.

I sprinted up the front walk. As I reached the door, I glanced back over my shoulder. Chris was slumped on the car hood, his hands covering his head. Was he mad? Crying?

God.

I quelled my own hysteria. The front door was open a crack, which was weird. Maybe Liam had heard us drive up. Maybe the Materas had decided to stay out longer after the play. Maybe their car broke down. Please, please, please.

Chapter 19

*L*iam's voice filtered down the Materas' hallway. "Please," he pleaded. "Don't hurt me."

"Take it off." David's voice.

At the end of the hall Elise stumbled backward out of her bedroom, face paralyzed with fear.

"Please," I heard Liam say again. "I was just fooling around."

My brain engaged. Elise turned and saw me racing toward her, but her haunted eyes strayed back to the bedroom. To whatever fright scene had horrified her.

I veered around the doorway in front of Elise. Liam stood at her full-length mirror, stripping out of a white negligee. Luna, I should say. Her eyes met mine and held for a long instant before cutting over to David.

David, who was poised at his nightstand with a butcher knife raised in his hand.

"Don't!" I charged into the room and threw myself against Luna. She stumbled backward. "It's my brother. Please. She was just fooling around."

David's eyes seared my flesh. "Your . . . *brother?*"

"Please," I said again. "Don't hurt him."

David repeated, "Your brother?" Unbelieving. Taking him in. Her. Slowly, David's hand lowered.

I whirled on Luna, eyes slit, screaming silently at her, How could you?

She didn't react, or wasn't receptive to nonverbal threats. Probably because she was struggling to remove the negligee over her head. It'd gotten stuck on Elise's black bra. Luna tugged one last time and ripped a length of lace on the front of the nightgown. "Sorry," she said. "I'll pay for it." She folded the nightgown and set it on the bed, then unhooked the bra in back. I tried to shield her, but I could feel David's eyes on her. On him. On us. Liam slipped his sweatshirt over his head and shimmied into his jeans.

Jamming his feet into his shoes, he staggered past me. Or tried to. David blocked his escape. "The earrings." He extended a stiff hand. Liam yanked off Elise's pearl earrings and, with trembling fingers, deposited them in David's palm. David closed his fist, crucifying Liam with a look.

Liam charged for the door. Elise jumped out of his way like he was a mass of open sores.

"He was just goofing around," I said, popping the cap back onto Elise's tube of lipstick. "I had an emergency and had to leave for a little while." The lie sounded rehearsed even to me. "I called Liam to come and stay. I wasn't gone that long."

Elise didn't answer. David glared at me in the mirror. The set of his jaw scared me.

"I'm s-sorry," I stammered, stepping away from the dresser, around the bed, keeping David in view, backing out the door. "It won't happen again."

"You're right about that," David said. He set the knife on his bedstand and yanked out his wallet. Removing a ten dollar bill, he threw it at me and added, "You're not welcome in our home anymore, Regan. And your brother . . . My God, he needs help."

A knife twisted in my gut. It might as well have been the real thing. I watched the money flutter to the floor, then blindly turned and ran.

Rage fueled my feet as I propelled down the basement stairs. Liam's door was closed. I burst in. Stupid Dana International was singing on the CD player and I punched off the power. Opening the lid, I removed the CD and flung it against the pockmarked wall. "Thanks a lot!" I screamed at him. "You just lost me my job."

He blinked from his fetal position on the bed, hands folded flat under his cheek. There were traces of Elise's red lipstick on his cracked lips still. "Do you think he'll call here?" Liam asked quietly.

"How should I know? Is that what you want them to do? You're lucky they didn't call the cops and have you arrested." Or committed, I thought. "David could've killed you. I wish he had." I stormed to the door.

"So do I," Liam said.

Anger roiled in my stomach. He was so wasted. So pathetic. I whirled. "You are pathetic," I spat at him. "God! I hate you."

I hadn't made it to my room before Liam was on me. He touched my shoulder and said, "Do you really think they'll call the police?"

"Liam!" I wheeled again. "I don't give a shit. I needed that job. I *loved* the Materas. They were, like, family. I *loved* that job. It's the only thing I had that was mine." I slapped my chest. "Mine." My voice broke. "It was the only place I had to go to get away from *you*." Tears welled in my eyes. He didn't get it. He never did.

I lashed out to shove him away, but Liam clamped hold of my wrist. "You're muddy. And you're missing a shoe," he said.

"Get out of my face," I ordered him. A fuse ignited in my core. "Get out of my life. I hate you. I hate what you are. I wish you'd never been born."

Liam dropped my arm like it was on fire and reeled back a step. The look on his face . . .

I slammed my bedroom door on it. On him. Shut him out of my life.

⟜

Sunday morning I felt so sick I didn't even get out of bed. I lay there, staring into space, waiting for the phone call to come. The basement door would fly open and Mom and/or Dad would put an end to this charade. This game. How could this be happening to me? It wasn't real life. It was a TV show: Disaster Island. There is no immunity idol. I lose every challenge. I humiliate Chris by making him fall off the porch. I bust his car window. I get him busted at home by his soon-to-be stepdad. I dump and destroy his CD collection. I get him a speeding ticket. I hurt his feelings. Every time we're together, that's all I do — hurt him.

God. I squeezed my eyes shut. He had to hate me.

Same way I hated my brother. He was always there, invading, interfering, ruining my chances for any kind of ordinary existence. It was always him, his needs, his wants. What about what *I* wanted? A regular family. A circle of friends. A best friend. A boyfriend. Was that so much to ask?

I wanted a childhood I could look back on and remember with . . . If not fondness, then happiness at least. Joy. I wanted my own memories. Everything I remembered about me interleaved with Liam. His life. Her struggle. Where were my memories? Where was my life?

Just once I wanted to be able to hold a conversation with a person without having to watch every word I said. Or worry about saying too much, divulging the truth, giving her away. I wanted to be free of this secret, this lie, this brother who wasn't a boy.

I couldn't *believe* Liam lost me my job. Okay, I shouldn't have gone out with Chris; I should've been more responsible; it was all my fault —

No, it wasn't! I refused to shoulder the blame. Liam was out of control. He'd taken advantage of me. He'd humiliated me. He'd risked my life. For what? For his pleasure, his stupid desire to dress up.

"I'll never forgive you," I vowed out loud, hoping he could hear me through the wall between our bedrooms. "Never."

A soft knock sounded on my door. "Re?"

I rolled over in bed.

He knocked louder. "I know you're in there. Smoke's coming out from under the door."

I retrieved my remote and turned on my CD player. I cranked up *La Traviata*.

Guess he got the message.

Sometime later my eyelids fluttered and I jerked awake. Liam stood over me, staring down, smiling tentatively. "Mom and Dad asked where you were at breakfast and I told them you had a hot date last night. I said you hadn't come home until dawn. I wish you could've seen their faces." He lowered himself to the edge of my mattress. "Dad, especially. So, how was it?"

I willed him away. Far away. Hadn't the Materas called? Why wasn't Liam behind bars, or in a straitjacket?

Liam said, "Look, Re. I'm sorry." He placed a hand on my shoulder.

I elbowed him off. "Sorry isn't good enough, Liam. You're destroying my life. Do you know that? Do you have any idea? I don't claim you as a brother. Or a sister, whatever. Get out of here."

He didn't move. Instead, he quipped, "What time do you want to go shopping today?"

God! He was so dense. I threw back the covers and straggled out of bed.

"Please, Re. I have to get something to wear tomorrow night. To meet Teri Lynn."

"Get your makeup and crap and clear out of my room," I said. "I don't want to see one single trace of you when I get back." I snatched my robe off the floor and headed to the bathroom.

When I emerged from my shower a few minutes later, Liam was hovering outside the door.

"What?" I practically screamed in his face.

He tilted his head. "Shopping?"

"I'm not going shopping with you." I spoke deliberately, as if to a child, right in his face. "Get it? Do. You. Get. It."

Liam swallowed hard. "Then I'll go alone."

"What a concept." I smashed him against the wall.

The next time I woke it was dark. Pitch black. I squinted at my clock. One fifty-three. A.M.? If Luna had been in my room, there was no indication, no sense of her. She'd packed up her caddy and lighted mirror, at least. That's when I heard it. Muted at first, then louder, clearer. That sound, so familiar. So frequent.

Liam, crying.

Gut-wrenching sobs. Hiccuping. Keening into his pillow. He used to cry almost every night. If Mom or Dad had ever heard, they'd never let on. I tried to comfort him once, years ago, by holding him and soothing him, but he either wanted, or needed, to suffer alone.

Fine. Let him.

What brought on this latest crying jag? I wondered. Was

Liam upset at me because I wouldn't go shopping with him? Like he really expected me to. It was probably what I'd told him earlier. Namely, the truth. Had Mom or Dad confronted Liam about the Materas? If David or Elise had called I'm sure I would've gotten busted, too. Everything was my fault. No, it wasn't. Everything was Liam's fault. His whole life was one long fault line. So what? He'd screwed up my life. He didn't care.

His sobs intensified. I felt myself weakening. It hurt my heart to hear him cry. But his tears were eternal; they'd never go away.

He'd said it himself: he was wrong. He didn't fit. And there was nothing I could do — nothing anyone could do — to make him right.

Chapter 20

*M*onday morning. Breakfast. Another meal with the surreal O'Neills. Mom chittered at Handy Andy about the cut-rate wholesale florist she'd found who'd do the entire Sorensen wedding for less than half what her regular florist charged. Dad chuckled to himself at the funnies. Liam and I erected shields to shut out the world. And each other.

The kitchen phone rang, and Liam and I jumped. Dad grumbled, "Who's that so early?" He scooted back his chair.

I practically tipped mine over to beat him to it.

Mom beat us both, rushing into the kitchen, ending her call with Andy. She caught the phone on the third ring. "Hello?"

I held my breath.

"Oh, hello, Elise." Mom signaled to me. Then her hand froze midair. "No, she didn't," Mom said.

Forget it, I thought. Forget how I wanted to end the charade. The vision of its conclusion — the bloodbath, the aftermath, Mom and Dad finding out this way — it was too horrible to imagine.

"I see," Mom said flatly, turning away from us.

Oh God. I should've told her. But, where to begin?

"Yes, thank you. No."

I couldn't meet Liam's eyes. I could sense him across from me, shriveling in his skin.

"Well, Elise, I don't think that's any of your business. If no one was hurt . . ." Mom listened, her spine stiffening. Without warning, she slammed down the phone.

Here it comes. Liam and I both braced for the explosion. Mom zipped her portfolio shut and lifted the handle, dropping her cell into her purse and shouldering it.

"Who was that?" Dad asked, shaking out the sports section.

Mom didn't answer, or pretended not to hear. She hurried past us toward the door.

Saved, I thought.

Too soon.

From the living room, Mom barked, "Regan."

I flinched and swiveled my head around.

"Do a load of laundry after school." She wrenched open the door. "And empty the dishwasher."

That was it? No nuclear fallout?

Dad set down the paper. "Where does Mother Goose take her trash?" he said.

Silence.

Dad repeated, "Where does Mother Goose —"

Liam and I droned, "To the Humpty Dump."

Dad huffed. "You heard that one. Okay, who do mice see when they're sick?"

"Hickory Dickory Doc," Liam intoned alone.

Under my breath, I added, "Maybe someone should make an appointment. Ask if he does head work."

Dad waggled a finger at me. "Good one, Re."

Like, I meant him.

"Your sister takes after her old man in the humor department, eh, Liam?"

Liam responded by burying his nose deeper into his physics

text. Surreal. This was unreal. What just happened here, besides nothing?

Dad scraped back his chair and stood. He moved behind Liam, wrestled him into a headlock, and knuckled a noogie on Liam's thick skull. "Ah, loosen up. Your old dad sacrificed a career in comedy writing to raise the all-American family."

Liam looked like he was going to burst into tears. His eyes were still swollen from last night's pity party.

Dad gave his head one final squeeze and released him. With his hands spread over Liam's bony shoulders, he said to me, "So, let's hear about this date you had, tootsie."

I grabbed my backpack and rose to leave.

Dad said, "Oh, come on." He trailed me to the door. "I'm not going to hang you from your thumbs for sneaking out. An all-nighter, though? At your age?"

If Dad only knew what people did at my age. Regular people. Ordinary people. People with lives. People who actually had friends to go out with. In addition to the fizzled fireworks this morning, I was a little surprised the cops hadn't been by the house yet. They should've found my purse by now, with my billfold and driver's license. And Aly's cell phone.

Shit. Aly's cell. I'd forgotten about it. She'd be pissed as hell at me for losing her cell.

"Actually," Dad pressed a palm against the front door to prevent my escape, "it's sort of encouraging to see a little predictable behavior out of one of you."

Predictable behavior out of *us*?

Dad searched my eyes. "I just want you to talk to me, honey. I'm your dear old Dad, remember? We go way back. Girly whirligig?"

My throat constricted. "I gotta go." I slipped under his arm and charged out. The day was foggy and drizzly, which fit my mood perfectly.

Halfway down the block a car slowed beside me and the window scrolled down.

"I'm not speaking to you." I pulled my parka closer and trekked on.

Half a block farther, Liam pulled up again. "I don't blame you for hating me."

Shut up, I thought.

"I just want to give you a ride. We don't have to talk."

I drew a deep breath and considered the options. He was still my brother; he always would be. There was no changing that. It was miserable out. I was cold. He owed me. Oh, how he owed me now.

I circled the Spyder and got in. "Turn off that techno crap," I ordered. "I hate your music."

He ejected the CD.

"Give me your house key. You lost mine."

He looked confused, but pulled to the curb and switched off the ignition. From his key ring, he removed the key.

"And tell Aly you lost her phone." I snatched it from him. "*You* have a job. *You* buy her a new one."

"Did I lose your shoe, too?" Liam asked.

I turned away. Expelled a short breath.

"Look, Re," he said. "About what happened —"

"I told you, I don't want to talk about it." I'd said everything I wanted to say.

Liam started the car again and we traveled the rest of the way to school in silence. The distance between us seemed to grow. Or shrink. I'm not sure which. We were planets at opposite ends of the universe, orbiting a dying sun. As we swerved into the parking lot, I suddenly remembered —

"Oh no!"

"What?" Liam startled, like he'd been lost in himself. Lost in space.

"I spaced a chem test today. I haven't even reviewed the chapters or the worksheets." I smacked my forehead with my palm. "Dammit. If I flunk this test, there's no way I'm even pulling a C in that class. Bruchac's such a bastard. He's using me as an example. Because of you," I snarled at Liam. "Ever since I poured sulfuric acid on my arm —"

"What?" Liam interrupted. "When did that happen?"

A lifetime ago, I thought. In someone else's one-day-long meaningful existence. "It was no big deal. He's just out to prove his point that girls are brain-dead. Did he pull that crap on you?"

"Oh yeah." Liam rolled his eyes. "He's a moron."

"You probably still got an A, though, right?"

He didn't answer.

Which was the answer. "I guess there's one advantage to not being a GG," I muttered.

Liam said, "I'm sorry about your job, Re. I just couldn't help myself. I didn't plan to —"

"Shut up. I don't want to know. It's not just the job. It's . . . everything." It's you, I didn't say.

"I know." He turned away. "Don't you think I know?"

Did he? Did he realize how much I'd sacrificed for him? How long? What it'd cost me?

Once when I was little Dad let me try on his hunting jacket. It was huge; it hung to the floor, and it stank. But what I remember most was the weight. As if that coat would break my knees and drag me down and trap me inside and smother me. That's how it felt with Liam. Like I was trapped. Suffocating.

Was that fair? No. Life wasn't fair. Liam proved that.

A carload of cheerleaders and jocks emptied out by the door and headed inside, jostling and jockeying for position on the walkway. "I do not want to be here today," I thought aloud. "I hate it here."

Liam said, "We could go to the mall."

I shot him a death look.

"Joking," he said, shirking his left shoulder like I was going to hit him. I might. He added, "I took your advice and went alone yesterday."

That shocked me. "How'd it go?" Don't ask me why I cared.

He didn't reply. Yes, he did. His face told the story.

"Oh God. What happened?"

He exhaled a long breath. "You don't want to know."

"You're right. I don't." Go ahead, freeze me out. I grabbed the door handle.

"I only wanted to try on a dress." His voice went flat. "They didn't need to call security."

My eyes squinched shut.

"Hey." He brightened. "Do you want to come tonight? Meet Teri Lynn? She's buying me dinner at the Palmer House."

I twisted back and shook my head. "Expensive."

"I'm sure she wouldn't mind if you came along. You could eat whatever I didn't want off my plate."

I sneered at him. "I'm sure you two need to talk. Compare the size of your Adam's apples, or whatever it is trannies do when they get together."

Liam laughed. He actually laughed. I'd made him laugh.

It felt better than making him cry. But not much.

⌒

As I trudged down the hall, feeling wasted and depressed, I spotted Chris. He was the last person I wanted to run into today. I slowed to a stop. He was leaning against the bank of lockers opposite mine talking to Shannon and a couple of her ditzy friends. They laughed at some joke he made. Chris raised his head and fixed on me.

He pushed off the wall and headed my way. I panicked. I couldn't deal with him. Saturday night was too raw, too sucky. I veered off down the opposite corridor toward the nearest girls' restroom.

"Regan!"

I started running. Made it. I locked myself in a stall and waited. Waited until the earth stopped spinning. Until the roar in my head subsided. Until I could stop breathing, stop shaking, stop wanting him so bad.

⁓

When the final bell rang in my Skills for Living class, it jolted me awake. Or aware. I didn't even remember the day passing. I did recall my angel food cake flopping. The sticky mess I shoveled into the trash, then rinsed out the tube pan and hung up my apron. Mrs. Torres smiled sympathetically as she marked my grade for the day. I think we both knew culinary arts was not in my future. I wished I had a future.

There was a surprise waiting for me at home. A box on my bed. It was wrapped in flowery paper and topped off with a shimmering pink bow. My room smelled of roses. Littered all over my desk were eye shadow creams and mascara tubes and lipstick.

Damn her. Damn Luna. I meant it when I told her to stop using me.

She must've dressed in my room and left early for her dinner with Teri Lynn. She probably wanted to slip out before Dad got home. Still, she could dress in her own room. Buy a mirror.

I tore off the wrapping and opened the box. Inside was a stack of stapled papers. A cover sheet with my name printed in pink ink lay on top. Underneath my name was written, "These look familiar?"

I scanned the first sheet. The temperature lab. Second sheet, the hydrogen peroxide lab. The worksheet on hydration. I riffled through the sheets and stopped on the test we had today. The one I totally blew. Showing up for class was a vague memory. Liam hadn't failed the test. He'd gotten one hundred percent. Plus twenty-five extra points for answering the bonus question correctly.

Figures.

As I fanned through the pages, I saw he'd gotten A's or A+'s on everything.

There was a smaller note at the bottom of the cover sheet. Liam had printed, "I hope this makes up for what I did." He'd drawn a little heart. Next to it he'd written in curlicue cursive, "Love ya, Luna." An arrow indicated more on back. I flipped it.

"P.S. These are probably worth a small fortune. Erase my name before you auction them on eBay."

My jaw unhinged. He was right. People would sell their souls for a set of answer sheets to Chem I. Chris would. Stop thinking about him. He's history.

Bruchac *was* an idiot. He didn't even make up new test questions each term; just rearranged the order. Did he think people wouldn't clue in?

The bigger question was, Would I take advantage of Bruchac? Would I cheat to save my soul?

No.

But to salvage my G.P.A.?

Yes.

She tiptoed down the stairs around eleven. I was still erasing Liam's name from all the Bruchac Papers, while in the background a rerun of *Liar, Liar* played on The Movie Channel. Luna hadn't changed her clothes. She wore a red suede skirt with a silk blouse, a striped scarf draped around her neck. The scarf was pinned in front with a cameo brooch. A little too Mrs. Doubtfire for my taste.

"How'd it go?" I asked absently.

She sank down beside me on the sofa, leaning back and closing her eyes. Tears glistened between her lashes.

"Not good?" I set the Bruchac Papers on the coffee table. As mad as I was at him, I wasn't immune to her pain. "What happened?"

She sniffled, opened her eyes, and blinked at me. "It was incredible, Re," she breathed.

Incredible. As in unimaginable? Horrifying?

Luna exhaled audibly. "It was just . . ." She blinked again and a tear slid down her cheek. "Teri Lynn is living my dream."

My heart fell. "I'm sorry."

"No." Her hand shot out and clasped mine. "I mean, it's so fantastic. To know it can happen, that it's possible. That *I'm* possible." Her lungs filled hungrily, as if tasting life for the first time. She pushed to her feet and kissed the top of my head. "Thank you, Re," she said, sort of wistfully, before floating off to bed.

Thank you for what? I wondered. Wishing her gone? "Thank *you*," I called after her. "For the present."

From the doorway, she blew me a kiss.

"Oh, and Aly called earlier. She said to remind you about the senior breakfast tomorrow. She's picking you up at seven."

Luna's door lock clicked. I wasn't sure she'd heard, she was blissing out so bad.

⟋⟍

Liam was back the next morning at breakfast. In boy role. Something about him had changed, though. He seemed softer around the edges. His eyes weren't vacant and dead anymore, as if they'd retained a glimmer of light from last night. He seemed looser, too, more relaxed, almost comfortable in his body.

I was relieved, glad for him, but worried. When I'd finally drifted off to sleep around midnight, I'd had a dream. A premonition that Liam was going to do something dangerous again. Impulsive. Reckless. The dream was hazy and I couldn't invoke a clear image this morning; couldn't conjure up what he'd done or where. Only this ominous foreboding remained.

A car honked outside. "That's Aly." Liam jumped up and glugged down the last of his milk. On his way past Mom, he looped an arm around her shoulders and said, "You look lovely today. As always." He kissed her on the cheek. "Have a good one, Pops." He waved to Dad.

Dad choked on his Cheerios. The front door closed and he said to Mom, "What's he on? Some of your happy pills?"

"What's that supposed to mean?" Mom snapped.

Yikes. I prepared to exit stage right.

Mom said, "You know, Liam's eighteenth birthday is next Saturday. Has he mentioned to either of you what he wants?"

Dad blew out a breath. "Like he'd tell me."

They both angled their heads my way, eyebrows raised. Yeah, I considered telling them, Liam wants to be a girl. Can you arrange a small reception for his sex reassignment surgery? Maybe a little Post-op Party by Patrice? And Dad, you could redecorate the basement. She's partial to pink.

"Not to me," I mumbled.

Mom sighed. "I suppose we could give him money — again. Not that he needs it."

Dad lifted his coffee cup. "I guess you'll have to write the check since it'll be coming out of your account."

Mom's fiery glare scorched the length of the tablecloth.

"Outta here," I said, and jettisoned through the fire exit.

⟶

Liam intercepted me on my way to first period English. "Are you coming straight home from school today?" he asked.

"Yeah, I guess. Unless I have to stop by the bank to make a rather large deposit." I exaggerated a grin.

"I'm going to tell Aly."

My backpack thudded to the floor. As I squatted to retrieve it, all the blood drained from my face. "Liam, no," I said on the way up. Speaking to air.

He was halfway down the hall.

I sprinted to catch up. As I caromed around the corner, I had a head-on with a body. Chris Garazzo's, to be precise.

"Regan, hey." He clutched my arm to steady himself. I must've jerked because he let go fast. "Sorry. I, uh, want to talk to you," he said.

In my peripheral vision, I saw Liam duck into the media center. "Not now." I sidestepped Chris. "I have something to do." More important than you, was the interpretation. I didn't look back as I hammered down the hall. To save my brother from himself — again.

He was just slipping into a carrel. "Liam." I perched on my haunches beside him, gulping for air. "You can't tell Aly."

He blinked at me. "Why not?"

"If you don't know . . ."

He pulled out his physics text and said, "She already thinks I'm gay."

My jaw dropped. "She told you that?"

He cast me a withering look. "She isn't stupid, Re." Flipping open a spiral, he licked his finger and leafed to a blank page, then printed his name at the top, the date underneath.

No, but you are, I thought. "Don't, Liam." The warning bell rang and I straightened to stand. "Don't do this to her."

His mechanical pencil poised over the page. "To her?" He shook his head. "You don't get it, do you?" he said, sounding angry.

He was angry? "Liam —"

His cold stare froze me solid.

Releasing me from the icy grip, his eyes skimmed down the page of his physics text and he added, "I'd really like you to be there. For moral support in case I need it. If you don't want to, though, I'll understand."

I hissed a breath between my teeth. It's not that I don't want to! I wanted to scream. But that's exactly what it was. When he told Aly the truth about himself, I wanted to be on any other planet.

Chapter 21

*S*he was in the basement with Liam, cursing and squealing, "You pig! Get off my ass." Alyson smacked his arm. When my foot creaked on the bottom stair, I saw him lean away from her, looking smug and grinning evilly.

"I've decided to call this game Aly Oops," he told her.

She slugged him in the arm, hard.

Please, I prayed to God, tell me that megabrain of his picked up Pentium speed during the day, that it executed the code called Understanding and Logic.

"Re, there you are." Liam dropped his joystick and scrambled to his feet. Mine were weighted to the stair tread.

"Hey, Regan." Aly acknowledged me with a wave over her shoulder. Liam's death screech wailed from the speakers overhead — *Aaah!* "Whoo hoo," Aly cheered. "I baked your butt." She continued to punch her joystick for a moment before realizing Liam wasn't playing. "The game isn't over yet, is it?" She swiveled her head upward. "We're only in eighth grade."

Liam's eyes locked with mine. Please, I mouthed. Don't.

"I want to tell you something, Aly." Liam blinked down at her.

My stomach hurt. I skittered to the sofa and dropped onto it like a body bag, doubling over and trying to swallow the rising bile in my throat.

Aly said, "Okay." She set her joystick down and glanced over.

I felt her questioning eyes on me. All I could do was burn holes in the carpet and hold my breath. Hold out hope he wouldn't go through with this.

Aly spun on her rear and hugged her knees. "So, what?"

Liam said, "I like your hair that way. I always have."

Aly reached back to feel her ponytail. "Thanks. I wear it this way like, eight days a week." She crossed her eyes.

"I know. I love it."

I peered up to see Liam touch the top of Aly's head. Please, God, no, I prayed.

"What I wanted to tell you . . ." Liam swallowed hard. He folded his arms around himself and let out a shallow breath. "What I've wanted to tell you for a long time, Aly, is . . . um . . ." His voice trailed off and he turned to me.

No. No way.

"Well, spit it out," Aly said. "Christ. Do you have a brain tumor or somethi — Oh God." Her hands covered her mouth. "You don't —" Her voice muffled. "Liam —"

"No." Liam placed a hand on her shoulder. "No, it's nothing like that. I'm not sick. I'm . . . a girl."

The air in the room stilled. Stopped. The walls closed in. Aly went, "Huh?"

Liam said, "That's it. I'm a girl."

That was it? Hadn't he thought more about how he was going to reveal the truth about himself? Aly wasn't going to understand "I'm a girl." I'm sure.

Liam let out a little laugh. He sauntered over to the TV and took a swig of his soda. He set it down and said, "What you see on the outside? This," he swept a hand down his body, "isn't me. The real me is on the inside."

"Well, duh." Aly cocked her head. "That's real deep, Liam. It's true for all of us, isn't it?" She rolled her eyes at me.

Really. He was blowing this. He was so inept.

Liam met my eyes, pleading.

No, Liam. No.

Please, Re, I could feel him begging. Help.

God. Why me? "What he means is he's not really a guy." I said the words so fast they all ran together. "He's a girl. He's trans. Get it?"

Aly frowned a little. "Trans what?"

Right. She didn't know the lingo. "Transgender," I told her. "He's a girl in a boy's body."

Her expression didn't change, but the height of the ceiling did. The weight of the world came crashing down. My heart began to hammer in my chest.

"I don't understand." Aly blinked up at Liam. "This is a joke, right?" She scrabbled to her feet. Punching Liam in the gut as she passed, she said, "You guys." She retrieved her Sprite from the coffee table and flopped onto the sofa next to me.

"No joke," Liam said. "I'm a trans girl. A T-girl. The way you're a genetic girl, a G-girl."

"G-girl, T-girl. What the hell are you talking about?" Aly gulped her Sprite.

Liam held my gaze. "Maybe I should just show her."

"No —"

"Show me what?" Aly cut me off. "Your boobs? Your T-boobs?" She snorted and drank again.

Her hand was shaking. She was shaking. Liam noticed, too. He perched on the coffee table opposite Alyson and folded her hand between his. "My name is Luna," he said softly. "I want you to know me. The real me." His thumb traced the length of her slender index finger. Liam gently placed her hand in her own lap, stood, and headed for his room. He closed the door behind him.

Aly said, "What's he going to do?"

I mashed my lips together, wishing to God I didn't have to tell her. Wishing none of this was happening, that it was a dream, a nightmare, that I'd wake up to my actual life. My real life.

Aly said, her voice unsteady, "I thought he was going to tell me he was gay. I thought he was telling me he had AIDS."

"Oh God, Aly. No." I swiveled to face her. "It's nothing like that."

She was so white. "I mean, it's okay if he's gay. Gay people get married, right? They have kids. He could change."

Was that the hope she'd been holding onto? All these years? She was deluding herself. Even if he was gay —

"He's not gay," I said. "He's trans. He's not what he appears. He'll show you. He's going to change into her girl role. Except, it's not really a role. It's who he really is. Luna. Who she is."

Aly looked so confused, so lost.

I was doing as bad a job at explaining as Liam had. I tucked a leg under me and took a deep breath. "I know this is hard to understand. It's even harder to explain, but Liam feels like a girl. He is a girl, really. Problem is, she's a girl who was born with a boy's body. I don't know how it happens, or why. Luna says it's hard-wired into her brain to be female. It's who she knows she is, same way you and I know. It's instinctive. Natural."

Aly stared at me as if I'd just told her her best friend had died. Which, I suppose to her, he had. That disbelief-before-reality-smacks-you-in-the-face look. Denial. Fear of facing the truth.

I forged ahead. "It's horrible because you want to be this person you are in here," I pressed my heart, "and here." I touched my temple. "But you can't because you don't look the way you should. You look like a guy. And that's what people expect you to be. Every day you have to put on this act, play a role, and the only time you can ever be free is when you're alone, when nobody's watching and you can let yourself go. In your world, your private world, you can present yourself the way you want the world to see you and treat you. That's how Liam explained it to me. Does it make sense?"

Delayed reaction. Slowly sinking in. Not wanting it to. Aly shook her head from side to side. "What you're telling me is, he's in there," she thumbed over her shoulder, "putting on girls' clothes?" Her voice rose.

"More than that. He's transforming. She is. You'll see."

"He's a . . . a cross-dresser?"

"No! God. Don't call him that." My face burned. "It's not the same. Liam's dressing because he wants you to see what he sees on the inside. His true identity. Hers, I mean. Luna's. There's all kinds of psychological mumbo jumbo and names for this stuff. Dysphoria, Gender Identity Disorder, I don't know. She can explain it better than me."

"She?" Aly smiled sardonically. She raised her Sprite to her mouth and tipped the can. It was empty so she put it down.

"That's another thing. When she's dressed, she wants you to address her by her chosen name — Luna. And use 'her' and 'she' It won't be hard. She really is a girl."

Alyson's smile stuck to her face.

"Don't you remember that time at her ninth birthday party when she asked for a bra?"

"No," Aly said.

"Or that time at my slumber party when she absolutely loved having her nails polished?"

"No," Aly said faster.

She remembered; I know she did. "There's always polish around her cuticles, Aly."

Aly shook her head.

There had to be other traces of evidence, other instances. All the time she and Liam spent together? Luna couldn't have hidden from Aly entirely.

Aly bent forward and began to scrape the side of her Sprite can with a fingernail. "If this is some kind of game you two are playing —"

"It's not a game."

She looked at me, hard.

"Aly, you had to have seen."

Her mouth opened and words spilled out, but I was distracted by Luna, who had emerged. She pressed a finger to her lips and slipped into my room, carrying two pairs of shoes to try on.

I tuned into Aly. "I'm sorry, what did you say?"

"When did you know?" she repeated. "How long have you known? When did he tell you?"

Tell me. Did he tell me?

"Hurry up, guys. All the good prizes are going to be gone." Dad comes out of the hallway, fastening his watch band. I'm sitting on a kitchen stool while Mom is French-braiding my hair. Liam's leaning over the counter, reading a comic book. Or pretending to. I can feel his eyes on me. He's always watching, watching.

"Pat, come on!"

"Oh, hold your horses," Mom says. "I don't know what the big rush is. You never win anything anyway."

"Hey, I represent that." Dad punches his fists into his sides. He winks at me and I smile. He wins games all the time. He just always gives me the prizes.

We're on our way to the school carnival, which is fun. For me and Dad. Liam's in sixth grade and he thinks it's babyish. Mom goes because all the moms do. It's what moms do. Dad spends about four hours at Whack-a-Mole with me, then drags Liam over to the baseball toss. Last year Liam actually knocked over the stack of milk bottles on his first try and won a huge stuffed panda. Which I begged and pleaded to have. He's so stingy, though. He never gives me anything.

The only thing Dad's ever won at the baseball toss is the free giveaway — a number two pencil engraved with "Eagle Elementary." He must have a drawerful.

Dad points to Liam. "This year, buddy boy, it's the O'Neill grudge match. Winner take all."

"If you ever lose your job, you can always sell pencils on the street corner." Liam smirks.

"Why you . . ." Dad threatens him with a fist, but he's grinning. "Come on, girls." Dad throws up his hands. "Let's gooooo."

Mom bands my braid and sighs wearily. Liam trails us to the foyer, then stands with his hands in his pockets as we start out the door. "I'll meet you guys there," he says. "I told Aly and Jessica I'd go with them."

"No," Mom snaps. "You're coming with us. I'm not leaving you here alone. We're all four going together." This surprises me. Dad's the one who's always griping about how we never do things together as a family. How everybody's too busy with their own lives, their own activities. He's the one who insists we sit down and eat breakfast together every morning. He calls it our family time.

Liam runs his shoe in an arc across the quarry tile. "I promised Aly I'd go with her."

Mom says, "I don't care if you promised Aly the moon —"

"Pat," Dad cuts in. "Let him go with his girlfriend." He slips an arm around Mom's waist to steer her out the door. On the front stoop, I see Mom twist back and narrow her eyes at Liam through the screen.

Liam steps out of view. I hear him murmur, "She's not my girlfriend."

Dad calls to him, "One o'clock, buddy boy. You be at that pitching booth at one. I've got money riding on this. And don't forget to lock up when you leave the house."

We drive the ten blocks to school. As we're pulling into the parking lot, I remember: "Mom, we forgot the cakes."

"Oh, for chrissakes. Jack . . . ?"

Dad groans. "Do we have to?"

Mom eyes me over the seat back.

"You're the one who signed up for the cake walk," I remind her.

Mom sighs heavily. "We'd better go back."

Dad grumbles under his breath, but turns the car around. When we pull into the driveway, Mom tells me to run in and get the cakes. She hands me her house keys.

The two angel food cakes are sitting on the dining room table where we left them. They're beautiful, and perfect. I balance one in each hand and head out. Just as I get to the door a noise in the house stops me, drawing my attention back. There's a presence in the house.

I hear the noise again — singing. It's coming from down the hall, from Mom and Dad's bedroom.

I set the cakes on the buffet. I should be frightened. What if there's a burglar in the house? For some reason I'm not afraid. Just . . . curious.

The door's ajar and I push it all the way open. My eyes fix on the girl who's sitting in Mom's vanity seat, spreading lipstick over her stretched-back lips. She has long blonde hair and she's wearing a sweater exactly like Mom's. It is Mom's. The new cashmere sweater Dad bought for her birthday last week. The radio's playing softly on the bureau — golden oldies — and the girl stops putting on lipstick for a moment to sing along. "First time, ever I saw your face."

I'm mesmerized. This girl, whoever she is, is in her own little world. She caps the lipstick tube and laughs suddenly. She speaks to herself in the lighted mirror: "I know. Could you believe he said that to her?" She clucks her tongue and flips a lank of hair over her shoulder.

I say, "Hello?"

The girl jerks around. She stands and knocks over the vanity seat.

It takes a moment to register who she is, and when it does, my jaw unhinges.

"Regan." My name escapes his painted lips like a whisper in the woods.

I want to laugh. I squelch the urge. Something tells me this isn't a joke. The sheer terror on his face, maybe.

We stare at each other for a long moment, neither of us knowing what to do, I guess. I take a step backward.

Liam surges forward. Not only is he wearing Mom's sweater, he has on her pearls and my black stretch pants and a pair of Mom's summer sandals. I don't know where he got the wig.

"Re, please." He catches my arm as I'm whirling to flee. "Don't tell Mom you saw me in here. Don't tell Dad. Please. Pleeease." He grips my arm. "Don't tell Dad."

At once I relax and turn around. "I won't."

He smiles, tentatively. "You can never tell anyone. Ever."

I look deep into his eyes — deep inside his eyes — and ask, "Who are you?"

He mimics this gesture of Mom's, where she runs her hand down the back of her hair, stopping at her neck. His head tilts to the left and he rests his cheek on his arm, his elbow on his breast. His . . . breast?

He's wearing a bra.

"I'm Lia." He smiles shyly, dropping his eyes to the floor. "Lia Marie."

"Okaaay," I say slowly.

She lifts her eyes and adds, "I'm a girl."

Chapter 22

The door to my room swung open. Aly and I both whipped our heads around as Luna stepped out. "Here I am," she said.

It wasn't a shock to me, of course. I glanced over at Aly and saw her scanning Luna up and down. What did she see? A girl, dressed in jeans and a velour top. The girl's cheeks were flushed, partly from blusher and partly embarrassment. Light blue eye shadow. Pale pink lip gloss. Nothing garish or outrageous. She'd styled the blonde wig in a ponytail to match Aly's.

"Let's finish our game." Luna strolled over to the computer. She curled cross-legged on the rug and added, "I believe I was beating the crap out of you. Oh yeah. A hundred thousand points to ten." The monitor beep-beeped to life.

Aly rose and crossed the room, then slowly lowered herself to the floor. She lifted her joystick and set it in her lap.

Luna said, "If you think just because I'm a girl I'm going to let you win, you are mistaken beyond belief. If anyone advocates equality of the sexes, it's me."

Aly went, "Ha, ha."

My heart sang. She was going to be okay with this. Everything was going to be —

"Oh God. You know what?" Aly shot to her feet. "I told my mom I'd pick up some milk on my way home. She's probably waiting for me." Aly grabbed her backpack and purse off the floor and charged up the stairs.

Luna called at her back, "E-mail me later?" The lights flickered and the door slammed.

Luna didn't meet my eyes. Smiling oddly, she maneuvered the game characters into position and fired her bazooka. Aly's scream split the air. Again. And again. And again.

By the time I hit the front porch running, Aly was backing down the driveway. I waved frantically for her to wait, but her eyes remained focused on the rearview mirror. "Aly, stop!" I yelled. I smacked my hand against her front windshield.

Her 4Runner lurched to a halt. I motioned Aly to roll down her window. It took a minute.

"Don't do this to her, Aly. She needs you."

Alyson stared at me, through me. "Don't do this to *her*?"

"Look, I know it's weird. Not weird, just different. But you'll get used to it."

"Why didn't you *tell* me?" Her voice oozed with anger. "I thought you were my *friend*."

"I am. Aly —"

Her searing glare cut to my marrow. Tears sprang to my eyes.

Aly hit the gas pedal and squealed into the street. Sand and salt spewed from her tires as she roared off, leaving me to eat her dust.

⁓

I was still questioning whether I'd betrayed Aly when I got to school the next day. Was I the one who should've told her? Did I betray our friendship? Was it my fault she couldn't deal with the truth? I'd been up most of the night thinking about it, agonizing. The look on Luna's face yesterday when Aly deserted her . . .

I'd warned Liam, hadn't I? I told him she couldn't handle it. Not yet. Not ever.

After Aly fled, Liam had shut himself in his room, doing what, I don't know. If it were me, I'd be burying that treasure chest. Burying myself. He wasn't crying. No sounds had penetrated the wall between us. All I could visualize was Liam lying prone on that naked mattress, staring at the ceiling, wishing himself gone.

Maybe I could've made it easier — softened the blow or prepared Aly. I could've dropped a few hints, given Aly time to digest the news. She might've been able to —

"To what?" I finished aloud. "Accept the fact that the guy she's been in love with all her life is really a girl?" How do you deal with that?

Why didn't Aly see it herself? Why didn't Liam see that Aly was more than a friend? Or wanted to be? Maybe he did see. He saw, but couldn't see what he was supposed to do about it.

Tell her, that's what. Not leave it to me. Not always leave it to me.

~

School. Again. I couldn't decide if I hated it more here or at home. I had nowhere to escape now. No job. No friends. I wrenched open my locker and an object fluttered to the floor. I picked it up. An envelope, addressed to me, note card size. Someone must've slid it through the vent in my locker.

Aly? My stomach knotted. What if it was a hate card? She'd written one of those once to this girl who'd accused her of stealing money from her purse. Which, of course, Aly would never do. She'd called this girl a pathological liar. Is that what Aly thought of me? Liam and me, we were both liars.

I couldn't deal with it. Not today. I just wanted to check out — permanently. Sliding the card into my chem book on the top shelf, I gathered books and spirals for my morning classes.

⌒

The lab experiment today was called Stoichiometry. Great. I couldn't even pronounce the title. I read over the instructions, which boiled down to mixing liquids and solids and determining the percent composition of each. The worksheet was one problem about figuring out the percent of each component in a Big Mac. Oh, brother. This was a calculation I'd need to know later in life, when I began my career as a high school dropout.

I couldn't extrapolate the equation. It made me mad, frustrated. Bruchac purposely created these impossible problems to trick me. As he wandered the room harassing people, I surreptitiously glanced around to see if anyone was watching me. Like they would. I removed Liam's Stoichiometry lab and worksheet from my backpack and slipped them inside my spiral. If it wasn't for the fact he was ruining my life, Liam would be the coolest brother in the world. Or sister. Whatever.

I opened the spiral and skimmed down the lab. Then closed the notebook. I couldn't do it; couldn't cheat. What gratification would there be in earning an A for work I didn't do?

I disgusted myself. I was such a nun.

There were five minutes remaining in the hour when Bruchac announced, "I have your tests graded. If the suspense is killing you, you can pick them up as you leave. Otherwise, we'll review the answers tomorrow." Did he intentionally zero in on me? Did he shake his head?

The masochists in the class, including me, trooped to the front. I waited until I was out in the hall to look at my test. All the way down the left side of the page next to every problem

Bruchac had scrawled in red ink, "Nope. Nope. Nope." At the top he'd given me twenty-five points. "For effort," he'd written. Underneath, "Why don't you ask your brother for help?"

Burn my nun's habit. Bring on the Bruchac Papers.

As I jammed the test in my chem book, the note card from Aly sailed to the floor. I retrieved it and studied the envelope. Reread my name on the front: "Ray Gun." It hadn't registered the first time. Dad was the only one who'd ever called me that. His pet name. How could Aly have known?

Duh. We'd practically grown up together. She'd have heard it a million times. She remembered that, but she blocked out Liam's bra? Denial runs deep.

I really did *not* want to know what Aly thought of me.

What *did* she think of me, though? Masochism may run deeper than denial. I sliced through the envelope and removed the card. On the front was a photo of Earth taken from space. The caption read, "Love makes the world go . . ."

It continued inside.

I opened the card. No words. Only the earth again, totally obliterated. What did that mean? There was no signature. Wait. On the back was scrawled a long message. "Dear Regan," it began.

"I know you never want to talk to me again and I don't blame you. I'm a total jerk and I know it. I don't deserve you . . ."

Who was this from? I skimmed to the bottom. "Chris."

Chris? He didn't deserve *me*? The writing was cramped, itty bitty printing. I read the rest. "You probably don't give a rat's ass, but I'd at least like to apologize in person. Will you meet me before 6th period in the gym? It's okay if you miss Skills for Living cuz girls already know how to cook."

I snorted.

"If you don't come I'll understand. I'll just leave your purse with Bruchac."

My purse! Did he go back for my purse? All that way? How sweet. Thoughtful. Apologize. *He* wanted to apologize? For what? I studied the note, reread it, absorbed every word. I loved his handwriting. Before sixth period.

Sixth period? That was now.

⁓

The gym was cut in half by a rolling wall divider. The half I walked into was split again with a volleyball net. No Chris. I'd missed him. Panic rose in my chest. He'd given up on me. As I reversed direction to try the other side, a sound snagged my attention. Scraping. Clanging. Metal on parquet wood. I turned around. This . . . this mechanical beast came barreling toward me. A full suit of armor: leggings, breastplate, helmet with feathered plumage.

My prince in shining armor, I thought. Stupid thought. The armor wasn't shiny. It was tarnished and bent and falling apart at the seams.

The visor raised and Chris's eyes twinkled at me. "Cool, huh?" he said.

I realized suddenly what the armor was about — he was protecting himself from me. He should. I was dangerous. "It looks hot," I said.

"It is. If I sweat any more, I'm going to rust shut." He lifted off the helmet and smoothed down his hair. We stood for a moment in awkward silence. Then we blurted in unison, "I'm sorry."

Chris frowned. "What are *you* sorry about? I'm the one who screwed up. I assume you got busted for getting back so late and that's why you're not talking to me. One of the many reasons."

"I'm the one who got *you* busted," I said. "I broke your car window. I scratched your CDs and made you get a speeding ticket." I hurt your feelings, I didn't say.

"You didn't do anything, Regan. Here I am with this totally hot girl I've been trying to get to go out with me for weeks. She finally says yes and my crappy car falls apart, then my driving about fractures her skull. Denny the dickhead scares the shit out of you. I risk your life driving like a maniac. I ruin your clothes. I get you busted. Stupid. I'm so stupid. I'm a spaz."

"No, you're not. It's my fault."

"It is not."

"Is too."

We looked at each other for a long minute, then cracked up.

Okay, it was funny, in a sadistic sort of way. But it felt good to laugh. In retrospect, the whole horror show played out like a comedy routine. Laurel and Hardy, the Two Stooges.

We stopped laughing, but couldn't stop smiling at each other. It was making me warm. "You have my purse?" I said.

"Oh yeah." He clunked a pivot. "This-a-way."

I trailed him to the rear of the gym. "Did you know the theater prop room is back here?" he asked over his shoulder. "I found it just now when I was waiting for you."

As he lifted off the breastplate and bent to unlash the leather thongs from behind the leggings, the room drew me in. It was larger than I'd imagined. I did know about the prop room. Last year the theater department organized a Shakespeare festival and Liam, Aly, and I bought tickets for *Romeo and Juliet*. Between acts, the two of them took off to find food while I shadowed a couple of players down the hall and into the staging area. They'd disappeared inside this room.

My eyes adjusted to the dimmer interior light. There were racks of costumes, headdresses, hats, wigs, a long table with mirrors for makeup. "Luna would die and go to heaven here."

"Huh?" Chris materialized at my side.

My face flared. "Nothing." Shut up, Regan.

"It's awesome, isn't it?" He reached for a top hat on the shelf and popped it onto his head. He admired himself in the mirror. Boys and mirrors.

I strolled down the racks of costumes, letting my fingers brush the fabrics: satin, brocade, chiffon. My hand came to rest on a velvet evening gown. Emerald green, strapless, with a hooded cape. For a moment I envisioned myself in this gorgeous dress, at a ball, dancing until midnight. No, not dancing. Sitting in the throne watching others dance. I might dance, if someone asked. Or I'd be on a stage, as Violetta, singing, "Ever free my heart must be."

And I thought Luna was a drama queen?

A rustling from behind brought me up short. "Don't look," Chris said, peering over the top of a Japanese screen. "Oh, man." His head retracted. "This is so me."

A smile warmed me from within. I felt so comfortable with him. Relaxed, even hopeful. Like maybe this time I wouldn't make a fool out of myself. At the end of the racks of costumes there was an umbrella stand and in it, a cache of weapons: swords, rifles, spears. All props, of course. I pulled out a cavalry sword from its sheath. Wow, it was heavy. This was no rubber dummy.

I slashed the air. Whish. Again. Swish. "En garde," I said, lunging. "Take that." I spun around and lashed the air. At that moment Chris stepped out from behind the screen and my sword whacked him on the shoulder.

He stumbled backward into a rack of costumes, which tipped over and crashed on top of him.

"Oh my God." I threw down the sword. "Are you all right?" Frantically, I dug through the dresses.

"Move away," he said. "Slowly. Move. Away."

I obeyed. Stumbling backward, my arms stiff at my sides, I thought, You've finally done it, Regan. You've inflicted the fatal blow.

As if animated, the dress rack elevated itself. Chris's face appeared between the velvet gown and a poodle skirt. He said, "We should take this act on the road."

At least he was smiling.

"Ta da." The costumes parted and he leapt out. "What do you think? Is it me?"

My heart seized.

Chris flipped a length of blonde wig over his shoulder and threw out a hip. "Why don't choo come up and see me sometime." He wiggled his hips. The fringe on the flapper dress swayed.

I felt dizzy. Nauseated. Had to get out of there.

"Regan, wait!" Chris called at my retreating back. "Where are you going? What did I do this time?"

That stopped me in my tracks. I turned around slowly. "Nothing. You didn't do anything. It's me. I'm —" What could I say? A prisoner in a parallel universe? I'm being held hostage by my life? Liam's everywhere I go, everywhere I turn. He's my living nightmare. There's no waking up.

Chris exhaled a long breath. "Here's a stupid question: Do you even like me?"

Do I like you? No, I don't like you. I don't think about you every moment of every day. I never relive the way it felt to have your hand holding mine, to be so close to you I could smell you, feel the warmth of you, breathe the air you breathe. I don't remember your arm around me, making me feel safe, special, wanted.

My eyes found his. He searched my face, probing for an

answer. I couldn't say it, I didn't dare. "Just once," he said, "I'd like to get inside your head."

I let out a short laugh. "You do *not* want to go there."

He laughed. Then I laughed. Our laughter, it lifted me. The lightness of it, the release. Like a shaft of sun piercing a long-darkened window.

Chris folded his arms loosely, then unfolded them, looking uneasy in the dress. "Could we start over?" he asked. "Just blank out everything from day one? Pretend we're meeting for the first time. We see each other across a crowded room —"

"A chemistry lab," I said.

"Okay." He arched eyebrows.

Why'd I say that?

"We feel the vibes," he said.

"The chemistry." I should shut up.

"Right," he agreed. "The chemistry. I say, 'Hi.'"

I ask, "How high are you?" God. Could I be a bigger dork? "Forget that. I say, 'Hi' back."

"Would you go out with me? I promise it'll be a safe place. No stupid raves. I'll get you back on time. Door-to-door delivery, guaranteed." He paused, waiting.

For what? Was he asking me out? For real? Was the game over? There was definite chemistry between us. I know we both felt it, along with the possibility of more developing. I wanted that. Like nothing I'd ever wanted before in my life. But could I? Should I?

"I say . . . 'Okay.'" It felt as if I was diving off a cliff, taking a header into a bottomless sea. Fear of the unknown, the unexplored. I was nervous, anxious. More about screwing up than anything else.

The bell rang, yanking both of us out of this fairy tale. Footsteps thundered through the gym and Chris yelped, "Yikes! I gotta get out of these clothes." He ripped the wig off his head. "I have practice in five minutes." He dashed behind the Japanese screen and popped his head over the top. "Is Friday okay?"

"Uh, yeah." For what? Whatever. "Friday's great."

He ducked down and added in a muffle, "I'll call you."

Casually, I strolled out the door, then broke into a run. I had the strongest urge to shout at the top of my lungs, "He likes me! Chris Garazzo likes me." As I flew past the cafeteria, the world a blur, a dream, a magic carpet ride, my eyes took in two figures next to the south stairs.

A voice ricocheted in the hall, "Freaking pervert."

I skidded to a stop. I knew that voice. Hoyt Doucet.

"Freaking fag pervert."

I turned to see Hoyt reach out and smack Luna's shoulder. He slammed her into the railing.

Luna?

What was she doing here?

Hoyt screeched, "You fucking pervert!" Loud. It attracted the attention of a couple of girls who were clomping down the stairs. Hoyt jabbed Luna's shoulder again and yelled, "Perv! You're a perv. I always knew it."

Luna spoke quietly, "Ow. Don't."

"Don't? Don't what? Do this?" Hoyt raised his arm and ripped off Luna's wig. Clumps of Liam's hair tore out with the bobby pins.

The girls above them eyed each other and giggled. They skittered down the stairs and scurried off, their laughter ringing in my ears.

Classrooms drained of people and the hall began to clog. There was a sudden back up at the juncture of Hoyt and Luna.

Over everyone's heads, Luna's eyes found mine. She opened her mouth to say —

"Regan, hey. You forgot your purse."

I whipped around. Chris had sidled up beside me. He was smiling, but his gaze drifted from my face to the crowd by the stairs and his jaw went slack.

"Thanks." I grabbed my purse from under his pullover where he was hiding it, naturally. He wouldn't want to be seen with a purse. "There's something I forgot to give you, too," I said. Taking his arm, I spun him around. My vision narrowed, honed, located the sign. EXIT. "Outside." I tugged on Chris's sweater, about ripping it off.

The door slammed shut behind us. I flattened myself against the brick, gasping to catch my breath and quell the imminent eruption in my stomach.

Chris was breathing hard, too. I'd made him run the length of the hall. Not far enough. Never far enough. I opened the flap on my pack and withdrew the thick folder. Handed it to him. "Here. You can use these next year." I pushed away from the wall and charged off in the opposite direction.

"Wait," he called. "Regan. I forgot to tell you there's a surprise in your purse."

I had to get out of there. Put as much distance between me and the school, between me and Chris, between me and Luna . . .

He'd seen her.

"When's a good time to call?" Chris's voice penetrated the roaring in my ears, the rumbling in my stomach.

Never. It's never a good time.

Chapter 23

"*H*ow *could* you!" I cried aloud. "How could you do that to me?"

The words echoed in my room, in my ears. How could you?

How could Luna show up at school? People knew we were related. Chris knew. Liam and I would never be dissociated now. Me and Luna. They'd always see me as Regan — the one with the transgender brother. I'd never be able to separate from him. Never have my own identity.

Even worse, people would think I was like him. Her. Different. I didn't want to be different. I wanted to be the same. I wanted to be accepted, loved, liked for who I was.

Who was I? I didn't even know.

I knew Luna better than I knew myself. I knew what she wanted — acceptance, love. The same exact thing as me.

She had to be aware, though, that this transition affected not only her. There were consequences for everyone in her life. For me. It hurt me to see people staring at her, pointing at her, laughing at her. What if they laughed at me? Or made jokes. She'd be the butt of people's jokes. I would. What if Chris laughed at me? What if he looked at me differently now?

I couldn't stand that. It embarrassed me what my brother was. He humiliated me. He betrayed me. How could he?

He betrayed me.

A voice inside my head said, "Really? Who betrayed who?"

Shut up. What did that mean? Liam's the one who never thinks about anyone but himself.

Herself.

The voice asked, "What does Liam's transition have to do with you?"

Everything. It embarrasses me. He embarrassed me. She did.

"Embarrasses you," the voice repeated. "Wow. She's out there putting herself on the line and it embarrasses you? You left her in danger. You left her with Hoyt."

I stood for a moment, examining myself in the full-length mirror. The length of me, the breadth of me, the depth. Lack of it. How shallow was I? Embarrassed? I left Luna in Hoyt Doucet's filthy hands. I left her in danger. How could I do that to my own brother, sister? I deserted her when she needed me most.

A dark veil descended over my eyes. "You traitor," I said it aloud. "You hypocrite." Without warning, my knees buckled and I crumpled to the floor. "You coward."

I *was* a traitor. I *was* a coward. I abandoned Luna in her hour of need. I betrayed her the same way Aly had. Luna trusted me. She believed in me. She counted on me for her *life*.

What kind of person did that to someone? Someone she loved? What kind of sister was I? Friend? Human being? I promised her — I promised myself — I'd always keep her safe. Then, when she was at her most vulnerable, I failed her.

I failed myself.

How small a person I was. I felt ashamed. I was weak. I'd given in to the fear. My reputation was more important than defending my brother against attack. What reputation? I didn't even have one.

It scared me, this whole transition thing. Every time she went out in public I was terrified what people might say or do. Hoyt.

Others like him. What if the violence extended to me? The bigotry? And hatred. I couldn't deal with it. How could anybody deal with it? I didn't have the strength, the character, the strength of character.

"No," the voice said. Then louder, "No! Your fear is justified. Anyone would be afraid. You're a person. You're human. Yes, you thought of yourself first. You ran. But if you'd come to her rescue this time, you'd be doing it forever. Nothing would ever change."

That was true. Nothing would change if I was always rescuing her. And something had to change. We couldn't go on this way. We were hurting each other.

The last sight of Luna crystallized clearly in my mind again. Help me, Re, she'd pleaded with her eyes.

No, I'd responded. I won't.

And in that moment when she realized I wasn't there for her, she'd looked inside of me and known the truth. She'd seen me for the coward I was.

She knew, she knew she was utterly alone in the world.

The tears started slowly, then built until they gushed from my eyes in a torrent. They'd never stop. Never.

I cried for her.

I cried for me.

I cried for a world that wouldn't let her be.

⁓

I don't remember going to bed, closing my eyes, falling asleep, but then Luna was there, bouncing around on my mattress. Crush me, I thought. Bury my shattered bones. An unmarked grave where no one will ever come visit.

Her hair draped across my face. "Thank you," she said in my ear.

She was cruel. I gulped an audible sob.

"What's wrong?" Luna climbed over my dead carcass and slid off the bed. She kneeled on the floor beside me, her face level with mine. "Re?" she said softly.

"I'm sorry." My voice was raspy. That's all I could say, I'm sorry. It sounded as hollow as I felt. I was so confused; I couldn't reconcile my feelings. I loved my brother, but I hated this transition.

"You did what you had to do," she said.

No, I didn't have to. It was my choice. "I didn't mean to leave you there with Hoyt. Not on purpose."

"I know. I'm sorry I put you in that position. I didn't think you'd be there after school. I wasn't thinking. It was selfish. I've been expecting too much of you —"

"No."

"Yes," she insisted, squeezing my forearm. "Yes, Re. I'm always in here crying on your shoulder, asking your advice, taking up your time. It isn't fair to you. All these years, I haven't been fair to you." She sat back on her haunches. "I've been so self-centered, so self-absorbed. I haven't taken your feelings into consideration. I've leaned on you too hard. Depended on you too much."

No, I wanted to argue. I wanted to say, I'm your sister. You *can* depend on me. You should. But the words wouldn't come. I couldn't force them out. "Why did you dress at school?" I asked her. "Why did you have to do that?"

She lowered her eyes. "You said it: I had to. I had to test myself. To see if I could go through with it. I needed to know that I had the self-confidence, the will to do it every day."

She was going to do it every day? I'd never have a life. She didn't get it; my feelings meant nothing to her.

Luna reached over and smoothed my messy hair back off my face. I flinched at her touch. "I'm sorry if I hurt you," she said quietly, "or humiliated you in front of Chris. I was only doing what needs to be done. This is life or death for me, Re. If I don't transition, I don't want to live."

All the blood drained from my face. How could she say that? She couldn't mean it.

Our eyes met and understanding flowed between us. Total comprehension.

Life or death.

I got it. I finally got it. The change had to come in me. My acceptance of Luna, my support of her transition, my seeing her as a real person.

"Did Hoyt hurt you?" I asked.

Luna exhaled an irritated breath. "That moron. No, I survived." She clenched my arm. "That's what I'm trying to tell you, Re. I survived. I lived. I proved myself today. I *want* to live. I can. You did that for me. You made me stand on my own two feet, gave me the push I needed; you required me to face it alone, which is what I have to do eventually."

My tears welled again. I hated that she had to do this alone. I hated her struggle, her battle, her war with herself, with me, with everyone in the world. This was just the beginning.

Luna stood and padded across my room to the full-length mirror. Pulling the silk-screened tee she was wearing over her head, she examined her left shoulder under her bra strap. "Oh, lovely," she said. "I'm going to have an ugly bruise. Do you think foundation will cover this?" She twisted around to show me.

It was a huge welt, big as a fist. Hoyt had left his mark on her. I hoped he was proud of himself, beating up on a girl. Luna may have to survive this transition, I thought, but she wasn't alone in the world. Throwing off my covers, I said, "Go get your makeup. Bring your stuff back in here. We'll fix it so good no one will ever know."

⁓

The mirror on the medicine cabinet was cracked down the middle. I had to bob my head around to get a full view as I braided my hair. It wasn't as long as it used to be, and I hadn't worn a French braid in years, and I'd forgotten how to plait it . . .

Liam's hands covered mine. "Let me," he said.

I relinquished the mess to him.

He smiled at me in the mirror. One side of his face was higher than the other, split in half. I noticed behind him by the door he'd dropped a duffel. A surge of panic rushed through me.

As if reading me, Liam said, "I won't put you through that again. I'm not going to dress at school anymore. It's enough to know I can. I don't particularly relish the thought of getting pounded to a pulp every day. I'll drop you off if you want."

Relief flooded through my veins. I didn't want to feel relieved. I wanted her to be herself, to know I'd support her. I wanted not to care so much about me.

Liam banded the end of my braid and added, "I'm going to the mall to buy myself a birthday present. Do you want anything? Hey, you found your other shoe."

I followed his eyes to my feet. "Yeah." I couldn't smother my grin. "Chris found it." He'd washed it off and buried it in the bottom of my purse. Inside the shoe he'd stuffed a tiny music box that played *Twinkle, Twinkle Little Star*. How sweet was that?

Liam wiggled his eyebrows. "Do I hear wedding bells?"

"Shut up." I shoved him out of the bathroom, shutting the door on his smirking face.

~~~

As I was heading to the cafeteria for lunch, Alyson materialized at my side. "Would you give this to Liam?" She handed me a present, adding, "Or Luna, or whoever he is today."

Had she heard about yesterday? That kind of news would have spread like an e-mail virus. I was bracing for the fallout, but so far nothing. If people were avoiding me, it'd be hard to tell.

The present was wrapped in *Rugrats* birthday paper. My gaze lifted to Aly. She didn't look so good. Her eyes were red and bloodshot.

"It's men's cologne," she stated flatly. "Tell him I would've gotten him perfume if I'd known. He can exchange it." She slapped the receipt on top of the present and took off.

"Aly," I called.

She was speeding away, halfway through the atrium before I caught up with her. I grabbed her arm. "I just want to say one thing."

She turned, and nailed my coffin with a glare.

The entire spirit squad flounced by us, laughing and joking around. We both waited until they passed. I lowered my voice and said, "He's still the same person you've always known. Just happier as a girl."

She opened her mouth, and shut it. Shaking her head at the skylight, she said, "But I'm not the same. What does this make me? A lesbian? I don't think so." She broke away from me and stalked off.

I shouted at her back, "If you really loved him, it wouldn't matter."

She lowered her head and ducked into the nearest restroom. That was cruel, Regan, I admonished myself. How would you feel? You're so noble.

I wanted to go after Aly, but didn't know what else there was to say to her. And I couldn't stand to see her cry.

My eyes dropped to the box in my hand. The receipt. Wow. She'd spent sixty-five dollars on his present. That was another factoid I'd never divulged to Aly — every bottle of men's cologne Liam had ever received as a gift got flushed down the toilet.

Sixty-five dollars. His birthday was Saturday and I hadn't bought him a thing.

Hmm. I could exchange this cologne for a bottle of Passion, I thought, Luna's favorite perfume. I'd tell Liam it was from Aly, that she was beginning to come around.

No, it would only cause him more pain when he found out the truth. And he didn't need any more hurt in his life. No more lies. I'd give him the perfume as a present from me, even if Luna already had three gallons of it stowed in her treasure chest.

Chris called that night. Shocker. He said he'd been trying to find me all day, that he'd waited at my locker before and after school and I never showed. A thrill rippled through me. He actually waited for me.

"Are you blowing me off — again?" he intoned.

"No, of course not." Was I? Maybe. Probably. Yes. He'd seen Luna. How would he react? He'd look at me differently now. He'd see Liam as a freak.

"Were you absent?" Chris asked. "You're not sick, are you?" He sounded worried.

Worried about me. "No." I smiled to myself. "I didn't go to my locker this morning. Or after school." I didn't stop there all day for fear of what I'd find. Messages. A mob. Clones of Hoyt. "I left right from class so I could go buy my brother a birthday present."

Chris didn't respond.

Was he going to ask? Make a joke about Liam? He wasn't talking. Was he still on the line? "Hello?"

"So, um," Chris cleared his throat, "where did you get those chemistry papers?"

I expelled the breath I'd been holding. "Don't ask."

"Don't you want them? Or did you already make a copy?"

"No. I decided if I'm going down, Bruchac can kiss my ass. I'll just repeat chemistry next year. Or take something else. Maybe genetics. I hear girls are good at reproduction."

Chris laughed. He actually laughed. It made me laugh. Broke the tension. He said, "There's a problem with Friday night."

My heart stopped beating. I knew it. It was over. He couldn't deal.

"My mom is having this rehearsal dinner and she wants me and Pam to be there."

Good excuse. I wondered how long he'd been working on it. "Regan?"

"Yeah. No problem," I said quickly. Eclipse. Hang up the phone. Need to implode.

"So could we change it to Saturday?" he said. "I know it's short notice and you probably have plans . . ."

My head was spinning. Plans? What plans? "No problem," I said.

"Yeah? Okay, cool." He sounded happy. Relieved. He couldn't be as happy and relieved as me.

"What time should I pick you up?" he asked. "I was thinking we'd go to a movie. Maybe eat first."

Eat? As in handle silverware? "You don't want me anywhere near knives," I told him.

"I'll take my chances," he said with a smile in his voice. "I'm not afraid of you. Remember, I have armor."

"Did you a lot of good last time. Be afraid," I warned him. "Be very afraid."

He laughed again. So did I. It went on like that for two hours. Just stupid stuff. Jokes. Laughter. Chris didn't mention Liam. Neither did I. The subject never came up. The time wasn't right.

When would the time ever be right?

The answer to that one was easy. I guess I just wanted to pretend for as long as possible that it wouldn't ever matter.

Chapter 24

*L*iam was still in the shower when I peeked out my bedroom door Saturday morning. Good. I could sneak into his room and deposit my birthday present on his mattress.

Or not. I'd changed my mind about his gift. The new box was so tiny, he might sit on it. Instead, I left the present on his treasure chest, along with the card I'd addressed to "Luna-tic." He wouldn't miss that.

Mom was in Code Blue crisis when I got upstairs.

"What do you mean they double-booked? They can't *do* that!" she screeched into her cell phone. My ears squinched. Even Dad put down his newspaper and frowned at her. "Well, it's first come, first serve. What?" She listened, her chest heaving. "Dammit, Andy! Where are we going to find a place *now* for a wedding reception two weeks *away*?"

God, take another Valium, I thought.

A box of Krispy Kreme Doughnuts sat open on the counter and I helped myself. The traditional O'Neill birthday breakfast, after Mom stopped baking cakes.

"*Who* got food poisoning from our caterer?" Mom hyperventilated. "Well, my *gawd*."

Food poisoning? I dropped the doughnut back into the box. My stomach was breeding butterflies, anyway. Eight hours and counting till Chris. What was I going to wear? I'd trolled through my closet twice already and all the clothes on my floor three times. Nothing screamed Hot Date. I needed Luna's expertise.

Mom was still flaming about her caterer getting closed down by the health department when the door to the basement opened and my brother emerged. Rather . . . my sister. "Good morning." Luna strolled through the kitchen. Dad had his back to her, but Mom's eyes fixed on the apparition. She shrieked, "Andy, we can't have beans and franks!" She rotated on her chair so she was facing away from us.

Luna selected a lemon-filled doughnut and brought it to the table. Her outfit was new — a short jean skirt and yellow sweater set. She'd chosen the brown curly wig. As she slid into her seat, she began to sing softly, "Happy Birthday to Me."

Surreal. I swallowed down my panic, for her sake. Of course this would be the next step in her transition. She had to do it sometime. Still . . .

She met my eyes and winked. Her face held a mixture of emotions: strength, defiance, fear. Make that terror.

"Happy birthday, Luna," I said, lifting my OJ in a toast.

"Thanks," she replied, toasting me back with her milk.

At some point Dad must've checked in because he turned his head and spluttered, "What the —"

"Get hold of Ellen Rosenberg and tell her we have a problem. Explain the situation. No, better yet, let me do that. You start calling around to every hotel and community room and estate we've ever used and find out what's available. Call me back." Mom punched the off button. She huffed and swiveled around to us. Her focus fell on Luna and she looked at her, through her, the way your eyes settle on an object you don't really see. Your mind is somewhere else, anywhere else. Luna smiled at her. It was almost imperceptible, but Mom's head shook from side to side. Her gaze lowered and she flipped open her Daytimer on the table.

Dad said, "What is this? Some kind of senior prank? You pulling a stunt this weekend?"

Luna licked her lips. Her cranberry-colored lips. Clasping her hands in her lap, she said, "Dad, I'm a transsexual."

My breath caught. I'd never heard her say that word. It was always transgender. TG or trans. Transsexual. It took it to another level. More of an official declaration.

She added, "I'd like to change my name to Luna, with your blessing. And yours, Mom." Luna addressed the presence at the other end of the table. What was with Mom? Back to Dad. "It's the name I've chosen to represent the person I truly am."

In response, Mom murmured to herself, "Food poisoning? Am I liable for that?" Dad threw back his head and laughed.

Luna found my eyes. And died inside.

Dad wheezed, "Good one." He reached over and whapped Luna's shoulder. "The joke's on me."

"No." Luna's gaze penetrated him. "This is who I am. This is who I've always been."

Silence. The air in the room changed. Dad's face sobered. Hardened. Mom flipped a page.

Dad's head spun my way. "You lied to me! You told me he wasn't gay." He pointed an accusatory finger. "I asked you point blank and you lied to me."

"Why does this always come back on me?" I shouted. "First Aly, now you —"

"What did Aly say?" Luna interrupted, looking hopeful.

I blanched. "Nothing. Forget it."

Luna blinked a couple of times and blew out a breath. "Leave Re out of this," she said to Dad. "It has nothing to do with her."

Pressing a hand against her chest, she added, "This is about me, Dad. Me."

Dad's face registered . . . what? Denial? Revulsion? "What. Are. You." His tone of voice made me shrink in fear.

Luna swallowed hard. "Like I said, I'm a transsexual. TS, if you prefer. I was supposed to be a girl, and I am, but I was born in the wrong body. Think of it as a birth anomaly."

"A *what*?" Dad shrilled.

"Nothing," Luna mumbled. She picked up her doughnut and raised it to her mouth. Her hands trembled as she bit into it. She chewed and chewed and chewed. A tiny glob of lemon stuck to her upper lip.

Dad morphed. Into what, I don't know. His face, his body, they seemed to grow, contort. Mom's cell rang. She grabbed for it. "No, Andy, that won't work. There's no wheelchair accessibility at the Burnham-Grant." She stood and marched off toward her bedroom.

She actually left. Was she blind? Deaf?

"Mom!" I called.

Luna said to me, "Please pass the napkins."

I lifted the napkin holder and handed it across the table to her. She forced a thin smile. "Thanks."

Dad's lips receded over his teeth like a snarling dog. "You're sick," he hissed. "You are sick."

Luna set down her doughnut and wiped her fingertips. She scooted back her chair and replied calmly, "I'm going out now. I have an appointment with a manicurist."

I said quickly, "Would you like me to come?"

Luna met my eyes. The answer: Would I ever.

I braced the table to stand, but Dad blasted me with, "Where do you think *you're* going? Sit down!" He shot to his feet and thundered past Luna, who was moving toward the foyer, extracting her car keys from her purse. Dad impaled himself against the front door. "You're not leaving this house dressed like that. You look like a . . . a clown. Go downstairs and change."

Luna's spine fused. "No. This is who I am. This is how I choose to live the rest of my life."

"Not in my house you don't. Not if I can help it." Dad's fingers clenched in a fist and he drew back his arm.

I toppled my chair, racing to throw myself between them. I heard myself screaming, "No, Dad, don't! Stop it."

Dad spread out his left hand and thrust it at me. Though his hand never made contact, the force hit my chest like a brick wall. I gasped for breath. "Stay where you are, Regan. This is between Liam and me."

"It's Luna," she said.

Dad's fist balled tighter. Hard, white-knuckled. His elbow extended farther back, arm vibrating.

I couldn't move; couldn't speak. I was frozen in time and space. I imagined the crushing blow to Luna's face, lethal in its intent, in its execution. Dad was big, strong. And more angry than I remembered him ever being.

Luna held her head high, waiting. Almost daring him to do it. Seconds ticked away. Years.

Then, slowly, Dad released his fist.

My lungs collapsed.

Luna reached around him for the door knob. "Excuse me," she said.

Right in her ear, Dad said, "If you walk out that door, don't bother coming back."

"Dad!" My voice was raspy.

Luna poised for a long moment, her hand on the knob. She stared straight ahead into the solid wood, into the nothingness.

Please, God, I prayed. Make this not be happening.

Dad said, "I mean it, Liam."

Luna's arm fell to her side. Every bone in her body seemed to disintegrate as her shoulders slumped. She said, "I realize I've been a big disappointment to you, Dad. I'm sorry I couldn't be the son you wanted. I'm sorry." Wrapping her arms protectively around herself, she plodded through the living room toward the basement stairs. Defeat hung in the air like nuclear waste.

"I hate you," I spat at Dad. "I hate you!" Pivoting, I stalked down the hall to the master bedroom, where Mom was still on the phone. Still!

"Hang up," I commanded her.

Her eyes flickered over me.

"Hang. Up." The venom in my voice startled even me.

"Andy, I have to go," Mom chirruped. "I'll call you right back. Try that conference center in The Springs, okay?" She disconnected. Sighing wearily, she asked, "What?"

"What?" I repeated. "Mom. Clue in. Do you know what's happening here?"

Her eyes fell to the phone in her hand. "I don't have time for this. Not today." She lifted the cell to her ear.

I walked over and snatched it out of her hand. I threw it across the room, where it cracked the wall.

"Regan!"

"Mom!" I practically yelled in her face. "Why did you leave? Liam is transitioning. Do you understand what that means?" Of course she didn't understand. "She's changing her sex."

She blinked about a dozen times in rapid succession. "Why does he have to do this now," she said. "I can't deal with this to-day. I've got a wedding with no reception hall and a caterer un-der investigation by the health department —"

"Shut up."

Mom's jaw went slack. "What did you say?"

"I said, shut up. Listen to me, for once. Liam needs you. Luna needs you." We all need you, I didn't say. We always have.

"Luna." Mom clucked her tongue. "Where did he get such a name?"

I couldn't believe what she did next. She walked across the room and retrieved the phone off the floor. She began to punch in numbers.

"Mom, for God's sake —"

"I can't handle this, Re!" she screamed, sounding on the verge of hysteria. "I can't handle it today."

"I couldn't handle that," Mom says. "Poor Carol. I don't know what I'd do if Jack ever left me. I'd never be able to take my college classes and manage a house and raise two kids on my own. And she has four." Mom shakes her head. "Poor Carol."

She's talking to our next door neighbor, Mrs. Camacho. They're sitting on lounge chairs in our backyard, supervising us kids, me and Katie and Liam, as we splash around in the kiddie pool. Katie calls out, "Watch this, Mommy." She clambers over the edge of the plastic. Standing in place, she winds up, then leaps in, sploshing water over us.

"That's nice, honey," Mrs. Camacho says. She continues her conversation with Mom. "He emptied their joint savings account, too."

"He didn't!" Mom's eyes narrow. "That bastard."

Liam calls, "Mommy, watch me." He imitates Katie, only making a bigger splash, and almost drowning me. But I don't care; it's fun. We all giggle.

Mom says, "He could've at least taken the kids."

Mrs. Camacho laughs. They both do.

Katie stands up and yanks on the rear end of her swimsuit — again. She high steps out of the pool and runs across the grass. "This is too itchy, Mommy." She tugs the elastic lace around her leg, stretching it out.

"Oh, come here. I knew the lace on these legs felt too stiff and

stickery." Mrs. Camacho tells Mom, "She just had to have this Hello Kitty swimsuit."

Liam asks me, "Can you do this?" He skims like a salamander along the bottom around the perimeter of the pool. I copy him. When we've come full circle, we see Katie skipping back.

She's naked.

I stand up. "Can I take mine off too, Mommy?"

Mom waggles a limp wrist. "Go ahead."

I strip as Katie jumps back in.

Liam pretends to tread water, but I know he's really sitting on the bottom. He can't swim yet. He looks at Katie, then me. I show Katie how to be a salamander and we skittle around the pool. A movement makes me look up. Liam's trunks are around his ankles and he's kicking them off. For a minute he just stands there in the water, looking at himself.

Katie points to him and giggles. I giggle, too.

Liam grabs his penis and starts to pull. "Take it off," he says, almost in a whisper. He sloshes toward Katie and repeats, "Take it off."

"Okay." She gets up.

I hear Mrs. Camacho ask, "What is he doing?"

"Liam!" Mom shrieks. "Get out of there." Her shrill voice makes us all wither in fear. Mom races across the lawn. She grabs Liam's hand and jerks him out of the pool.

"Take it off," Liam says to her.

"Take what off? Where are your trunks?"

"Mommy, take it off." Liam pulls at himself again.

"Stop that." Mom slaps his hand away. "That's nasty." She retrieves his swim trunks from the lawn and shakes them out. Liam backs away from her. "No," he whines. "I want it off. Take it off, take it off, take it off." He starts slapping at his penis and stamping his feet, throwing a fit.

Katie and I huddle at the far side of the pool.

"You stop that, young man. You stop it right now!" Mom orders.

"No!" Liam shouts. "No, I'm not a young man." He's acting like a baby and it makes me and Katie snicker behind our hands.

Mom grips Liam's arm and hauls him toward the sliding glass doors. "You go to your room. Don't come out until you can behave yourself." She drags him inside the house.

"Are you girls okay?" Mrs. Camacho squats beside us. We both nod.

"It isn't nice to touch each other down there," she says softly. "Do you understand?"

I nod hard.

Katie says, "He made me do it."

"No, he didn't." I frown at her.

Mom comes back outside. She exhales audibly and says to Mrs. Camacho, "I figured I was due. He's been such an easy child, so much easier than Regan. Jack keeps saying, 'Any day now, he's going to turn on the testosterone.'" She rolls her eyes. "I guess he chose today."

Mrs. Camacho smiles. "Boys. I'm glad I don't have any."

They resume their seats; pick up their conversation.

Katie says, "Let's play Samantha dolls."

"No." I salamander off. I'm mad at Katie now. She's a liar.

The phone rings in the house and Mom pushes up off her lounger. I hear the sliding screen open and close. A second later the air explodes with Mom's scream. "What have you done? Oh my God. Put that knife down." She appears behind the screen, clutching Liam in her arms. "Connie, I need to run Liam over to the emergency clinic."

Mrs. Camacho rushes across the yard. "What happened?"

"He cut his . . . his leg. Will you watch Regan?"

"Of course. You want me to call Jack?"

"No," Mom replies quickly. "No, I can handle it. He doesn't need to know." Mom says something else, but all I see is the blood running down her leg.

She knew. I stood in Mom's doorway, staring at her back as

she paced around the room with her cell suctioned to her ear. She'd always known.

Why hadn't she helped him? Been there for him? Why hadn't Mom acknowledged Liam's difference? She could've made his life so much easier. She could've raised him as a girl. Why didn't she?

Dad. Of course.

He didn't know. She should've told Dad. All these years he'd tortured Liam with the sports, the sports. His unrealistic expectations. He'd made Liam feel like a failure, feel inadequate as a son.

Which made Dad feel inadequate as a father.

Mom could've given Dad time to come to terms with it, accept Liam for who, and what, he was.

Another memory resurfaced, along with a question. After that time Liam stole Mom's pills to commit suicide and I'd flushed them down the toilet, why hadn't Mom interrogated us? Gone crazy? Asked where all her pills went?

Unless she knew.

Unless she left them out on purpose. She had a purpose. She gave Liam easy access. "Here, Liam," I could hear her thinking. "Help yourself. Something to help you sleep. Something to ease the pain."

Slowly, numbly, I backed out of her room.

My God. My mother was a monster.

Chapter 25

I didn't tell Luna. I didn't want to discuss it. I didn't want to confirm it. Luna had been through enough today. It was her birthday. She'd removed the wig, but was still dressed in the skirt and sweater, clicking away on her laptop, coding her game, or whatever she was doing. She was back in her element. Back in her world of make-believe.

I didn't want to leave her alone — not today. Not like this. I wouldn't. Settling on the sofa, I grabbed the remote control and switched on the TV, surfing for an all-night movie marathon.

"Don't you have a date tonight?"

Her voice made me jump. I thought she was totally spaced.

"Maybe you should start getting ready. It'll take you that long to do your hair."

I sneered at her. "I think I'll stay home and rag on you."

Luna swiveled all the way around on her desk chair. "You don't have to baby-sit me, Re," she said.

"I'm not." My face flared.

"Yes, you are. Are you still punishing me for losing you your job?"

I threw the remote at her. She caught it midair. "Wow," I said. "You should go out for baseball."

She didn't crack a smile. "You're doing it again. You're very good at it, you know."

"What?"

"Making people feel guilty."

I let out a little huff. She should talk.

"I'm all right," she said, tossing the remote back to me. "Stop worrying about me. Don't you dare cancel your date with Chris because of me. I'll be really, really upset if you do." She pouted, poufing out her lips.

The lights flickered. Luna and I whipped our heads around in unison. The creaking on the stairs announced the last person I ever expected to see here again.

"Hey." Aly stood on the landing. She looked . . . determined?

"Hi." Luna shot to her feet. "Hi, Aly."

Aly's eyes darted up and down Luna's body. "Happy birthday," she said, her wavering voice betraying her confidence. "Hi, Re." Aly smiled in my direction.

"Hi."

Before Luna or I could react — however we were supposed to react — Aly waltzed over to the PCs and picked up a joystick. "We have a game to finish," she said. "I need to figure out how to get out of that fucking alley." She flopped on the floor at Luna's feet.

Luna widened her eyes at me. I shrugged. Was that hope surging through my veins? It was filling Luna, too. She seemed to grow taller; her skin less sallow, eyes more focused.

Aly gripped the joystick in her lap with both hands and let out a long breath. "I don't know how long it's going to take me to be okay with this." She spoke to the empty space between us. "It's hard. You know?"

Luna lowered herself slowly to the floor beside Aly. "I know," she said quietly. "Take however long you need."

Aly heaved a tremulous breath. "Could we finish this game, please?" She jammed her joystick into Luna's middle and snared another one for herself. "It's giving me nightmares."

Luna switched to Play mode, then settled more comfortably on the rug. She smoothed her skirt over her bent legs. Aly said, "Start us when we're nine. I want to play that birthday again." She turned her head to look at Luna, for the first time, eye-to-eye contact. "You can't be serious about that outfit," she said.

Luna's back stiffened. "What. What's wrong with it?"

"A sweater set? Please." Aly refocused on the screen. She pressed a button and her clone's scream split the air — *Aaah!* In its echo, Aly added, "I hope you're not getting fashion advice from Regan."

"Hey!" I cried.

Aly didn't acknowledge, but I could sense her smile. My heart burst apart with song. I loved Aly. I loved her more than I ever had. I loved her like a sister.

⁓

We were sitting in the movie theater, Chris's arm snaking across my shoulders, when the last conversation I'd had with Luna replayed in my mind. Aly was gone after having finally won a game of Aly Oops. I think Luna let her win. Luna was hunched on the floor, screwing together the casing on a mother board, and I asked if she'd help me pick out something to wear.

"I can't, Re," she'd answered. "I have to finish this. There isn't much time left."

What did she mean by that — there isn't much time left? For who? Why?

"Where are you, Regan?" Chris tapped my shoulder.

"What?" I jerked to the moment.

"You really go away sometimes, you know that?" His voice was a whisper in my ear. The movie had begun. When had the movie begun? "Is anything wrong?" Chris asked. "You don't really seem like you want to be here tonight."

Perceptive. All that had happened today with Dad and Mom and Aly weighed on my mind. It preyed on me. I couldn't get Luna out of my head, out from under my skin. I never would. She wasn't as happy about Aly's acceptance as I thought she'd be. I expected her to be dancing on the ceiling, singing Dana International. Instead she was moody, uncommunicative, distant.

"Regan?"

What? God. "I'm sorry," I said to Chris, lowering my head. "It . . . it isn't you. I do want to be here with you."

The couple behind shushed us and Chris removed his arm from my shoulders. He stood, jammed our tub of popcorn in the crook of his arm, and took my hand. "Let's go."

I didn't resist.

Out in the car, Chris said, "Do you want to talk about it?"

Yes, more than anything in the world I wanted to talk about it. I wanted to tell him what was going on, reveal the truth about Liam. I wanted to get it out there, get it out of me, deal with it, see how he would deal.

My brain said, "Speak," but my mouth wouldn't work. I couldn't do it. This secret had been with me so long, it was a part of me now. If I let it out, I'd be opening myself. To hurt, ridicule, loss.

Chris said, "I have an uncle who's gay."

"So?" I whirled on him. Liam's not gay! I wanted to cry. I wish he was. It'd be easier, more acceptable. Better understood, at least.

"I'm just saying, I don't have a problem with . . . you know."

He didn't know. How could he know? I couldn't tell him. I couldn't form the words.

This was too new to me. Trusting someone. I wasn't ready. I was scared. If I told him the truth, I might lose him, and I'd only just found him.

Chris was watching me, waiting.

I wondered how long he'd wait. Letting out a long breath, I said the only words I could manage, "I . . . can't . . . yet."

"Okay," he said quickly. "No problem. I'm cool."

He was. He was so cool. If we sat here another minute, though, I wasn't going to be. "Could we go?" I asked.

"Whatever you want, Regan." He cranked up the car and drove me home.

As we pulled into the driveway next to the Spyder, Chris turned off the ignition and shifted to face me.

"I'm sorry," I said before he could blast me. Before he could tell me how sorry he was he'd ever met me. How he decided I wasn't worth the wait. "I'm sorry." Why was I always apologizing? For me, for Luna, for everything wrong in the world.

The basement lights were out, which spooked me. Liam wouldn't be in bed already. Chris reached over and took my hand. "It's just family stuff," I mumbled. "It's not you."

"Hey," he said. "Family shit can wear you down."

That was an understatement. I was suddenly angry. Here I was with this incredible guy who made me feel special and bought me dinner and took me to a movie and wanted to spend time with me and all I could think about was what my brother was doing, what he was thinking and feeling. How I shouldn't have left him alone on his birthday, not tonight. Not the way he was acting. "There isn't much time left," he'd said.

"I'm a good listener." Chris cocked his head and tried to engage my eyes. "You tell me your shit and I'll tell you mine. My family's so dysfunctional, I bet it beats yours any day."

I snorted. "How big a bet can you make?"

His eyebrows arched. He wasn't pressuring me, but I felt pressured. I wasn't ready. "I have to go." I had to get out — now.

Chris scrambled to open his door and catch up with me on

my dash to the porch, to Liam. My eyes drifted to the sky in search of the moon, the stars. Nothing. No lights shone. An eternity of darkness. Chris touched my hand. If he tries to kiss me, I thought, I'll burst into tears.

He didn't. Only laced his fingers through mine and squeezed gently. "Call you tomorrow about next weekend?"

He still wanted to see me? He *is* a masochist, I thought. If I nodded, it was only because my head felt so heavy I couldn't hold it up.

The first thing that struck me was the disassembly, the expansion of space. Objects had been moved, rearranged. Liam's PCs were on, all four of them, blinking screensavers. Not skyscrapers this time. Numbers. A string of them, scrolling across the monitors. The coffee table where he usually kept his laptop had been cleared; in fact, the whole room looked like Supermom had swept through. Somebody else's Supermom.

Liam — Luna — must've spent all evening cleaning. Cleaning. As in clearing out? Leaving this world?

I barged into his bedroom. He lay curled on the mattress, snoring. Still had on the skirt and sweater. The digital clock on his dresser glowed 9:02. I eased the door shut, breathing a sigh of relief.

Unfortunately Luna's cleaning bug hadn't extended to my room. It was a slum, as usual.

I dropped into a chasm. Deep and dark and jagged-edged. My body felt as if it'd been pushed off a cliff and hit every outcropping of rock on the way down. Bruised and beaten, so exhausted. I lay on my bed and closed my eyes.

Chapter 26

*F*lash!

My eyelids flew open and I shielded my eyes from the blinding light.

"Wake up, Re." A hand touched my shoulder. "I need you to do me a favor."

I squinted at the blurry figure looming over me. Luna. "What time is it?"

She checked her watch. "Four-thirty."

"In the morning?" I dragged myself to a sitting position. The bleak night seeped in through my window. No moonlight still. Only the harsh glare from my overhead globe.

"I need you to come with me." Luna handed me a stack of neatly folded clothes. *My* clothes, apparently for me to put on.

She was dressed to a T. Suit jacket, matching skirt, heels.

I yawned. "The mall doesn't open for a few hours yet," I grumbled.

She pulled back my comforter. "Hurry. We should leave in ten minutes."

She left me alone to dress. When I emerged from my room, she was waiting for me by the stairs. "We're going to have to sneak out. Dad's been up watching TV all night."

"I know," I said. We'd evil-eyed each other when I came in from my date. Shortest date in history. Dad and I weren't exactly on speaking terms. He wasn't actually watching TV, either. Just lying on the couch, arms folded, stiff as a corpse.

"He finally fell asleep," Luna said. "I don't want him to wake up and catch us." She shouldered her purse. "Or stop us."

"Where are we going?" I tiptoed behind her up the stairs. No creaking. She must've disengaged the sound effects.

We slipped past Dad, no problem. He was out cold, an empty beer on the rug by his hand.

Luna punched in the Spyder's security code and we climbed in, easing the doors shut. At the roar of the engine we both cringed, but no lights came on. No doors flew open. Luna backed to the street.

I waited until we were on the Interstate before speaking. "Wherever we're going, you're bound to get noticed in that getup. Wow."

She beamed. It was true. She looked gorgeous. Her suit was tailored, expensive, white wool, with a navy blue blouse and matching pumps. She had a new blonde wig, shoulder-length with bangs, which made her look totally glam. This must've been her birthday present to herself.

Her eyes reflected the streetlamps along the highway as she concentrated on the road. But the sparkle seemed to originate within.

Something else sparkled. "Hey, do you like them?" I indicated my ear. I'd forgotten about my birthday present to her.

She touched her right earlobe. "I love them." She turned and smiled. "Thank you. They're perfect."

I'd chosen a pair of gold earrings, half moons. Opposing halves that formed a whole when pieced together.

Past the city limits, we picked up speed. Traffic was sparse this time of morning. Plus, it was Sunday. Wasn't it? Last night seemed a lifetime ago. I wanted to talk to Luna about Mom and Dad, but wasn't sure how to broach the subject. Or what there was to say. They'd been tested as parents and failed. Zero percent.

We flew by so fast I almost missed it. The sign. "We're going to the airport?" My head swiveled all the way around to confirm.

Luna's expression didn't change.

My heart raced. It hammered against my chest.

We veered up the ramp for departing passengers and Luna located a parking space in the short-term lot. Opening her door, she swung out both legs and stood.

"What are we doing here?" I said, following her out my side.

She opened the trunk and reached in, extracting a bulging suitcase and a carry-on bag, then her laptop in a leather brief-case I'd never seen before. She handed me the carry-on and laptop.

My heart was breaking ribs. "Clue me in. What's going on?"

Her high heels clicked on the pavement as she headed for the elevators.

"Luna —"

"Oh, shoot." She spun in place. "I forgot my coat. Will you run back?" She handed me her keys. "The door code is 6940128. Can you remember it?"

No, I thought. I can't think.

"Re?"

"Say it again."

"6940128."

Replaying the numbers in my head gave them a rhythm — 694, 0128. 694, 01, 28. The coat was in the back seat covering an envelope. On the front of the envelope was written, "Mom and Dad," in Luna's pink ink. My throat constricted. Next to the envelope was a box from Nordstrom's and a card attached with my name on it.

I slammed the door shut. This was not happening.

She was standing at the ticket counter, to the side, being questioned by a security guard. Oh God. She was nodding her head at him, looking freaked. As I hurried toward her, the guard motioned another official over and talked to him a moment. They both turned away from Luna and sniggered into their chests. An arrow pierced my heart.

As I reached the counter, the first guard handed back Luna's driver's license and said, "I'm sorry. I can't let you board."

Luna snatched up her laptop and luggage and hustled toward me. "What a hassle," she said under her breath. "I have to change back."

She scanned the area, then took off down the corridor toward the restrooms. I jogged behind her, eventually snagging her suit jacket. "Would you please tell me what the hell you're doing?"

"Isn't it obvious?" she said, barely looking at me. "Would you guard my stuff until I get back?"

She dumped her briefcase and carry-on at my feet, then ducked her head and disappeared in the women's restroom with the suitcase. I decided to kill her when she returned. A ticketing agent approached and I said, "One of the toilets just overflowed in there."

She made a face and scurried away.

A few minutes later Luna came out dressed in slacks and a blouse, without the bra, without the wig. She'd wiped the lipstick clean, but the eye makeup remained. As she bent to retrieve her briefcase from the end of my limp arm, she said, "It took me forty-five minutes to get this eyeliner on straight and I'm not taking it off."

She stormed back to the ticket counter and checked in. This time they let her through.

Rendezvousing with me again, she eyed her coat that I was dragging on the floor and removed it from my hand, brushing it off. She stuck her boarding pass in the pocket of her briefcase and checked her watch. "There's still an hour before my flight. Do you want to get something to eat? I'm starving."

"No." I seethed. "I want you to tell me what you think you're doing."

Surveying the vicinity over my head, she replied, "I'm going to Seattle. Teri Lynn has an extra room where I can stay until I get settled. She's going to speak to her therapist on Monday to see if he can take me right away."

"For what?" I fairly screeched.

Luna finally looked at me. "For evaluation. To begin my change. To start the Harry Benjamin standards of care. Depending on how strictly this doctor adheres to the rules, I may be required to live as a woman for a year to complete my real-life experience. Then I'll need two letters from psychotherapists to recommend me for SRS. Which shouldn't be a problem." She glanced around again. "Come on. Let's get a croissant." She sped off down the corridor.

I scrambled to stay up with her, but my brain lagged behind. It was trying to process everything she'd said. She was going to Seattle. For SRS. She was leaving.

She veered into a coffee shop and stood at the counter, studying the menu on the blackboard. She ordered a latte and a chocolate-filled croissant, then queried me.

It was all I could do to shake my head no. No, no, no.

Luna told the clerk, "Make that two croissants. And an orange juice."

Luna paid and I trailed her to a booth. Not too many people here at five-thirty A.M. on a Sunday. Maintenance crew. Couple of Skycaps. I gazed out the window where a small engine plane was taxiing down the runway. Across from me Luna gobbled her croissant, but I couldn't eat. My stomach hurt.

As if thinking out loud, she said, "I need to get my own prescription for estrogen, too."

"What?" Was that the hormone she was taking, estrogen? Luna rattled on about antiandrogens, laser hair removal, breast implants if she still needed them.

If? I glanced at her chest. Was she growing breasts?

Estrogen. It stuck in my head. Wasn't Mom taking estrogen? She'd said something about a prescription. "Are you stealing hormones from Mom's medicine cabinet?" I said. Or was Mom doing what she was so good at, pretending not to notice? Giving him the opportunity. "Is she trying to kill you again?"

"What?" Liam made a face. "What are you talking about?"

I turned away.

"Mom never hurt me. She wouldn't —"

"She knows about you." I whirled back. "She always has, hasn't she?"

Luna closed her eyes and dropped her head. She let out a sigh. "Did I ever tell you about the time she caught me in her room?"

"No," I said. "When?"

Luna raised her hand and took a sip of coffee. "It wasn't the first time. I always thought I was being so careful, but you know me. I get lost in the mirror and the hours just slip away." Luna smiled somberly. "The last time, I guess I was ten or eleven. I don't know where everyone was, but I do recall what I was wearing. Mom's negligee and bra and heels and this wig I'd purchased at a yard sale. I was doing my makeup when, out of thin air, Mom appeared. I almost poked out my eye with a mascara brush." Luna blinked at the memory, her eyes far away.

240

"She told me to stop. Mom said, 'You'd better stop right now.'" Luna imitated her perfectly. "Like I could. Mom didn't really understand. About the need, you know? I hated not telling you, Re. I thought you should know that Mom knew. But she warned me, 'Don't you ever tell anyone, Liam. Especially not Regan. What if it came up in conversation and your father heard? What if he saw you like this? Do you know what it would do to him? Do you know what he'd do to *you*?'" Luna's lips parted and she expelled a shallow breath.

God, Mom. Thanks a lot for trusting me. No wonder Luna was scared of Dad. Yeah, she knew what he would do: shut her down or shut her out. Exactly what happened.

"That's been the hardest part," Luna went on. "Having this unspoken truth between Mom and me. Knowing it was 'unspeakable.'" She shook her head slowly. "Yes, Mom's always known. She just hasn't known how to cope with it. Or me." A slight smile creased Luna's lips. "Well, she did give me her favorite tapestry bag for my fourteenth birthday." Luna chuckled into her chest.

I didn't laugh. It wasn't funny.

Everything Luna said swirled around in my head, mixing with my own thoughts and memories. I was more confused than ever about Mom. Was she a monster, or a martyr? Or just a mother. Had I jumped to the wrong conclusion about her? I hoped so. God, I hoped so.

Luna babbled on about all the surgical procedures she planned to have — an Adam's apple shave and a facial contour. I tuned in to hear her say, "I can't wait to grow out my hair. I'm so sick of wearing wigs."

"What about school?" I interrupted. "You're just going to blow it off? And college? All your scholarships."

"I can't think about that right now." She downed the rest of her coffee. Setting the cup on the table between us, she added, "I think I have enough credits to graduate. And if not, I'll take my equivalency exam. But college . . ." She shook her head again. "It's not time yet. I need time for me."

"Yeah, you," I snarled. "It's all about you. It always is."

Her eyes found mine, but I couldn't hold them. My vision blurred, scattered, to the ceiling, the floor, the counter, menu, signs, phones, anywhere but her. I couldn't deal with this. I didn't want to.

Luna reached across the table and touched my arm. "This has been a burden on you, hasn't it, Re?"

"No." A lemon lodged in my throat.

"You know I'm doing this as much for you as for me."

"What do you mean?"

"I think you know."

I didn't. I didn't know. My pulse quickened. My heart exploded. "I take it all back. Everything. I didn't mean any of those things I said to you. You can use my room whenever you want. You can dress at school. I don't care. I don't want you to go. I don't want you to leave."

"I have to," she said.

"No, you don't!" I was practically screaming. My chest hurt. My throat burned. How could she? How could she do this, just pick up and go? She had a life here. She had me. She had . . .

"What about Aly?" I said.

"What about her?"

"You're going to leave without telling her?"

"I e-mailed her."

"Oh, you e-mailed her." I mocked Luna. "That should make her feel good, feel important. She's okay with it. Or will be. She just needs time."

"It's time I don't have," Luna said, squeezing my arm. "I can't wait. For anyone."

No. She couldn't do this! I jerked away. "How can you leave?" I said again. "How can you go?"

She tilted her head and said softly, "How can I stay?"

Our eyes held for a long, hard minute. Then, folding her arms around herself, Luna added, "We'll end up hating each other."

"I could never hate you. You're my brother."

"Not you. Dad."

Dad. It always came back to him. She was right. I couldn't keep it in anymore; I burst into tears.

"Oh, Re." Luna slid out her side of the booth and came around the table. She scooted in next to me.

"Please," I sobbed, "don't go. He'll come around."

"Maybe," Luna said calmly. "I hope so. But I need to do this now."

My tears intensified. She looped an arm around my shoulders and I fell into her. I let her hold me. "This isn't their fault, okay?" she said.

She'd read my mind; I hated them so much.

"It's nobody's fault. I don't want you blaming them. This is what the goddess meant for me to be. I just haven't figured out why."

My tears couldn't be stanched.

Luna arced across the table and grabbed her briefcase off the seat. She dug out a packet of travel tissues and removed one. Shaking it out, she handed it to me. "Don't leave me here," I pleaded. "Take me with you."

She ran her hand down the back of my head. "No."

I added in a whimper, "What am I going to do without you?"

"Live," she said. "Be happy."

"I can't!" I cried. I collapsed onto her lap, a heap of flesh and bone and blubbering mass. "I can't."

"Please, Re," she whispered hoarsely. "Don't do this. Don't make me bawl. Once I start . . ."

I felt her chest rise and fall. She rubbed my back, held me until I could raise my head enough to blow my nose. People were staring at us, but I didn't care. I didn't give a damn what anybody thought.

An announcement echoed in the concourse: "America West Flight 337 bound for Phoenix and continuing on to Seattle/Tacoma will begin boarding in just a few minutes. Ticketed passengers should proceed through security."

Luna gently pushed me off her and removed the boarding pass from her briefcase. My stomach churned. "That's not mine." She stuck the ticket back into the front pocket. Smiling at me, she said, "Let's talk about something cheery. Tell me more about your hottie new boyfriend."

I swiped the corners of both eyes with my palms. "He's not my boyfriend."

"Yet." She wiggled her eyebrows.

A lady with an oxygen tank rolled past our booth and frowned at us. I curled a lip at her. "Where'd you go last night?" Luna asked.

"What? Oh. Out to dinner. To the movies."

"What did you see?"

"I have no idea."

"Mmm."

I elbowed her. "It wasn't because of that. We didn't stay long."

"Mmm," she went again.

I clucked my tongue.

There was another announcement about security regulations, not leaving your luggage unattended. Luna asked, "Are you going out with him again?"

My brain shifted into gear. I was concentrating so hard last night at dinner on not slopping spaghetti sauce all over myself that I'd completely forgotten what Chris had talked about. His invitation. His mother's wedding. "Yeah," I said. "Next Saturday. His mom's getting married and he wants me to come with him to the wedding, then afterward to the reception."

"Ooh, that sounds like fun."

"Yeah, loads." A thought barreled through my brain. "Wouldn't it be a total freak-o-rama if Mom was her wedding planner?"

Luna laughed.

I crossed my eyes at her. Panic rose in my chest. "What am I going to wear? I've never even been to a wedding. How do you act? What do you do?"

"There's a box for you in the car," Luna said. "Open it when you get home. Throw out everything you own and start over. Put some color in your life, Re. You need it. As for how to act, that's easy. Be yourself."

"Be myself. Right. I don't even know who I am."

"United Airlines Flight 875 to Seattle will now begin boarding at Gate Four. Passengers who have not already done so should proceed through security —"

Luna slid out of the booth and stood. I staggered to my feet. She took my hand, both hands, and smiled into my eyes. "I know who you are," she said. "You're my baby sister, Regan. My beautiful baby sister. I've always been so jealous of you."

"Yeah, right."

"I have. You're beautiful."

I snorted.

"You are." She seemed surprised at my reaction. "Haven't

you ever looked at yourself?" She dropped my hands and fisted her hips. "Regan O'Neill —"

"Like I could get any mirror time."

"Look at me." She lifted my chin with an index finger. "You are beautiful. Inside and out. You're kind and generous, compassionate and caring. You're the most caring person in the world. You saved me; you know you did. If you hadn't been there for me, Re, all those years . . ." Her voice faltered. My eyes filled with tears. We both had to look away.

Luna lowered her head and spoke directly to me, only to me, when she added, "Don't you know, you're the girl I always wanted to be."

I bit my quivering lip.

Luna scurried around to gather her things. "We have to go." I collected trash from the table; tried to collect myself. We followed the signs to the security checkpoint and queued up together at the end of the line. The man and woman in front of us both did a double take at Luna. She smiled at them and said, "I hope my eyelash curler doesn't set off the metal detector."

They dropped their stares. I smacked Luna. She stepped out of line and pulled me to the side. "I almost forgot." Jamming her hand into the front pocket of her slacks, she retrieved her keys, grabbed my wrist, and set the keys in my palm. "It's yours."

My jaw unhinged. "What?"

"I won't be needing it. I'll probably buy a new one. Maybe a VW. A rusty retro Bug I can fix up." She grinned.

Was she joking?

"Do you remember the code for the door lock?"

I remembered. It was a song now.

"In case you forget, I coded it into the screensavers at home. The numbers are scrolling across all the monitors."

She was giving me her Spyder? No way.

She folded my stiff fingers over the keys.

"Next, please." The security guard waggled her fingers at us. Luna faced me square on. "Don't say good-bye," she ordered, her voice threatening. "This isn't good-bye. It's hello. I think of it as a new beginning because that's what it is for me. A rebirth. I'm starting my life over. The next time we meet, you won't even know me."

"That's what I'm afraid of," I murmured.

"Oh, Re." She exhaled exasperation, as if I were a child. Which is exactly the way I felt. Small. Lost. In trouble. She set down her briefcase and removed the carry-on from her shoulder. Laying the coat across the cases, she clenched my arms and said, "You're not losing me. I'll always be here for you. You got that?" She shook me a little. "I'll e-mail you every day, and you'd better e-mail me back. We could chat live, say at midnight?"

"Forget it. I plan to be sleeping — for once. But I will e-mail you. I promise."

Luna and I looked into each other's eyes, then spontaneously embraced. We held each other as if our lives depended on it. "I love you," she said.

"I love you, too."

She broke away and picked up her gear. For a harrowing moment as the guard checked her ID and boarding pass, I feared she'd be detected. Rejected.

Would that fear always be with me? Be with her?

The guard let her through. Luna took two steps and wheeled around. Her eyes found mine and she smiled. An aura framed her, a glow. Her whole body seemed to be backlit as she blew me a kiss.

I felt it land, a brush of butterfly wings against my cheek. It lifted me up, away. All at once the weight of the world dissolved and I felt myself expand, grow. The same way Luna must feel to be free, I realized. She'd freed us both.

I watched her until she passed beyond the metal detector and headed for her gate. She walked tall, proud.

I was proud. To be her sister. Her friend.

Suddenly, it struck me — I'd never see my brother again. Liam. A hole opened in my heart. A hollow place, a cavern. "It's okay," my inner voice said softly. "He'll be okay. He's happy."

I wanted that. More than anything in the world, I wanted my brother to be happy.

A part of him would never leave me. His strength. His courage. The essence of who he was as a person.

I took a step back, then another. I turned around. I walked, walked faster. Ran. Toward the door. The exit. The entrance. "Good-bye, Liam." I spoke the words aloud so their music filled my head: "Hello, Regan."